Healing Wounds...

The Redemption Legacy

Healing Wounds...
The Redemption Legacy

By Daniel D. Dirscherl

Table of Contents

"The pursuit of justice without vengeance is a noble cause. The quest for revenge through the guise of justice is a lie... know your heart."

DDD

Preface

The following is an astonishing tale, a true story, and a plea for help all rolled into one. It's an unbelievable story that meanders through time and lives, and causes most who hear it to shake their heads in disbelief. It's the chronicle of the untimely and mysterious death of my father, Robert John Dirscherl Sr. which took place in Dunedin, Florida in 1977; and my family's thirty-five year quest for answers and justice.

Although news reporters have labeled Dad's death *"The Most Bizarre Unsolved Murder Mystery in Tampa Bay History"*; those who hear it realize it's much more. It's a story that has come to a halt several times, yet for some reason won't go away. It seems the truth doesn't die easily…it smolders, sparks, and reignites, coaxing those diligently searching to eventually find it.

My family's challenges investigating and explaining the mysteries surrounding our father's death have plodded on now through four decades. Our search has been daunting, and has led us into realms of existence we had never before experienced, or even believed might be real. Our journey has taken its toll on friends, families, and the inherent quest for the truth. At times it seems the simple option would be to give in to the frustration, end our mission, and surrender to the lie. I think as you read on, you'll understand why that can't happen, and why I wrote this book.

I suppose this story is technically a nonfiction murder mystery, but that label doesn't do it justice. Family, friends, and a quest for truth and justice encouraged me to share our story, and I decided to put it on paper for several reasons: First, I want to tell my family's story through the eyes of one who has personally experienced some of the unexplainable events and occurrences. Many people have heard parts of the story, but I wanted to get all the information together and share the entire account as I know it before my head exploded. I wanted to relay the facts through a first-person lens, so people could experience my family's perplexing journey, and our personal struggles to uncover and expose the truth.

A second goal is to share this story hoping the right person might read it and be able to help us conclude our decades-long quest. In 1997 and 2008, our story aired on the television show Unsolved Mysteries. Although that national publicity opened fresh leads and helped uncover new facts; law enforcement authorities, forensic pathologists, state's attorneys and medical examiners have not been able to (or perhaps not been willing to) close this case in an explainable and credible manner. Perhaps you or someone you know can help.

Finally, and most importantly, I wrote this book to glorify God. I realize this statement may cause a percentage of readers skimming this preface to shut the book, never to open it up again. Some people don't believe there is a God. Others may associate God with religion, and that's a topic that can raise some haunches, cause even the most spiritually confident to question life-long view points or sacred beliefs, and initiate arguments most would rather not be involved in. This isn't meant to be a book about religion, but it is a book that discusses beliefs in general; how they converge, how they diverge, and how they significantly impact each of our lives.

While investigating my father's death, I realized over the years how strongly personal beliefs shaped, and are still shaping the outcome of this case. I also realized how beliefs help shape everything else about us. In my humble opinion, beliefs are one of the most powerful forces in the universe. They affect every culture, every human being, and potentially every decision ever made. In essence, beliefs shape our lives and realities while time and actions generate our life's history.

As I tell this tale through my eyes, I share some of my personal beliefs. Though some of these beliefs may differ from yours, it is not my goal to impose them upon you, or to argue my beliefs are more truthful and accurate than yours. I simply share them because they play a major role in this story, and help explain how this amazing experience touched and shaped the lives of many.

Although my father's death significantly impacted my life, I have four siblings and extended family whose lives were also altered forever. While I planned to tell "our story", I soon realized that trying to share the critical case details and all my siblings' emotions, experiences, and points of view through my eyes would have probably resulted in a monstrous chronicle that encompassed way too much, and said less. As I share personal and significant events from my life, I don't mean to diminish my family's roles or pain, or detract from my father's legacy.

I also want it known that the intent of this book is not to ridicule or embarrass those you read about. It is intended to share some specific truths without the quest for revenge or humiliation. Unfortunately, at times the painful truth cannot always be avoided.

While I'm not a previously published author, famous philosopher, nor do I have a doctorate in anything, I hope I'm able to convey an understanding of how important beliefs are; my beliefs, your beliefs, the expert's beliefs, and human beliefs in general. You're about to read a story that may touch your heart, ignite a few deep emotions, and perhaps help you understand the truth a little more clearly; at least the truth concerning this mystery and our experience discovering it.

This story is about uncovering the truth surrounding my father's death, and the struggle to clear the name of one Robert John Dirscherl Sr. To some he was a father, uncle, grandpa and friend. To one he was a loving husband. But in the flash of a moment, and to one other individual, he became a murder victim. In that moment, justice, righteousness and life went haywire. Fortunately the truth still remains; hidden for a time, but now unfolding. The following pages are my attempt to explain our bizarre search for that occasionally elusive entity…the truth.

Please make yourself comfortable, strap yourself in, and keep your arms and legs inside the ride at all times…things may get a little bumpy.

Chapter 1

The Unthinkable

The date was March 13th 1977; it was a cool spring morning in
Florida and it was beautiful. Our house sat on a corner lot at 1111
East Lotus Drive in a middle class neighborhood in the small town of
Dunedin; a quiet, scenic hamlet whose western boundary hugged
sugar-white beaches, and whose eastern border stretched towards
Tampa Bay. Dunedin offered residents and visitors a close-knit
community, endless opportunity, and the proverbial "Good-Life"
surrounded by semi-tropical playground.

It was a crisp, breezy Sunday morning, which meant this
fourteen-year-old boy would be up fairly early and off to church with
Mom and Dad. While perhaps a pious ritual, realistically it meant I'd
be off to Mass to squirm in the pew for the traditional inattentive
hour, where a congregational response or liturgical reading would
occasionally interrupt my daydreaming of the day's escapades. Then
it was back home to execute the daily adventures. That's how my
Sunday was supposed to go. Unbeknownst to me, my plans were not
what fate had in mind. It seems fate, or life, or destiny had other plans
for this fourteen-year-old still slumbering in a warm bed.

As usual, Mom and Dad were up early, drinking their coffee,
planning the day, and getting ready for church. Dad had been to the
post office to pick up mail and then dawdled around the house in his
usual way, searching for small projects he could complete, or minor
repairs he could mend before the traveling salesman hit the road the
next day. He spent some time out back chatting with a neighbor and
skimming love-bugs out of the swimming pool as he burned time
before church.

We, like many Catholic families in the area were members of
Our Lady of Lourdes (OLL) church in Dunedin; had been since the

late 1950s. And this Sunday Dad was the service Lector during the nine-o'clock Mass. He was actually scheduled to lector at the five-o'clock evening Mass the previous night, but accidentally put contact lens cleaning fluid in his eyes instead of eye drops, so he had to switch services.

Mom helped him with the pronunciation of a word or two that he would use during his readings. They shared their coffee and Sunday paper and discussed after-church plans and details surrounding Mom's bowling tournament which kicked off shortly after church ended. Dad prodded Mom that perhaps they should wake me so I could start getting ready for church. He asked her if there was any iodine or medicine he could use to treat his itching athlete's foot. Mom reminded him there was some Doctor Scholl's foot spray in the cabinet, so Dad headed to the master bathroom off their bedroom while Mom took the Sunday crossword puzzle and headed to the bathroom off the kitchen. Little did they know this nonchalant dialogue would be their last words to each other. Minutes later Dad would be found lying dead on the bedroom floor with a close-range shotgun blast to the chest.

I was still asleep in my bedroom at the other end of the house. Although the shotgun round's detonation produced a concussing blast, I didn't even hear the shot. A few minutes later Mom's scream woke me in an instant and I left my bed in a flash, sprinting through the house directly to my parent's bedroom; almost as if I were being lead, feet barely touching the floor. I didn't yet know why she screamed, but it was blood-curdling, and I knew immediately down in my gut something horrible had happened. I reached the doorway in a full sprint, turned and attempted to stop my momentum. There at the foot of the bed was my father, lying on the floor in a pool of blood, mouth wide open as if he were gasping for air, and the look of shock in his widened eyes as he gazed at the ceiling. The bed was still unmade, and the bedspread was pulled back showing its underside. His favorite shotgun was lying in the middle of the king-sized bed, muzzle pointing towards the headboard.

Instant shock enveloped my entire being. My brain short-circuited as it tried to decipher this preposterous scene. My reasoning abilities attempted to process this visual enigma, but the overload locked me up and I froze for what seemed like minutes. I now realize the lapse was only a second or two, but during those moments I aged immeasurably, time was in its pause, and the world I knew no longer existed. Then just as quickly as my brain stopped functioning, the synapses instantaneously began re-firing.

I realized I was supposed to do something…but what? I heard gurgling noises coming from his throat as if he were trying to breathe. I grabbed a pillow off the bed and put it under his head. I screamed at him over and over "Dad! Dad!" I shook him, thinking I could shake life back into him. I think deep down I knew it was useless, but I didn't want to surrender to the truth and accept the finality of that reality. No! He wasn't dead…this can't be happening. "Dad! Dad!" I screamed, but to no avail. While the noises I heard were signs of life to a teenager in denial, it was actually just blood bubbling in his throat and chest cavity. He didn't blink, he didn't look at me, and he didn't breathe.

In the adrenaline-filled panic of the moment, time went haywire…nothing like a normal few minutes. Mom yanked the phonebook out of the bedside table and dialed the police. I assume I was there kneeling next to Dad as she spoke to the police dispatcher, but I don't recall hearing her converse. I remember staring at Dad's chest, seeing his white knit shirt now completely bright red. I remember kneeling next to him, almost unable to move, frozen stiff. I stared at him and to this day recall the look on his face. His eyes and mouth stretched wide open, and his expression encompassed what I can only describe as an extreme look of astonishment and disbelief.

My mind was trying to comprehend the scene but shock was playing its protective role. The classic signs were there; tunnel vision, auditory exclusion and my inability to move. I was experiencing tachy-psyche, and the moments ticked away. The time warp was in full effect, helping me cope with this outlandish situation.

The next thing I knew I was rushing out the front door in my underwear to meet the paramedics. They sure didn't seem to be in much of a hurry; at least that's how my brain saw it. I pleaded with them to hurry, but there was no reason to rush. My father was dead.

You'd think a 12-gauge shotgun going off inside your house would wake a sleeping fourteen-year-old. I know today at forty-nine, I'm easily awakened by the furnace kicking on, or the newspaper delivery guy making his 4:30 a.m. rounds. How could I have not heard that shot? And why did I immediately leap from my bed the moment Mom screamed? Was this specific moment in time determined by randomness, or was there precision woven into the moment? Was there a reason I didn't wake when the weapon discharged?

My memory of that morning lost all fluidity; no long memories that flow smoothly from beginning to end. Time ran more like a camera taking quick snapshots every hour or so. I don't remember the police arriving, but I remember there were a bunch of them on the scene. I don't remember if I put pants on, or if I was still wandering around in my underwear. I do remember seeing the half dozen or so police cars parked in and around the yard, and then Mom and I were herded out of the house by police and sent to Ted and Mary's next door. I don't know how much time had passed, but the police had already told us that Dad had committed suicide. The shock of the scene was still controlling my consciousness, so this information from police that it was a suicide didn't really sink in…it was just fuzzy static hissing in my mind.

While standing outside, I gazed up the street and saw a familiar blue Mercury Montego headed towards the commotion taking place at 1111 East Lotus Drive. It was the Humann family (that's their last name, not a reference to their species) slowly cruising towards our home, now turned crime scene. They were on their way to church, and as they were driving down Highway 580, from about a quarter of a mile away they could see through the adjacent field that the Dunedin Police Department was now parked at our house. As they pulled to a stop, I remember wandering up to their car with tears rolling down my face, trying to explain Dad had been shot and that he was dead. I don't remember my exact words, but I remember the expressions on their faces; they too were in shock. The Humanns headed off to church in their state of bewilderment, and mom and I were directed into the next door neighbors' house while the police conducted their investigation at ours.

I don't remember much about the rest of that day. I guess my sprint to the bedroom took place at about 8:05. Mom's call was received by the dispatcher at 8:07, and the first police unit arrived at 8:10. Besides the horrible bedroom scene, meeting the paramedics at the road, seeing the Humanns pull up, and spending a few minutes inside Ted and Mary's house next door, I don't remember much about the gaps that make up that day. The hours between 9:00 a.m. and about 5:00 p.m. seemed to have vanished. I don't think the police even questioned me, although I would think they must have.

Mom and I were whisked out of the house, the police were gathered and were investigating the scene, but now some very unpleasant notifications needed to be made. My siblings were still unaware of the horrible happening that took place in the master bedroom of the home they grew up in.

Mom and I knew that Dad was dead; we didn't believe it, couldn't wrap our heads around it and didn't understand why it happened. But we saw Dad lying on the floor, the police had shown up and this nightmare was still unfolding. I'm not sure how police determined Dad's death was a suicide, but it was almost immediate. The determination of suicide was made literally within minutes of police's arrival, and it was thrust upon us during the frenzy of this surreal moment.

Mom and I had just experienced the shock of a lifetime and were beginning to process and deal with it, but there were other family members, my brothers and sister, getting on with their Sunday routines, who didn't have a clue about what had happened in that bedroom mere minutes ago. Their lives were about to come crashing down as the painful notifications were made.

I'm not sure which one of them got the first call, but I think it was my brother George. George, his wife Donna, and their three young kids were living near Lake Tarpon in the subdivision of Tarpon Woods. They too were in the midst of their Sunday morning routine getting ready for church when the police dialed their number.

The drive from their house in Tarpon Woods to Lotus Dr. was about ten miles. If I know George, the ten mile drive that MapQuest now says takes about sixteen minutes, probably took him eight or nine. He was working with Dad, traveling the state of Florida selling hospital furniture for Hill-Rom. Spending much of their time in a vehicle meant large, comfortable, powerful cars were the Dirscherl norm. At the time, George was driving a dark green 1973 Pontiac Grand Ville powered by a 455 4-barrel. I have no doubt his sensory overload, the urgency of the moment, and the Pontiac cubic inches got him to our house quicker than was legal.

To this day, George doesn't remember who called him that morning at his home in Tarpon, but he flew out of the house by himself, leaving Donna and the kids behind; he doesn't remember much after that. The only memories he can put together are arriving at our house and the police not letting him go inside. They immediately told him Dad was dead, and he vaguely remembers them mentioning it was a suicide. George's brain was now entering this strange world that he wished was make-believe. He doesn't remember anything else except standing in the side yard of the house on Lotus Drive...the rest is just a blur.

My brother Guy and his wife Barb were living in an apartment just off U.S. Highway 19 near Sunset Point Blvd. They were in bed when the phone rang and Guy still can't remember who was on the other end of the line when he heard the senseless words. His best guess is that George called to break the news. He doesn't remember exactly what was said, but it was clear that something very bad had happened and to get there now.

Guy and Barb quickly dressed, jumped into their bright red Toyota Celica hatch-back, and flew north on U.S 19, hung a left on Highway 580, then pulled up to the scene from a TV police drama. The only snap-shots of the day Guy remembers are seeing a large black police officer he went to high school with now standing in the yard, not letting him into his old house, but instead directing him next door to Ted and Mary's. He recalls images of stunned people sitting around their house not saying much. He can't recall how long this went on, and the only other thing he remembers is Barb and him heading back to their apartment that evening with me along for safe keeping.

There are hours missing in this day, but I too remember the snap-shot of people sitting around Ted and Mary's living room, wringing their hands and pondering this suicide explanation. While we couldn't believe Dad was dead, this explanation from the on-scene experts just didn't make sense. Mom, George, Guy and I were now aware of the situation. But there were still two siblings living out of state that needed to be notified; one in New Hampshire, and one in Germany.

My oldest brother Bob Junior, whom I knew my whole life as Kookie, was the next to get the call. And he, like George and Guy can't recall who phoned him. Kook (pronounced like cook) and his wife Dianne were living in Plaistow, New Hampshire. Dianne was seven-plus months pregnant with their soon-to-be daughter Kara, and had another Robert Dirscherl running around the house; this one was about to turn two years old, and he was Robert John Dirscherl III. The stunned New Hampshire family soon boarded a flight headed for Florida.

Kook remembers that on the hours-long trip he had time to think and process the call. He rationalized and was certain that a mistake had been made and somehow Dad was not dead. When they got to Florida, he had to go to the funeral home first and see Dad's body. He needed to see physical evidence to confirm the horrible rumor. It was true; but parts of his psyche still didn't fully accept the painful reality. At the funeral service it began to sink in, and he got really sick and had to go outside to get it back together. For almost two months, Kook dealt with Dad's death the way many deal with this type of loss. He just blocked out everything that had happened, slipped into a state of semi-denial and didn't really grieve.

Almost two months after Dad's death, and back in New Hampshire, he was driving home from work and had just that day, bought a new Lincoln Mark IV. Dad was a Lincoln guy, so Kook was excited...he couldn't wait to tell Dad about it. That's when reality arrived...while driving down the New Hampshire freeway; he finally admitted Dad was gone. He pulled the Lincoln over to the side of the road, sat there and bawled. It's like that portion of his mind that had been hibernating for two months finally thawed in an instant. A flood of memories and emotions ran through his mind. He realized how unique his relationship with Dad was and how there was no way to replace it. Memories rushed over him of things he did with Dad and the discussions he'd had with him that just couldn't be shared with anybody else. He realized that a very big part of his life was gone and there was no way to get it back. He wasn't even going to be able to share the great news of his daughter Kara's birth the following week, and share Dad's unique perspective on raising a girl. The recognition of losing that critical part of his life was so powerful, he sat on that interstate for almost an hour crying over the devastating realization of how his life changed when that shotgun discharged.

Four kids had been notified; one to go. The last child to learn of Dad's death was the first-born, the eldest child, and the only daughter; my sister Kandy. Kandy was married to her high school sweetheart Pat, who had joined the Air Force in the mid 1960's. Like most GI's, he moved to a new assignment location every few years. In 1977 they were stationed in Germany at Hahn Air Base; a small military community nestled into the beautiful berg-filled countryside.

They had two young daughters, Lindy and Terri, who were fourteen and eleven. Hahn was a great assignment for Air Force personnel and their families, as the beautiful countryside, friendly

German people, and closeness of the Air Force community made it a true home away from home.

During the prior summer, Mom, Dad and I went to Germany to visit Kandy and her family. We were there for the Fourth of July in 1976 while everyone back in the states was celebrating the U.S. Bicentennial. It was a wonderful experience traveling through Bavaria and the Netherlands with family, and it was the last vacation I would spend with Dad.

It was now Sunday, March 13th 1977, and a life changing phone call had to be placed halfway around the world. Someone had to break the news to Daddy's Little Girl that her father was dead. George volunteered to make the call. He was a young salesman and had made numerous uncomfortable phone calls before. When speaking with important clients, or handling stressful conversation, he was always able to maintain a calm demeanor and sureness on the phone line. This wasn't one of those calls. This wasn't a conversation he could initiate with small talk, then work his way up to the bad news like, "Oh by the way Mr. important client, your order is going to ship two weeks later than I promised."

This was one of those rip the band aid off quickly calls, and it had him nervous. Who would answer the call? How would he start the conversation? What words would he use? He wasn't looking forward to this call…but he knew it had to be made. He was hoping Pat would answer so he could pass the news through him, to perhaps somehow lessen the shock of Kandy hearing the horrible news over the phone. George anxiously waited for the lines to connect and hoped to hear Pat's long-distance voice. Instead, Kandy answered with a cheerful "Hello?"

After a very quick "Hi Sis," George asked to speak with Pat. Quite puzzled, Kandy passed the phone to her husband and watched a curious phone conversation unfold that would alter her life forever. Kandy saw her comedic husband's expression change instantly. She remembers the color drained away and his skin became ashen. She immediately thought something had happened to one of his family members. The short call ended, Pat hung up the phone and broke the news to his wife; her father was dead, and it was a suicide with his shotgun.

Once again, a family member's rational thoughts and normal cerebral functions were short-circuited as Kandy's mind and being entered the confused world where reality and surrealism meet; a world where actuality and truth just can't be, but they are. Her safety response was denial. She immediately transformed into a woman who was now angry at her brother for a cruel joke…the cruelest of jokes. How dare he jest about something like this? She was pissed and needed to straighten out her little brother. George had always loved to tease his big sister, but today he had gone too far. A very small part of her subconscious absorbed the real and horrible news, while the majority of her being denied the truth and resided in the make-believe world where George's call was a cruel prank.

The small lucid part of Kandy's mind knew she had to get to Florida because her father was dead, but that part was overwhelmed by the denying sister who needed to get to Florida to straighten out her little brother. The two parts of her mind were at odds, and a battle was raging as reality blurred. Although there was packing and planning and phone calls and travel, the mental overload she was experiencing warped her memories just like it had done to her brothers and mother.

Kandy had a unique way of dealing with the loss of her father. She rationalized the following: "Daddy traveled for a living, he was gone five days a week. He was just on a business trip and would be home soon." This is how she dealt with his absence…not just that week, but for years after. When she and her family would come back to the states years later, she continued to pretend Dad was just on the road hawking his hospital furniture for Hill-Rom. To this day, she still gains comfort by semi-pretending Dad wasn't killed that Sunday decades ago. Her words say it best… "Deep down I know my father is gone, but I like being in my world better."

Pat called his Commanding Officer, arranged emergency leave, and Sis and her husband flew home from Germany. The Dirscherl brood was home; family was gathering and preparing a funeral. People were numbly going through the paces of dealing with this unexpected death. Business executives from Hill-Rom were flying in to pay their respects while friends and relatives were trying to come up with the right words to comfort Mom and the family.

I don't remember much about the weeks following Dad's death. But I do remember sensing an overshadowing uncomfortable feeling whenever anyone gathered. It was a strange guilty feeling; a feeling of shame, or disgrace, or embarrassment. It was the stigma of suicide that was beginning to permeate our lives, and it became the proverbial "Elephant in the Room." If you haven't experienced it, you may not understand it. It wasn't extremely obvious, or overtly cumbersome...it was just there.

At times I wish I could recall those missing memories more clearly, but apparently they're buried and blurred by the protective effects of shock and those tachy-psyche symptoms I encountered. The tunnel vision and auditory exclusion are physiological responses to intense adrenaline and shock. They're designed to help us focus on a threat, or help us survive a stressful situation by speeding up the mind and effectively slowing down time. This amazing process happens in an instant and serves its purpose well. Unfortunately, the process seems to cloud memories, can scatter information, and frustrate someone trying to recall details.

Today we live in a time where information is available in the blink of an eye. We're now conditioned to Google anything, and locate answers in a fraction of a second. Unfortunately my memory can't be Googled. Although the information, memories, and details are in there somewhere, some remain locked away out of my mental reach.

Some details are episodic memories born through visual stimuli, routed through my hippocampus and stored inside my functioning grey matter, and can be recalled vividly and clearly on demand...however other details are deeply buried in my subconscious.

What are those details? Do they even matter?

As we began to investigate the investigation, we discovered that paying attention to details reveals critical facts and helps expose the truth. Failing to uncover those facts or dismissing important details can warp the truth and lead even the most confident investigators astray.

Chapter 2

The Good Life

Dad was drafted into the Army in 1941 while still a senior in high school. He was off to basic training, then more technical training as a supply officer. He wound up on a frozen rock in the Aleutians…the chain of Alaskan islands stretching into the Bering Sea. While in the Army, luck came his way and he was selected to play on a traveling Army basketball team that roamed military posts putting on exhibition basketball games. It was like a USO team, and he even wound up playing the Harlem Globetrotters. Once he was done in Alaska, he was reassigned to Seattle and decided it was time to wed the love of his life. Robert John Dirscherl and Virginia Rose Bigham were married on November 23rd, 1944 which was Thanksgiving Day.

In 1945, Dad's military service was done and he and Mom were living back in their hometown of Batesville, Indiana. Kandy was born in September of 1945, and in 1946 Dad and his new bride's brother-in-law partnered up and opened a bar in the small town. The pub was named The Ship, and it was the place in town where folks smoked, drank and relived memories of the recent war and the experiences of an amazing era. It was also the place where Kandy would accompany her father to work, staying busy wandering around the adults or occasionally yanking the arm of the slot machines. Mom was spending more time at home because in 1947, the second child Robert Junior arrived on the scene.

The growing family thrived in the Midwest town of Batesville, and in 1949 added a third child to the Hoosier population. George was the newest Dirscherl. He and his brother and sister created childhood memories in the picturesque town. Dad sold The Ship, and began working for Hillenbrand Industries, then in 1953, the Dirscherl household expanded with a fourth child they named Guy.

The kids grew, but so did the dangers. These were the years in Batesville when bouts of Tuberculosis attacked the population. Another debilitating disease lurked through the streets and cut down children in their prime; Poliovirus was making its rounds, sickening the un-expecting, crippling other children, and killing some. The virus caught the Dirscherl kids and life was never quite the same. Kookie, the oldest son was hit the hardest. He wound up with Paralytic Polio and at age two, annual surgeries began every summer; his last one at age thirteen. George and Kandy were a bit luckier and caught the non-paralytic strain, which made them ill, but didn't cause the crippling effects that manifested in their brother. Guy was lucky and was spared the illness.

Dad's duties at the office evolved and he was placed in charge of Sales. But there was a Florida sales territory opening up and Dad was interested. The family had twice vacationed in the Pensacola area and the draw to balmy Florida had entered their bloodstream. This was the opportunity to make the big move and head south to the land they had dreamed about. In 1958, Dunedin Florida became the Dirscherl Home.

The family of six lived and grew under the Florida sun, and life could not have been better. Dad was traveling the state selling hospital furniture, and Mom was the typical suburban housewife at home raising a close knit family through the late 1950s. They had become an established family in the Dunedin community and at Our Lady of Lourdes Catholic church. The 1950s rolled into the 1960s, and in 1962 an unexpected pregnancy surprised the household…Me.

I'm the baby of the bunch; not just by a little, but by nearly a decade. My parents had four of their kids within an eight year period. After taking a break in the human reproduction process, nine years and seven months later I popped onto the scene. My sister Kandy (actually Kandace Joan) was the first-born and the only girl. Mom and Dad loved games, thus the name Kandace…which actually stands for Kings and Aces (K-and-Ace). While waiting to go into labor, Mom and Dad played poker. When the time arrived, Mom was holding Kings and Aces. Apparently it was a winning hand.

Two years later, Robert John, the first boy arrived earning the "Junior" status. He was nicknamed Kookie. Another two years and the folks were at it again, perpetuating the Dirscherl blood line with a second boy they named George, who was born on George

Washington's birthday. Good thing it wasn't Dolly Madison's birthday, or the first three kids may have been Kandy, Kookie and Cupcake.

My flanking sibling is my brother Guy, who is nearly ten years older than me. Guy came along four years after George and was supposed to be the last of the offspring. Since theoretically he was supposed to be the end, Mom wanted to name him a short, three-lettered name. As was the gaming way, Mom wanted chance to play a part in the naming process. Everyone wrote down three-lettered names and put them into a hat. Not sure who wrote the name, but the small piece of paper drawn out of the hat read G-U-Y. The final planned Dirscherl boy would be named Guy Lloyd.

But as we know, accidents happen…especially in the Caribbean. I was conceived during a vacation to Jamaica, and in 1962 the family needed to come up with a name for me. Dad's closest friend and business associate was Daniel Hillenbrand. I was named Daniel after him, but wound up with only a middle initial instead of a middle name. Dad had been called Dixie while in the Army and wanted to share that heritage with me. While Dad wanted my middle name to be Dixie, Mom refused. So I wound up Daniel D. Dirscherl. Thank you Mom.

Childhood Memories

Living on the water had been Dad's dream. Our corner dream home on Lotus was edged with its own private beach and bordered a small lake loaded with fish, turtles, eels and alligators. In 1966 we installed a 16' by 32' swimming pool between the house and the lake, so the water was literally six feet outside our back door (which meant jumping off the roof into the pool was a natural inevitability). The pool and lake were great, but if we needed bigger water Dad would load up the boat and take us out in the local bays to fish for trout, flounder and redfish, or go snorkeling for scallops. If we felt the need for larger game, we'd head out several miles into the Gulf of Mexico to troll for King Mackerel or go Grouper digging near the reefs.

My dad's best friend would accompany us on many of our Gulf fishing trips. His name was Lucky Roberts and he lived just down the street. He and his wife Lucy didn't have any kids, but our families hung out together so much, they basically became the pseudo-adopted aunt and uncle, and Lucky the crazy fishing buddy of the family. Lucky's boat was named "Lucky Lucy", while Dad skippered our boat, named "On the Rocks". There were numerous boating adventures that created indelible family memories.

When I was about eight or nine, I remember being several miles out in the Gulf when the weather turned ugly. We watched the clouds darken and swirl and begin to drop funnels. The excitement and anticipation grew as one funnel dropped and touched the water. We were in our boats in the middle of the vast expanse, watching one of the scariest and most beautiful entities take shape before our eyes. The boat radio was going crazy with chatter about the waterspout that was stretching between water and cloud. We were all amazed, and Dad was prepared to run perpendicular to escape its slow path, but we were all kind of paralyzed by its magnificence and just idled there and watched. Then Lucky's voice broke over the radio with an excited... "Hey Bob, let's go get a closer look!" I think Dad's exact response was, "Not No, but Hell No!" They bantered back and forth for a few seconds, and then it was gone. The rush of adrenaline we were experiencing began to dilute, and our emotional buzz quickly wound down like the energy of the liquid vortex. There's nothing like a boating encounter with a waterspout to get the juices flowing.

Another great boating memory etched into my mind was the day we caught seven sharks. What made it so memorable was that they were caught on the same pole, by the same person, at the same time. On this adventure Dad's friend Don Schroder hooked up on a big fish, which he fought and finally brought near the boat. It was exciting to realize we were going to try to land about a six foot shark. A few moments later the fins and teeth were in the boat and the thrashing creature attempted to destroy anything in reach. It's quite a frenzied few moments when you have a six foot shark in the boat that doesn't want to be there. Adrenaline peaks, people are jumping over and around the thrashing animal and little kids are continually being told to stay back.

As we watched the shark thrash about on the boat floor, we all realized there was also a smaller shark in the boat. The words "Where the heck did that come from", were quickly followed by, "How did that…hold on…there's another one!" We quickly realized the shark was giving birth in the boat. With every few thrashes it seemed the dangerous baby-machine would eject another shark pup at our feet. While not quite as cute and cuddly as a litter of puppies, it was my first memory of seeing a live birth. I was amazed to see life begin…even if it was a cold, slime-covered gray fish.

While that boating memory was an entertaining and amazing experience, one of my most sobering memories was the time the catch of day was an unexpected monster from the deep. I wasn't along for the fishing trip, but I remember the fishermen's arrival home. The "On the Rocks" and the "Lucky Lucy" crews had been out in the Gulf fishing when Lucky hooked a leviathan. He fought and fought and thought he had hooked a huge fish. But this catch wasn't a massive grouper or king mackerel. When the mystery creature reached the surface there was a loud blast of air and an unexpected head looking up at him; Lucky had hooked a Green Sea Turtle, and it was huge. It weighed over four hundred pounds and somehow was landed and brought home alive.

I remember there was quite a commotion brewing in Lucky's front yard when the fishermen returned with their catch. I was about seven years old and I remember climbing up the boat trailer which was now parked in his driveway. I peeked over the gunnels and saw the huge turtle trapped in the boat. The dilemma…how do you remove a live sea turtle from your boat when it weighs four hundred pounds, has a head as big as a basketball, and a beak powerful enough to easily separate your hand from your arm? You call your buddy with a tow truck, of course.

Someone assigned the turtle the name Gladys, and once named, it was my instant pet. The bizarre memory of the tow truck removing the huge creature from the boat rolls into cheerful memories of climbing on Gladys' back and riding her around the yard. Granted, it wasn't a speedy, or very long jaunt, but there I was, poised like Neptune, grinning ear to ear as Gladys struggled to drag me a few feet across the lawn. My small relative size to the turtle meant she was huge to me. She was the size of a car door and her head was much bigger than mine. She had huge, sad black eyes like the eyes of horse. Gladys was my newest, coolest pet…a friendly big ole turtle.

After my quick ride, and a few more photos of the catch, the giddiness and happy scene ended in a moment of horror. I remember Lucky holding a large knife to the turtle's throat, and with one long draw of the blade, opening a gash in Gladys' neck. A dark pool of turtle blood spilled over the driveway. Gladys struggled for a few seconds, and then it was over. There was this massive animal, lying still in a spreading puddle of blood.

What a shocking way to lose my new pet and experience death. I cried for an hour. I'd seen fish and small animals killed for food. We bird hunted and fished, and ate everything we took. But the death of this large animal, whose eyes I had just stared into, was different. It left an understanding with this young lad that death could be shocking, violent, and final. The turtle was butchered and eaten and gone forever, but was never forgotten.

When you head out into the Gulf of Mexico with bait, poles and excited expectations, you never know what kind of memories might be created. While I loved the salt water excursions, and the chance and mystery of fishing borderless waters for who knows what, the familiar lake behind our house maintained the strongest allure on me.

My older brothers swam and played in it a lot, but the lake was usually off limits for me. Through the eyes of a seven year-old, it was a large lake; but driving by it these days I realize it's more of an overgrown pond that has lost much of its magic. But back in the day, it was an amazing memory maker, and it shaped much of my childhood.

Our house was one of those houses where kids would congregate...whether it was my friends or my brother's high school buddies; there were always a handful of kids at our house. We'd play football in the yard, ride mini-bikes, or play with our pet capuchin monkey named Doc. But when the Florida heat and humidity got the best of us, we'd always wind up out back cooling off in the pool which sat mere feet from the lake.

For some reason I was always drawn to the lake, and was constantly trying to sneak a short swim; that is if Mom wasn't watching too closely. If she caught me I always had the stand-by excuse ready that I had to retrieve the football, fishing rod or t-shirt that had "accidentally" fallen in. The lake had this mysterious draw on all of us. Although we had a beautiful clean shimmering pool to swim in, for some reason we were lured to the mysterious dark water. It was tannic brown and shadowy, and Mom didn't really like any of us in it. In the early days there were up to a half-dozen gators calling it home, and we knew it.

During my lake-swimming years there were only two alligators living in the waters...we named them George and Elmer. But hey…my friends and I were grade school daredevils…we had to jump in and occasionally tempt fate. I might initiate the taunt of the day by challenging my buddy Sparky… "I dare you to swim across!" The return challenge might be, "Okay, I'll go all the way across it, but I'm not swimming back….and you have to go down and touch the bottom!"

Crap! That was the freakiest challenge for me. I was a fast swimmer, and could get to the other side pretty quickly. But grabbing a breath, pointing my toes towards the bottom, and submerging like a dart through the murky depths was sure to launch major panic. It brought about that primal fear you get when you're swimming in water over your head, waiting for that large, unknown thing to bump your leg as it passes by. I hate that feeling. I knew as I plunged towards the bottom in the darkness I was going to encounter that thing; perhaps a large snapping turtle or Elmer the alligator who finally had me where he wanted me. Or perhaps a land locked shark that somehow managed to enter and survive in the lake behind our house. It could be anything. The temperature would drop the deeper I went. I knew I was getting close and was about to complete the challenge placed before me. Usually I'd chicken out before hitting the mushy weed-covered bottom and of course shoot back to the surface claiming victory…making up amazing details to tell my friends. Then somebody would say they saw Elmer coming and we'd all quickly return to the safety of the warm clear swimming pool.

If we got bored just swimming in the lake or pool, there were always a gaggle of fishing poles stashed just outside the back door. With a quick yell to Mom asking for a couple slices of bread, we'd race to bait our hooks with dough balls. In a matter of seconds we'd be pulling blue gill, shad and the occasional bass out of the lake. What do you do with a spastic fish that needs back in the water? You toss him in of course… not in the lake, but in the pool for your friends to chase. There is nothing more difficult or more memorable than chasing live fish in your swimming pool and catching them with your hands. Initially it's impossible, but I learned to strategize at a young age. I'd let my friends go at it like banshees; it was a crazy sight to watch as kids would surface with their mouths wide open screaming at the others, barely taking time for a breath, then submerging and continuing the quest. After a few minutes of diving, screaming, splashing and chasing, my friends would tire out and slow their attack; this was my time to pounce. I was a master at trapping the weary prey in the corner of the deep end. Not so much because I was a superior hunter, but because I soon realized if you let your friends tire out themselves, the chlorine in pool would take care of the speedy little blue gill. To this day I still talk to old grade-school friends who bring up those fish-chasing days and speak of it with a kind of giddiness.

It was a great time and place to grow up. If we weren't dodging alligators in the lake, battling sharks in the gulf, or jumping off the roof into the swimming pool to chase fish, we were catching snakes and armadillos in the front yard, or playing with the pet monkey. It really was a tropical paradise.

Decisions

After finishing eight years of Catholic schooling, 1976 meant I'd be attending public high school. I was in ninth grade when Dad died. As 1977 rolled on I began to experience my new life without a father. Since Dad died when I was young, I realize Mom felt that I had been robbed of the Father-Son relationship my brothers enjoyed with Dad, and she may have tried to over compensate a bit. I don't fault her for that; I know she was doing it out of love. She wanted me to experience some of the same things my siblings did, but Dad wasn't around to share them with me. She spoiled me a bit and gave me a lot of freedom, hoping I would enjoy my teen years like my siblings had.

Mom was working in the Phone Center at A.C. Neilsen's and I was beginning to hang out with a crowd who liked to party and push limits. Fortunately in November of 1978, I began dating Kim Ann Dielschneider; a beautiful blonde beach-bum who was sweet, athletic and had a pure heart. Best of all, she liked me...at least a little. Today she admits she didn't fall in love with me immediately, but I eventually wore down her defenses and convinced her I was the guy for her.

We dated, broke up, dated, broke up, etc. But we really were in love and would always run back to each other. We hung out with a group of kids nicknamed the Hoodlums. When some of the guys headed out to do something silly, I would usually pass because I wanted to spend time with Kim. Numerous times I was accused of being "whipped" because I wouldn't run with the guys. But while some of them would head out looking for, and usually finding trouble, I was with Kim, occasionally staying out of it.

I don't want to sound like I'm condemning them and exonerating myself. I too made some bad decisions as a teen, and got into my share of trouble. I, like the most of the Hoodlums was a pretty good kid who periodically made some bad choices. Fortunately the consequences that came with my choices didn't ruin my life…or end it. Having Kim at my side reduced my involvement in stupidity and fostered our decades long relationship. We dated for four years prior to marrying, and as I write this book just celebrated our 29th wedding anniversary. Thirty-three years together and it feels like we just started dating.

A teenaged kid with no father figure, no real responsibility, and time on my hands equals bad juju. I knew some of my decisions were bad, but I rationalized they weren't that bad. And hey, I was a teenager; I was supposed to challenge authority and get into some trouble. That may be a comfortable mantra to proclaim as a teen, but it isn't necessarily an obligation or a smart rationale. I knew deep down these poor decisions conflicted with my sense of right and wrong.

I made it through high school and in 1980 graduated from Dunedin Senior High, then headed off to the University of South Florida in Tampa at the age of seventeen. I didn't really want to be there, but I didn't know exactly where I did want to be…except with Kim. I didn't know what I wanted to do with my life, but my waning maturity and adolescent decision making processes convinced me that higher learning at the University of South Florida was not in my immediate future. By mid 1981 I was back living with Mom and was enrolled in a few classes at St. Petersburg Junior College, and was working local jobs for auto part stores and car lots; I loved being around automobiles.

In the summer of 1982, my brother George hooked me up with a friend of his who was looking for a young energetic salesman to expand a new line of surf wear into the Texas market. George stuck his neck out and recommended me for the job. I had a chance to start my life as an adult, as a salesman in Texas. My territory was the state of Texas…all of it.

Prior to taking the sales job, I had visited the local Air Force recruiter and had completed much of the preparatory procedures to join the Air Force. But after realizing my new sales job was based on a seven percent commission and the company expected a million dollars in sales from me, simple math meant I'd be ending my plans with the military and pursuing a sales career like my dad and brother. I let the recruiter know my plans had changed, and I left him hanging as I headed for the Lone Star State.

I loaded up my Toyota Corolla Lift-back and headed for Houston. Mom convinced Guy to drive out there with me and help me get set up with an apartment. He stayed and helped for a couple days and then headed back to Florida. I spent the next six months traveling all over the state showing the new surf wear, and meeting some of the world's surfing stars and shop owners. Unfortunately my sales drive, coupled with my new freedom and immaturity meant I wasn't long for the sales business. I came back to Florida in August 1982, and Kim and I got engaged. We married four months later in December 1982, and the following month I was fired from my Texas surf wear gig. I crawled back to the recruiter's office and humbly begged for a second chance. I was put on a twenty-for hour notice to be ready, and on March 10, 1983 I received the call, and began my Air Force career.

After Basic Training and Technical School at Lackland Air Force Base (AFB), my first duty station was Minot AFB, North Dakota. Kim and I lived there for three and a half years (1983-1986) and she wasn't thrilled, being a Dunedin beach bum and all. It was cold, flat and far from home. But it provide sweet memories as well, since our first-born, Danielle Nichole (aka DeeDee) was born there in 1984.

In 1986 we were able to PCS (permanent change of station) to Tyndall AFB in Panama City, Florida and were stationed there for eight wonderful years (1986-1994). In April of 1989 we added a second blessing to our growing family; a daughter we named Shelbi after the automotive legend Caroll Shelby. We lived in two different houses while stationed at Tyndall, and both were right on the water. It was nice to be six hours away from family in Dunedin, versus stuck in North Dakota. Our time at Tyndall was wonderful except for a day in March 1991 that nearly took my life.

That memorable day was Saturday March 23rd, and I was washing my car when I received a call from a subordinate's wife asking for a ride to the airport. Her name was Wanda, and she told me she was leaving her husband Rodney and heading back to NY. They had no phone in their apartment, so her call seemed unusual. She didn't sound upset or angry, but her call came out of the blue and I had a funny feeling something was wrong; I just didn't know what it was. After debating a few minutes I decided I should ride over and see if my suspicious uneasiness was justified.

I arrived, knocked on the door, and Wanda yelled "Come in." Rodney was sitting in his recliner with a six-pack of Michelob at his feet, apparently trying to get drunk. As he sat there downing beers, he never looked at me. I could feel serious silent tension in the room, then Wanda blurted out that I needed to get him some help. Rodney calmly said "Go ahead, tell him." Wanda mentioned he couldn't keep his hands to himself. Rodney calmly said "That's one." Then Wanda stated that he never sent her child support when they were separated. Rodney mockingly said "That's two." He took another sip of beer, calmly looked at the wall clock, then glared at Wanda and said, "It's ten till four...you're not getting out of here alive in the next ten minutes." He then blurted he was fed up with her and claimed he could get a gun and "end everything."

At that moment Wanda got up from the couch to pick up their two year old daughter and Rodney leapt from his chair with a meat cleaver in one hand and a 10-inch butcher knife in the other, and aggressively moved towards his wife who was now holding their little girl. Apparently he had stashed the weapons in his recliner so they were ready when he finally got drunk enough to kill her.

I moved between them, pleading with him to drop the weapons and talk to me. He kept telling me to get out of the way, saying he liked me and didn't want to hurt me, but that he was done with her and ready to end things. We all moved to the landing at the base of the stairs and he reached over and locked the front door. I continued to talk and plead with him to drop the weapons, but he kept telling me to get out of the way, then he ordered us up the stairs.

The front door was locked; he was ordering us up the stairs and had mentioned getting a gun. We were trapped, I had no weapons, there was no phone in the apartment and the only place to go was upstairs. It didn't take a genius to realize things were not looking good. Wanda and the baby were both crying and had reached the second floor landing, as I was slowly backing up the stairs pleading with Rod to drop the weapons and think. I was two or three stairs from the top, when he started up towards us brandishing the butcher knife and meat cleaver. I knew I didn't want him to retrieve a gun if it was upstairs, and in an instant decided to use my one advantage of elevation. As he started up the stairs I did a flying drop kick down the stairwell and caught him square in the face. I hit the stairs and my vision went black. Rodney bounced off the front door and was stunned for a moment. As my consciousness returned, he leaned over me and began hacking on me with the butcher knife and meat cleaver. As my vision returned I pushed and kicked at him to stop the attack. There was blood squiring on the walls, and a moment later he stopped hacking. He had fractured my right wrist with the cleaver, sliced my foot, and nearly removed my left thumb with the butcher knife. In an instant he was gone, but I didn't know where he went. I scrambled up the stairs and into the master bedroom with Wanda and the baby. I looked for something to slide in front of the door, but the only piece of furniture in the room was a queen-size waterbed.

My hands were kind of a mess so I lied on the floor pushing on the door with my feet and legs to keep him from entering the room. We were trapped and I was waiting for gunshots to punch through the door. But besides the noise of my heart pounding in my ears, there was silence. It seemed he had fled the apartment and was on the run. I wasn't sure if he was gone or not, but after a few moments of waiting for something to happen, nothing did. So I climbed out the second floor window and found some folks with a phone and called the police.

While the immediate threat was over, Rodney's troubles and decision making worsened. He headed to our office at the base firing range and retrieved his 9mm Beretta duty weapon and loaded magazines totaling one hundred and twenty rounds. When the police stopped him after a high speed pursuit, he jumped out of his car in the middle of the road, took cover behind his vehicle and began firing as fast as he could. He used a technique called tactical reloading, which meant his weapon never ran out of ammo. He continued the rapid-fire assault firing seventy rounds at them from his handgun. The police returned fire but they ran out of handgun ammo. They eventually grabbed their shotgun and skimmed 12-guage #00 Buckshot under his car to bring him down.

I remember the ambulance ride to the hospital at Tyndall AFB. I was wondering where Rodney went and what was going on. While being treated in the emergency room, my boss and my wife came in with the base Special Investigators. The investigators first questions panicked Kim and me when they asked… "Where are your children?" Kim had left the kids at home with some friends, and the investigators told her to call them and to have them get out of the house. A few moments later Kim walked into the room and mouthed the words, "They got him." Our panic and adrenaline subsided and I was being prepped for another ambulance ride. My injuries required some immediate surgery so the Base medical folks sent me to Bay Medical Center in Panama City for some quick repair work. At least I thought it was going to be quick; unfortunately the emergency room was packed to its limits with weekenders from hell. There were shooting victims, a guy who had been hit by a bus, and numerous other victims who made my injuries look a bit less significant. I literally laid on a gurney pushed up against a wall in the hallway for almost six hours while the ER staff treated the other not-so-lucky visitors. Another shooting victim rolled into the chaos…it was Rodney, and as he rolled past me our eyes met for a second or two. I was relieved he was alive, but wasn't quite sure of our new relationship. A few moments later a technician came towards me and I thought I was heading into surgery. Unfortunately he was just replacing my blood-covered sheet with a new clean one, and encouraging me to just be patient. No pun intended.

The weeks of recovery weren't particularly fun for me as both hands were bandaged and several cervical and lumbar discs were damaged. Rodney survived, was convicted of assault, battery and attempted murder and would soon begin his time in the Florida state pen. While my injuries and the experience were not pleasant, things could have been a lot worse. Wanda, the baby, Rodney and I all survived, and our lives headed down one of life's unplanned forks in the road.

As I rehashed the experience in my mind, I wondered what I could have done differently. I also wondered why I decided to ride over there. Nobody asked me to go, it was just a feeling, or intuition, or something that led me over there that day in March. Was it just coincidence or was there a reason? March was gradually becoming my least favorite month.

Chapter 3

The Note

For the next couple of years, life at Tyndall was back to normal. I resumed my teaching career as an Air Force Combat Arms Instructor, providing small arms weapons and marksmanship training to the base populace and maintaining the base's hand-held and shoulder fired weaponry. On Monday March 15, 1993 I came home from work and was involved in the usual routine of playing with the girls and watching television, when I received a phone call that would change my life forever.

My brother Guy was on the line, and after a short, "How you doing?" he got right to the point.

"I received this anonymous letter in the mail today, and I'm just going to read it to you."

His thirty-five word recital echoes in my mind to this day. He began to read…

"I have AIDS. I am dying. I must make my peace with the Lord. I killed your Daddy 15 years ago. He found me in his bedroom. I had no choice. Please pray for me."

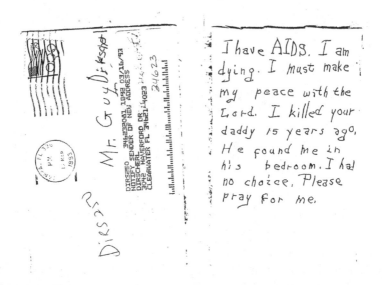

A numbing tingle sparked at the top of my scalp and raced down my body, and the tears began to flow. In a nanosecond my nervous system went haywire, my body began to shiver intensely and my mind jumped into overdrive as he finished reading the last words. This electro-emotional onslaught brought with it sixteen years of grief, pain, anger, and all the emotions I'd experienced and bottled up for the last decade and a half.

It was a strange feeling. I was shocked, and flabbergasted, but not surprised. The overwhelming sensation of "I knew it!" ran through me. My body still tingling, tears still flowing, I felt a strange warmth inside. A warm calmness that I don't think I'd ever experienced before. It's like my being was simultaneously in two completely separate places. One Me was on the phone with my brother, excited, tingling, and nervously pacing the room. The other Me, was pulled to the side and was experiencing a moment of peace, warmth and control. I'd never knowingly experienced an out-of-body experience, or anything I'd call supernatural, but the best way to explain this feeling was that God, or an angel, or perhaps the loving spirit of my father was there surrounding me, passing on that comforting reassurance that he really hadn't killed himself, and that good would somehow prevail. It was as if at that moment, everything in the world was okay; it was a feeling I had been hoping for for years…it was the peaceful feeling of truth and redemption. Two days later I drove home to meet with my family to discuss the obvious...what do we do next?

My mom, brothers and sister all gathered at Mom's house and discussed our options; we knew we had to get this letter to the Dunedin Police Department (DPD). The Chief of Homicide was a gentleman named Rick McBride, and as fate would have it, he was an old high school acquaintance of Guy's. Guy made the call to Chief McBride and explained our situation. The Chief told him he would meet with the family and see what could be done.

We also had an old family friend who worked for the DPD in an administrative role. Her name was Montein and she lived directly across the street from us when we lived on Lotus. Somewhat ironically she had become involved in our family's new mission. I say ironically because a few years prior, her father died in his driveway which was about fifty yards from the spot my dad died. Her dad had been lying on the ground drilling on his vehicle with an electric drill when he was electrocuted. Her father was killed on one corner of East lotus Drive, and here she was helping us solve the murder of our father who died on the opposite corner. We asked her if we could get a copy of the police reports regarding Dad's death, and she told us she could have them printed up; George and I drove to the police station and picked them up as soon as they were available.

A few days later Chief McBride came to the house with a Detective Farrell and picked up the confession letter and envelope, which were now in a zip lock bag. They seemed helpful and told the family they would check out the letter and see what they could come up with. I never had the pleasure of meeting Chief McBride, but the family felt comfortable with him on the case; he was professional and seemed eager to help.

With the confession letter now in the hands of the police, and a copy of the original police reports in front of us, the family was ready to begin the search for what really happened to our patriarch. Mom and her brood sat around the dining room table studying the reports, but as we read the words that were typed and hand-written by the investigators the hours and days following Dad's death, we were dumbfounded. How could we have been so asinine not to request these reports earlier? They were terrible; filled with dozens of inaccuracies, mistruths, assumptions, and poor investigative techniques. We also discovered that 10 to 12 crime scene photos, as well as a page from a report were missing. DPD had all the other crime scene photos from that day, just not the dozen photos of the crime scene at 1111 East Lotus Drive.

Our frustrations and questions began to mount. But at least the case was reopened and the Chief of Homicide was in charge. We were hopeful that something positive was going to happen…why else would this letter arrive? Who was this person bearing their soul and confessing their sin? The search for a killer was on.

I'd like to make a very important point here; one that I hope is gleaned as this book unfolds. It is not my family's or my intention to ridicule, deride, or belittle the Dunedin Police Department. In 1977, small town police departments were not operating at the miraculous investigative levels portrayed on current CSI television shows. They also employed mere humans who were subject to the vast array of flaws possessed by the rest of the race; subjectivism, imperfection, pride, false beliefs, etcetera. Police departments, like any other group of people are small microcosms of society at large. Some police officers are thorough, honest, humble and meticulous. Others are lazy, obstinate, mean-spirited, prideful, and unable to admit fault. Most police officers fall somewhere in the middle of these extremes and are simply good-willed imperfect servants, attempting to protect and serve their community.

I make this point to illustrate we understand mistakes happen. But when these mistakes alter the facts, undermine the evidence and wrongly establish a horrifying murder as an unexplainable suicide, someone needs to be held accountable and the truth needs to be brought forward.

It's human nature and an unfortunate reality that some investigators may not be totally objective when presented a conclusion before the investigation begins. The whole concept of objectivity is tainted, and the arena in which investigators apply their art and science is no longer sterile. Subconscious, if not conscious subjectivity can adversely cloud the facts while trying to prove the expected conclusion. According to the police reports, between 8:15 and 8:41 a.m., all investigators were briefed this was a probable suicide. I contend from this point on the case was subjectively investigated as a suicide and DPD failed to investigate key evidence or seriously consider the possibility homicide was the cause of death.

As we read through and studied the original reports, we discovered police did continue to work the case for several days; however their efforts to corroborate a suicide are clearly reflected in their documentation. They had prematurely determined Dad had killed himself, and whether they admit it or not, it's obvious their predetermined mindsets focused their efforts on closing this case as a suicide.

Understandably they asked friends and neighbors if Dad showed any signs of depression, or pain, or any other indications that he was preparing to kill himself. This type of questioning has its place when investigating a mysterious death. Unfortunately it is also easy to use leading questions and resulting answers to guide a subjective investigation to a predetermined solution.

Most parents use this technique several times during their child rearing days. Moms, you know the technique I'm speaking of. You're walking into the kitchen and pass your young son Billy walking out carrying a cup of juice. As you reach your recently cleaned kitchen you see a large juice puddle on the counter where it had obviously been spilled and left for you to clean up. After re-cleaning the counter, and jumping to the obvious conclusion Billy made a mess, you track down little Billy and begin the leading questions that you know will confirm your suspicions.

"Billy, did you just get some juice?" Billy replies as expected.

"That juice bottle is pretty heavy isn't it?"

"Yes Mommy, it's pretty heavy."

"It's kind of hard to poor too huh?" Billy begins to answer …

"Kind of, but that's why…" you cut him off and are on to your next question. You already know Billy made the mess and you have other things to do, so you finish your "investigation" with one last assumptive statement.

"I've told you before, when you spill something or make a mess you need to clean it up." Satisfied you've gotten the answers you were looking for, you turn to leave the room, already mentally on to a dozen other tasks, and you fail to hear Billy finish his answer…

"But that's why I asked Daddy to pour me the juice."

Facts don't seem to matter when assumptions become your truth.

This was the type of questioning the police used to substantiate their suspicions. They repeatedly asked friends, family, doctors and acquaintances if Dad was depressed. Was he in pain? Were their money or marital problems? Any answers that might be construed as concurring responses were documented. Any answers that were acquitting in nature were ignored, or led to a twist in the questioning until a bit of weak subjective support dribbled out.

When Dad hung out with his salesman friends, they talked about sales. Of course there were discussions and complaints about the travel and deals falling through; that's what sales-buddies talk about. The fact that for the first two months of 1977 Dad had earned three times the national average income was dismissed; that didn't support their finding. Friends who made any mention that he may have been a little depressed at times over the past year, also said there was no way he was depressed enough to kill himself. Unfortunately only the depression was logged in the reports, nothing was recorded about his jovial spirit or love of life.

Police also reported they found a note in the house that simply said "Bruce-will". This bit of evidence found its way into the suicide theory and bolstered their claim. The word "will" on a piece of paper found in the house seemed to imply to investigators Dad was involved with checking, changing, or writing a will because he was planning suicide. In actuality, the note was a reminder Dad had written to himself months prior to remind him to get with the family attorney because there had been changes to Florida law. The family attorney was my Uncle Bruce who had told Dad about the changes and recommended Mom and Dad review their wills. At least two police reports incorrectly stated the note was found in the bedroom where he died. Although the note was actually found in Dad's office, was months old, and Dad had not altered his will since 1969, investigators considered the paper with the word "will" on it another piece of evidence that supported a suicide.

One lead that seemed to steer the investigation was the fact that Dad's physical condition and pain were what caused him to take his own life. This issue became a major tenant of their case and led to their firm belief it was suicide. Dad did live with pain; he'd been dealing with it for years. He had developed arthritic bone spurs and pinched nerves in his cervical vertebrae that caused significant pain in his neck and arm. The vertebrae issue may have been amplified by a childhood fall from a horse and an injury suffered while in the Army.

Dad's spine problems worsened. The pain in his neck increased; impinged nerves were sending pain down his left arm, and he began to lose the strength in his left hand, and he was having problems holding on to a fishing pole. He could deal with the pain and discomfort, but if fishing was going to suffer, something had to be done. His visits to orthopedic surgeons and neurologists culminated in a hopeful neck surgery which took place in early 1975. The surgery included a discectomy and removal of bone spurs which would hopefully free the trapped nerves.

As surgeries go, this one was less than a complete success. The neck and arm pain did not completely go away, and the nerve damage caused his left tricep muscle to atrophy. His left upper arm became noticeably smaller than his right, and he began to lose strength and control of it. I remember him demonstrating how his arm became useless when lifted over his head. He would raise his arm up over his head, but when the tricep was required to maintain its position, his arm would collapse at the elbow, usually landing with a smack on the head. The nerves no longer fired and this tricep muscle was in decay. While this was a frustration at times, he learned to work around it and compensate for the disability.

Dad also wore a neck brace after the surgery. It was required immediately after the operation, but he continued to wear it sporadically when the neck pain flared up, figuring it might help relieve the enflamed nerve. While the pain and neck brace were inconvenient to Dad, to the DPD they were evidence of motive and a persuasive lead in their suicide investigation. There were prejudiced statements in the reports, including one from one of Dad's previous doctors' nurse who knew the surgery didn't help a whole lot. Her opinionated comments are logged in one of the police reports which reads… *"Nurse said there was no question of the man's death being a suicide."* Not only is she not qualified to make that factual determination, but she hadn't seen Dad for nearly two years. This was the type of hearsay and circumstantial evidence that was supporting DPD's suicide case.

Apparently the Investigators were getting the answers they were looking for and the case was closed as a suicide. It was pretty obvious to them the pain and depression Dad was experiencing led him to shoot himself before church that morning. According to DPD, after dressing for church, chatting with a neighbor while skimming love-bugs out of the pool, and recommending to Mom that I be awakened for church, he walked out the front door, then back in to the house, removed a slipper and shot himself in the chest with his favorite shotgun by manipulating the trigger with his big toe or the phone book.

After studying the police reports and looking at the facts, we discovered one major problem. Both of the police theories as to how he supposedly fired the shotgun were physically impossible.

Chapter 4

Crime of the Evidence

"The great enemy of the truth is very often not the lie... deliberate, contrived and dishonest, but the myth... persistent, persuasive, and unrealistic. Belief in myths allows the comfort of opinion without the discomfort of thought." ~ John F. Kennedy

Book'em Dano! Many of you probably remember that memorable order uttered by Jack Lord who played the cool, methodical police detective Steve McGarrett on Hawaii Five-O. The TV show originally ran from 1968 to 1980, and had millions of viewers waiting to hear the famous line of conviction. McGarrett's catchphrase still permeates the airwaves as a newer version of the show returned to primetime television in 2010. McGarrett's famous tagline was the contracted closure that brought the whole story to an explainable, tidy ending. It implied the gumshoes had collected the evidence, weighed the facts, and proven they had the criminal responsible for the crime. Amazingly the investigation was completed, culpability was determined, and the case was closed by the end of the sixty minute show. Steve McGarrett would turn to his trusted sidekick played by actor James MacArthur, and utter the famous line that would seal the deal…"Book'em Dano…Murder One."

Apparently in Dunedin in 1977, sixty minutes was also more than enough time to investigate a crime scene and determine a cause, motive and manner of a suspicious death. Perhaps it was because on the morning of March 13th DPD had already responded to another apparent suicide crime scene in the small town. Maybe it was their initial observation of my father's removed slipper and a shotgun lying on the bed that led them to a hasty judgment. Or, perhaps, just perhaps, the final paragraph of Patrolman James Allen MacKenzie's hand written report best sums up the suicide conclusion. It reads...

"In supposition of events, Mr. Dirscherl probably used the gun case to wrap the receiver area of the shotgun to muffle the sound of the shot and used either his left toe (and foot) or the telephone book to activate the trigger. Barrel length 30"and arm reach 26". The weapon was his favorite and his father also took his own life many years ago."

Patrolman MacKenzie's report was written just hours after the deadly shot was fired. The crime scene had been explored, photos had been taken, family and friends had been questioned, and theories were being etched on paper. Unfortunately some of the important words and presumptions being recorded were statements that mixed fact with supposition and physical impossibilities. This type of report writing tends to blur the lines between reality and fiction, and as we will see, can lead to an innocent man's condemnation...and to a murderer walking free.

The only truths in MacKenzie's last paragraph are: The gun was his favorite, and that of the barrel and arm length. DPD eventually realized it was impossible for him to use the phone book since Mom got it out to call the police after she found him. (This was before 911 was activated.) They also agree the wound and trajectory could not have been caused by triggering the weapon with his toe. Their hurried hypotheses created serious problems with their case that to this day have not been explained.

As my family and I methodically studied the recently procured twenty-five pages of police and medical examiner reports, we began to see how this investigation immediately forked down the path of suicide investigation. The police assumed they had it right, and subjectively convinced themselves and others Dad shot himself. Unfortunately for us the case would be closed as a suicide, and some family and friends were being coerced to believe it. The suicide ball was rolling and the experts were agreeing. The Medical Examiner's (ME) findings supported the police reports and the police were claiming the wound was self inflicted. But there was one little problem with their theory of how the wound was inflicted...that pesky physical impossibility issue.

So while the police reports were official records of the supposed events that took place in a Dunedin bedroom on a spring Sunday morning, they were full of erroneous and incorrect information that led to the official closure of suicide. In essence, Bob Dirscherl was inaccurately accused of killing someone; that someone was Bob Dirscherl. A Scandalous accusation was launched from misread evidence, an inadequate investigation and what many consider negligent behavior.

While most investigators solve cases based on the "evidence of the crime", we were struggling to overturn a case running in reverse; an investigation which began with a conclusion and worked its way backwards...as President Kennedy so eloquently stated...through the myth, persistent, persuasive, and unrealistic. We were in essence challenging a solution and a legacy based on that persistent, persuasive and unrealistic myth which had distorted reality, and morphed into a new and challenging paradox...the "crime of the evidence."

Police Reports

In order for you to understand the investigator's mindsets and reasoning, you need to read the observations and reports provided by the responding police officers and the Medical Examiner. Their observations and reports provide what is supposed to be an objective view of facts and details gathered at the scene of a suspicious death. After the puzzle pieces are gathered, science, natural laws, training, expertise and common sense are supposed to be applied to the evidence, eventually resulting in a fact-based conclusion. Unfortunately it appears the on-scene investigators rushed through the process and allowed their first impressions and assumptions to define the situation. Their rushed suicide conclusion was provided to the Medical Examiner, who is ultimately and legally responsible for endorsing the victim's death certificate.

As one reads through the reports, it appears police very quickly jumped to conclusions and failed to properly gather and weigh evidence, failed to properly process the crime scene and failed to test their predictions before stating an opinion...an opinion that would seal a man's fate and generate a tainted legacy that would endure for decades.

The place to begin is the first report provided by then Patrolman, James Allen MacKenzie. His report captures much of the investigators' mindsets, and set the investigation on its fateful path to infamy. The following transcription of MacKenzie's report narrative is replicated as accurately as possible. I'm not trying to be picayune about grammatical errors or his writing skills; I just want you to see the observations as recorded by the on-scene officers so you can weigh the evidence, and perhaps see as we did, how this case was investigated as a suicide. Again, my family and I are not out to persecute or belittle the DPD investigators. We just want this case solved on factual evidence and truth, instead of supposition and impossible methods.

(Report Abbreviation Legend: I/O = Investigating Officer, PRI = Person Reporting Incident, W/M = White Male, PTL = Patrolman, Det = Detective, D.F.D = Dunedin Fire Department, M.E. = Medical Examiner, N.F.A.T.= Nothing Further At This Time).

Keep in mind this report was completed just hours after the shot rang out. MacKenzie's report narrative reads as follows:

"R/e of a Gunshot wound at 1111 East Lotus Drive and that C&R and Fire Rescue were responding. I/O and Sgt. Hollis responded and were the first unit on the scene with Sgt. Hollis preceding I/O into the house where PRI pointed to where the victim was to be found. I/O observed a W/M laying on his back with his head facing South, feet facing North (see supplemental diagram). The W/M, Robert Dirschel, The Victim had on Blue Double Knit Pants, White Knit Shirt (Blood Covered) and One Bedroom Slipper (The other was south of the Bed which headed East). A Phone Book (Clearwater) was on the South East corner of the bed. On the bed was a 12 GA Shot Gun Double Barrel Over and Under (Mauser Bauer) with a Tan Gun Case entwined over and under the weapon.

PTL Wilber responded to assist and PTL Lawrence Provided Scene Security. Det. Sgt Shields and Det Robert Ayers Responded To Process The Scene. Fireman W. Hartley, D.F.D was the first Paramedic on the Scene And Checked For Vital Signs And Cut The Knit shirt open to see The Nature of The Wound. When he Saw A 30mm X 40mm Oval Entrance Wound over The Heart he ceased checking And the Scene was Not Disturbed Any Further. The M.E. Was Notified And Dr. Shinner Advised that he could Not Respond But had Coleman Services Transport And I/O Gave a synopsis TO The M.E's office.

The Victim Underwent Surgery To his Upper spine About Three Years Ago. This was necessitated by General Arthritic Degeneration.

The Surgery was Not Very Successful and The victim was and had experienced ever increasing pain Associated with his Neck and Spine. Also he was experiencing Numbness in his Right Hand and Left Hand, Arm and shoulder. He Drove as A salesman in his work And had To Wear A Neck brace which was painful and Uncomfortable. He was also very upset at not being as active as he had been in The Past. The Victim was also having a "bad" or "Poorer" Year in sales with his company Compared with his Past records. The Above Info Gained with Talking To DR. James Norton, DR. Arthur Smith, Ted Staramowicz (1125 E. Lotus, 733-XXXX, Next Door Neighbor for 13 years And Also A Salesman)

At The Time of the Shot, The Son Danny was Asleep in his Bedroom And The Wife Virginia was in The small Bathroom off of the Kitchen. She Thought a Door slammed Loudly, (Not A shot). She Left the Bathroom and was Reading The Paper for 10 To 15 minutes And reentered the Bedroom to get Dressed for Church And Found Him, Screamed And That Awakened Danny. Mrs. Dirschel Then Called At 0806 Hours. He had Dressed for Church And They All were Going out To Breakfast And Then to a Bowling Tournament. This Morning upon Getting Dressed he left the House, Walked To The Front Yard, Looked North Towards 1155 E. Lotus The Residence of Lucky Roberts, Reentered The House And shortly Thereafter shot himself.

Mr. Roberts was interviewed by Det. Ayers & I/O and he stated that he & Mrs. Roberts were having family troubles And Mr. Roberts had While Walking his Dog, stopped by The Dirschel House Last Evening And had Stepped inside momentarily And Mr. Roberts And Mrs. Dirschel And Then had A short Conversation on the front Lawn. Mr. Roberts stated That He & Mr. Dirschel had been close And That Mr. Dirschel was depressed About his position with the Company but not enough To Kill himself over.

Sgt. Hollis Located A Note Pad with The Note "Bruce-Will in it. I/O discovered that Bruce is An Attorney Bruce A. Beihl, in Bradenton, Fl. I/O Called Him And he Advised That No New will was drawn up but That A 10 year old will on was on file At his office.

The Victim Was Rolled over by Coleman And No Exit Wound was evident And Also The Property from The Victims's Pockets was Removed And Given TO George Dirschel (Son), See Supplemental Report, And PTL Wilber & Det Ayers handled the Property/Evidence Reference The Weapon.

In Supposition of Events, Mr. Dirschel Probably used the gun case to wrap the Receiver Area of the Shotgun to muffle the Sound of The Shot and used either his Left Toe (And foot) or The Telephone Book to Activate The Trigger. Barrel Length 30" And Arm Reach 26". The Weapon was his favorite And His father Also Took his own Life Many Years Ago. N.F.A.T."

Although the evidence and the crime scene implied a suspicious and unexpected death took place in this room hours previously. This report seems to wrap up the case leaving no doubt what happened. The report includes an alleged motive, ability and supporting evidence that Dad shot himself. MacKenzie makes his beliefs very clear when he states, *"This Morning upon Getting Dressed he left the House, Walked To The Front Yard, Looked North Towards 1155 E. Lotus The Residence of Lucky Roberts, Reentered The House And shortly Thereafter shot himself."* Unfortunately those beliefs are unsubstantiated. Was there a witness to this act, or was it more speculation? Was there empirical evidence, or was this a theory based on supposition? It all initially sounded quite convincing, but was it true? When investigating a crime scene like this, all the evidence is important and it should be recorded and reported, not just the bits that support a personal belief. As you'll see, truth and belief are not always the same thing.

This report states Patrolman MacKenzie and a Sgt Hollis were the initial police on the scene. Sgt Hollis entered the house first, and apparently they both headed directly to the bedroom, as there is no mention in the report of initially securing the scene, searching for a possible intruder, or checking other points of entry/exit. Apparently MacKenzie's report is the first police report generated, and what it fails to mention in physical evidence gathering and detail observation, it more than makes up for with guesswork, assumption and theorization. Instead of documenting crime scene observations such as blood evidence and unlocked doors and windows, PTL MacKenzie initiates a suicide premise, determines the victim's mental and emotional condition and wraps up the investigation with a self-inflicted wound theory that would pan out to be a physical impossibility.

MacKenzie's report states they entered the bedroom and observed Dad lying on the floor and his shotgun lying on the bed. He notes the position of the body, what Dad was wearing, and that one of his slippers was south of the bed. MacKenzie also reports there was a 12-gauge over and under shotgun on the bed with a tan gun case *"entwined over and under the weapon."*

Patrolman Wilber arrives later and captures the scene in his first rough sketch shown below.

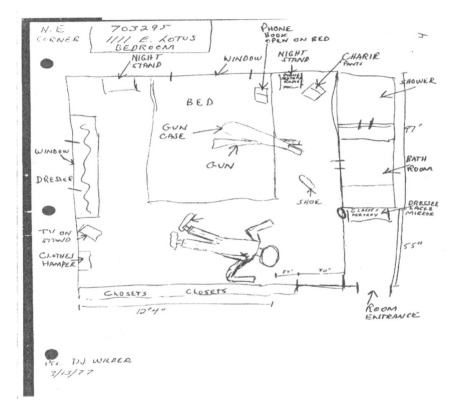

Wilber's second, neater sketch on the next page also shows the scene and the gun and case. Note both sketches show the gun lying partially off the bed, pointing south with the gun case lying on top of the gun, not *"entwined over and under the weapon"* as described by MacKenzie.

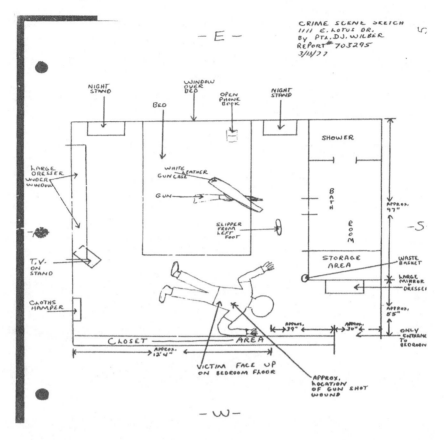

While the contrasting gun case positions may seem insignificant to some, it's an important point revealing inaccuracies and errors were beginning. Normally this error in recording physical evidence could play a major role in the investigation; details like these are critical. In our case, it really doesn't matter if they stated the case was entwined over and under, or if they sketched the case on top of the gun. I was the second person in the room after Dad was shot and I distinctly remember the gun lying in the middle of the bed, muzzle pointing east towards the head of the bed. This was one of those camera snap-shot memories I spoke of earlier. I don't recall the position of the gun case, but prior to Police arrival the shotgun was definitely not where Wilber's sketch shows it; lying off the side of the bed pointing south.

If I were a betting man, I'd bet the gun wound up there after an officer unloaded and cleared it. Perhaps one of them used the gun case to handle the weapon during clearing so they wouldn't transfer their own finger prints to the gun. I can't prove any of that, so it's simply a bit of circumstantial evidence showing the report and sketches are not compatible or accurate. Officer's possible concerns about transferring fingerprints to the gun were moot anyway, as apparently, according to their reports, they never fingerprinted the gun, the house, or the bedroom. Only Dad's hands were fingerprinted and bagged.

So we have a dead man on the floor with a shotgun wound to the chest. A slipper off one foot, a phonebook lying on the bed, and no obvious signs of forced entry into the house. Within minutes the suicide theory was building steam.

After finishing their crime scene investigation, the police interviewed neighbors, family, and a few friends. While nobody understood why Dad would have just walked into the house and killed himself, the Police's leading questions seemed to imply there was no doubt about what happened.

The questions about Dad having pain, or not being his old self led to assumptions and answers that helped support their case. In their minds they had it all figured out; it was definitely suicide.

There is no doubt MacKenzie was convinced the wound was self-inflicted. His police report appears to be the initial report, as three other officers prepared supplementary reports. Unfortunately this initial report which is supposed to be an objective record of facts and observations concludes with his unproven subjective belief and assumption that Dad had simply walked into the house, and by using a phone book or his toe, shot himself in the chest with his favorite shotgun.

Also note that the Medical Examiner who is supposed to respond to the scene of a suspicious death was unable to make it to this scene. This prospective independent observer wasn't able to examine the scene or observe facts and details that may aid in the investigation and help arrive at the truth. Instead, the police provided a synopsis to the ME's office about what they observed and assumed. We'll never know what that synopsis was for sure, but it most likely was based on the impossible toe or phonebook method.

So the ME is about to launch her autopsy based on flawed information supporting a self-inflicted wound. It seems the level playing field one would hope for in this situation may be tipping a bit…and not in our favor.

The next major piece of evidence in this death investigation is that of the fatal wound. Surely the wound would tell the tale of how the gun was held to Dad's chest and how the deadly shot was fired. We know the police weren't sure, as they stated he used either the phonebook or his big toe. And they didn't really say where dad was in the room when he fired the shot. Neither MacKenzie's nor Wilber's reports say anything about the blood spatter evidence at the scene.

Blood evidence can tell a lot about how a wound was inflicted. Unfortunately there is a huge amount of blood evidence we will never get the chance to investigate because the ten to twelve photos taken by Detective Ayers were lost or destroyed...they're simple gone. So we can't go back and look at where the blood droplets wound up, or how they landed on the bed, or the floor, or other places. We can't see the blood evidence showing direction of travel that must lead from the south side of the bed where Dad apparently was shot, to his final resting spot around the corner of the bed to the west side of the room...which brings to mind another interesting question.

If Dad shot himself on the south side of the bed, and manipulated the trigger with his toe, how was he positioned when he fired the shot? The initial police theory shared with us was that he may have leaned against the foot of the bed near the west side of the room where he was found, put the muzzle against his chest and fired the shot with his toe. When you see the description of the wound and the path of the bird shot through his body, you soon realize this positioning is physically impossible.

When questioned, the police stated they weren't sure if that was the method used. It kind of caused a problem when trying to explain the blood spatter on the south side of the bed. This quandary perpetuated the second theory that he probably used the phone book to push the trigger to the rear while standing at the south side of the bed.

There's one critical issue with that scenario that nullifies the theory. Since Mom removed the phone book from the dresser to call police before 911 service was available, Dad would have had to shoot himself in the chest by triggering the gun with the book, placed it back in the dresser, shut the drawer, then walked around to the foot of the bed, fallen down and died. I'm no investigative genius, but I think this chain of events is also highly improbable.

The mention of blood spatter on the bed sheets in other reports seems to indicate he was shot near the south side of the bed near the bathroom, most likely standing since blood was on top of a bed that was 32 inches high. If somehow he were able to stand at the south side of the bed and used his toe, did he then put his foot back on the ground and walk around the bed to the west side of the room to fall and die? Take a look at the sketch and understand the blood spatter was on the bed somewhere in the vicinity where the gun is lying. Since there are no photos and the written descriptions are not specific, we can only assume this is where the blood spatter is located. However the shot was fired, after the wound was inflicted he walked at least six to eight steps around the corner of the bed before falling to the floor.

Why would he shoot himself in chest near the bathroom on the south side of the room, then walk around the bed? I know there is no way to prove my thoughts here…but if I had decided I were going to shoot myself and was ready to die, I think once the trigger was pulled, and a near instantaneous fatal wound was inflicted, I don't think I'd walk around the room. Wouldn't a person ready to die fire the shot, then die where they lay, or stood, or kneeled, or hunched, or however they say Dad did this? It just doesn't make sense. That unanswerable question aside, we still have a gunshot wound supposedly self-inflicted, but the supposed methods are physically impossible.

This next report was written by Patrolman Donald J. Wilber, who was apparently the third officer to arrive at the scene. He was also the officer who prepared two sketches of the crime scene; the first a quick hand-drawn sketch, and a second neater sketch using a straight edge and measurements. The sketches are good quality and apparently capture what PTL Wilber observed. His hand written report is printed in capital block letters and reads as follows:

"UPON ARRIVAL AT 1111 E. LOTUS DR. WRITER WAS ADVISED BY SGT HOLLIS TO ASSIST PTL. MACKENZIE IN WHAT APPEARED TO BE A SUICIDE BY A SELF INFLICTED GUN SHOT WOUND. UPON ENTERING THE BEDROOM ON THE NORTH EAST CORNER OF THE HOME WRITER OBSERVED A WHITE MALE SUBJECT APPROX. AGE 45 TO 50 YEARS OF AGE LYING ON THE FLOOR AT THE FOOT OF A KING SIZED BED. WRITER OBSERVED WHAT APPEARED TO BE A 1" TO 1.5"

HOLE IN THE VICTIMS LEFT CHEST. SUBJECT (VICTIM) WAS DRESSED IN A WHITE KNIT SHIRT, DARK BLUE PANTS, DARK SOCKS AND A BROWN HOUSE SLIPPER ON HIS RIGHT FOOT. WRITER OBSERVED THE LEFT SLIPPER TO THE RIGHT SIDE OF THE BODY APPROX. 4' TO 5' FOOT AWAY AND ON THE SOUTH SIDE OF THE BED. OBSERVED ON THE BED WAS AN OPEN PHONE BOOK, SOUTH EAST CORNER OF BED, AN OVER AND UNDER SHOTGUN WITH A WHITE LEATHER GUN CASE LYING ACROSS IT. BARREL OF THE GUN WAS POINTING SOUTH AND EXITED FROM THE BED. WRITER THEN SECURED THE IMMEDIATE SCENE UNTIL THE ARRIVAL OF DET. SGT SHIELDS AND DET. AYERS. I.O. THEN ASSISTED PTL. AYERS IN GATHERING EVIDENCE AND TAKING PHOTOGRAPHS OF THE SCENE. UPON RECEIVING WORD THAT THE MEDICAL EXAMINERS OFFICE WOULD NOT BE SENDING ANYONE WRITER WAS REQUESTED BY SGT HOLLIS TO TAKE THE VICTIMS FINGER PRINTS.

Wilber's one-page report ends unexpectedly, and below the last word is the written instruction (*over*) implying there was a back page, but there isn't. Apparently when DPD copied the report to microfiche, they failed to copy the back page, or this is where Wilber drew his sketch...we simply don't know for sure. So Wilber's narrative ends here. His neatly drawn sketches show a birds-eye snapshot of the scene. They show an open phone book lying near the head of the bed, and Dad's left slipper on the floor between the bed and the bathroom entrance. They also reveal the position of the shotgun lying on the bed with the gun case draped across it. Also notice Dad's final resting place near the west wall of the room.

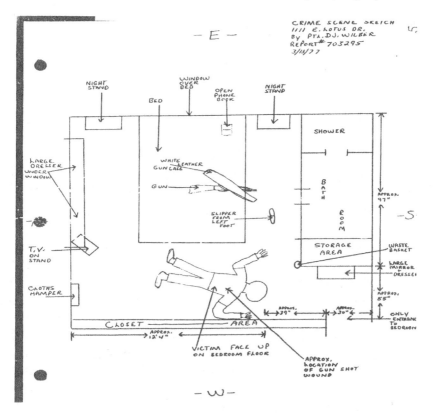

Shortly before heading into the bedroom Dad had asked mom for some medicine for his athlete's foot. Could he have removed his slipper and been treating his foot in the bathroom or at the edge of the bed when he realized there was an intruder in the bedroom? It seems to be a credible possibility.

Also note Wilber stated upon his arrival he observed the gun case lying across the weapon as indicated by his sketches. But MacKenzie stated the case was entwined *"over and under the weapon"*, and even suggests Dad *"probably used the gun case to wrap the receiver area of the shotgun to muffle the sound of the shot"*, but doesn't state that he or Hollis handled the weapon. So why was the gun case sketched by Wilber lying on top of the weapon if MacKenzie supposedly observed it wrapped around the gun? The facts aren't adding up.

As my family and I sat around Mom's dining room table going through the police reports for the first time, we were a bit confused when we reached the next report completed by Detective Robert Ayers. As we simultaneously began reading through the report, we realized one page didn't match the copy being read aloud by my sister. The report she was reviewing looked the same...both were Supplementary Reports, both were typed instead of hand-written, the title information in the heading and identification blocks at the top of the forms were identical, and both reports were approved with the hand-written initials GLS (Gary L. Shields). As we glanced at the reports, the pages looked nearly identical, until we began simultaneously reading the body of the reports. While our initial thought was that we made too many copies of the same report, we soon realized we were trying to compare two similar looking, but different reports.

I'm not certain why there are two very similar reports from the same detective. It's not as if one page is a continuation of the other. It appears as if one report was completed, then the second report was generated to add certain details and alter or remove other details. I'm not implying anything fishy took place here. It may simply be Detective Ayers wanted to improve his first report with a more accurate product. However we aren't really sure which report came first and which one is the rewrite. It's kind of confusing, but the information added and deleted provides a bit more insight as to the mindset of the officers. If my guess is correct, the report I believe Ayers wrote first describes his initial observations and explains his approach to the investigation.

This report begins with the opening sentence... " *I was called at approximately 8:15 a.m. on this date 3/13/77 to 1111 E. Lotus Dr. Upon arrival I met Sgt. Shields who advised me of the events and that the owner had apparently shot himself with a double-barreled shotgun and was lying in the Northeast bedroom.*" This honest documentation is probably the opening sentence of Ayers' initial report and reveals Det. Sgt Shields' belief this was a suicide from the get-go.

The other report from Ayers, the one that was probably the rewrite, begins a bit differently, and reveals a more objective narrative. He removes the subjective statement of an apparent suicide and documents a more detailed account. Its opening sentence reads... "*On this date, 13 March '77 at approximately 8:15 a.m., I was called at my residence by the Clearwater Dispatcher and advised of a suicide or possible homicide at the residence of Robert Dirscherl, 1111 E. Lotus Drive, Dunedin.*"

The following is a verbatim copy of the two reports provided by Ayers. Again, I'm not trying to boorishly criticize the report writer; I'm just sharing all the information available, which I think shows some interesting insight to the minds of those tasked with observing and reporting. The following is the verbiage from Detective Ayers' first report. Spelling and punctuation are replicated as he typed it:

"I was called at approximately 8:15 a.m. on this date 3/13/77 to 1111 E. Lotus Dr. Upon arrival I met Sgt. Shields who advised me of the events and that the owner had apparently shot himself with a double barreled shotgun and was lying in the Northeast bedroom. Approximately 12 photos were taken by myself of the entire bedroom at different locations. The body was removed from the residence at approximately 9:45 a.m. on this date. At this time, approximately 9:52, a search was made of the entire bedroom by Ptl. Wilber. The personal effects were removed from the body by the M.E.'s office. There was an undetermined amount of small change in the right front pocket which equaled $2.62. From the left front pocket there were credit cards and a five and one dollar bills. From the right rear pocket, the wallet was removed and $152.00. All of this will be turned over to the family by myself and Ptl. Wilber at this time. In the room at this time after checking it, the bed covers had been pulled back to show approximately 12 to 14 spots of blood also some were found on the top of the bed covers. The largest amount of blood was found next to the West wall approximately 13 inches from the bed. The green throw rug the deceased was lying on the time were found large splatterings of blood and large drops from the south side of the bed which went to the West where the body was located. The body was located approximately two feet from the end of the bed which runs in an East-West direction. The shotgun which was unloaded by Sgt. Shields and Ptl. Wilber, also a phone book that was lying on the bed will be taken to the station for processing. As the body was checked by the personnel of the Medical Examiner's office, it was shown there was no exit wound from the front to rear. At approximately 12:15 on this date, Ptl. MacKenzie and myself left the residence at 1111 North E. Lotus Dr. and preceded to 1155 E. Lotus Dr. to interview Mr. Roberts."

The next narrative was also typed by Detective Ayers, and is titled exactly the same way; same report number, same headings, and also states it is an original report. It appears to be a rewrite of the previous report with some changes to the details, and perhaps is an honest attempt to produce a better quality report. But which report is most accurate?

"On this date, 13, March, '77 at approximately 8:15 a.m., I was called at my residence by the Clearwater Dispatcher and advised of a suicide or possible homicide at the address of Robert Dirschel, 1111 E. Lotus Drive, Dunedin. I came to the Det. Unit Annex on Main St., picked up an unmarked unit and proceeded to this address where I was met by Det. Shields and Sgt Hollis and advised by both of them to take photos of the room and also of the victim Mr. Dirschel. Mr. Dirschel was lying in the Northeast bedroom. He was lying in a North to South position, his head being to the South and his feet to the North. He was lying approximately three feet from the bed and he was on his back, face up. There was a very large wound hole approximately one inch in diameter over the left breast heart area. On the bed there was a double barrel over and under shotgun. There was a few drops of splattered blood on the bed sheet and top cover. There was a large amount of blood on the South side of the bed. The bed was in a East, West direction with the head of the bed on the east side of the bedroom. The larger amount of blood being approximately two feet out from the bed. The other splatters of blood were trailing to the body. Ten pictures were taken by me of the room showing the bed, shotgun, body, etc. There was a telephone book with the top cover open lying at the head of the bed which was confiscated as information and brought to the Det. Unit to be processed. Prints were lifted by Ptl. Wilber and myself of the body and we also requested a copy of the victim's prints from the medical Examiner's office. They were called in and removed the body for a complete examination of the body. Ptl. MacKenzie and myself proceeded to 1155 Lotus Dr. E. where we interviewed Mr. Robert's."

This report provides the most details about the crime scene. When coupled with Wilber's sketch, it provides the best overview of evidence we have. Since the ten to twelve photos of the scene were lost by DPD, we have no way of interpreting blood spatter on the bed, blankets, floor, walls, or elsewhere. Unfortunately without these photos we are forced to rely on this report to glean what the evidence revealed. According to this report, Det. Ayers took the photos, Sgt Shields cleared the shotgun and assisted Patrolman Wilber with lifting finger prints from the body...the gun was not finger printed, nor was the house. Well, that's not completely true...the house was finger printed about 17 years later; but that's information for another chapter.

While it may take a reread of Ayers' two reports, there are some interesting and conflicting details. In his first report Ayers writes he took approximately twelve photos of the scene. In the second report he states he took ten photos. Not a big difference or big deal...and it really doesn't matter because all of the photos were lost by DPD and are no longer available.

Ayers also states in his first report, "*...approximately 12 to 14 spots of blood also some were found on the top of bed covers.*" But in his second report he states "*...there was a few drops of blood on the bed sheet and top cover.*" Since Ayers is the only officer to discuss blood evidence, one would hope it would be accurate. Was it a few drops, or a dozen or more?

Ayers also writes in the first report "*...The largest amount of blood was found next to the West wall approximately 13 inches from the bed.*" But in his second report he states "*...the larger amount of blood being approximately two feet out from the bed.*" Those distance inconsistencies are quite significant; nearly doubling the measurement/distance of the blood's location.

As a third example of conflict, Ayers' states in the first report, "*The body was located approximately two feet from the end of the bed.*" Then in his second report states, "*He was lying approximately three feet from the bed.*"

These measurement conflicts are just one more example of the sloppiness involved in the investigation and report writing. These detail ambiguities make it difficult to determine what really happened in that bedroom.

The next officer to file a report was Detective Sergeant Gary L. Shields whose report was also completed on 13, March '77. His report reads...

"*On 13, March, '77 at 8:25 a.m., I received a phone call at my home advising me of a possible suspicious homicide at 1111 E. Lotus Drive. I arrived at the scene at approximately 8:41 a.m. Det. Ayers and myself assisted Hollis and Ptl. MacKenzie in conducting an investigation to what we believed at this time to be a suicide. The victim, Robert Dirschel apparently placed a 12-gauge Mauser-Bauer over and under shotgun to his chest and by some means triggered the device to shoot himself. He was found lying in the Northeast bedroom of the house on his back with a gunshot wound thru the chest area. (See the crime scene drawing for details). While at the scene, I assisted in photographing the scene, collecting evidence, unloading the weapon and transporting these items with Ptl. Wilber to the police annex building where they will be processed on 14, March, '77 by Technician Smith. Also, while at the residence, I talked to George Dirschel the deceased's son. He stated to me that his father had been having problems with his neck and back. He has a medical history of back problems and he was in quite a bit of pain. He also stated that he had been depressed over the last month or so. Also while at the scene, I talked to Dr. Smith, a pediatrician at Mease Hospital, a friend of the family who advised that Robert Dirschel had been having more than an unusual amount of pain in his neck, numbness of his arm and great pain. This all goes back to the operation he had on his neck about two years ago and he had an arthritic condition in his spinal column. He also stated to me that Robert Dirschel had been in a depressed state over the physical discomfort he had been thru and also the fact that business over the last year was not up to par as it had been in the past years. Det Ayers while at the scene photographed the area before the body was moved and also after the body was removed. At this time the investigation will continue until there is further information to report.*

INVESTIGATION CONTINUING"

The next report was typed and completed by Detective Glenn R. Carlson. According to its headings it is a Supplementary Report written on 16 Mar 77, based on an investigation completed the prior day, 15 Mar 77.

"On the date indicated IO and Detective Sgt Gary Shields went to the Dirschel residence for the purposes of an interview with regards to the above captioned matter. The interview was conducted in the presence of Bruce Biehl, attorney for the family and was tape recorded by his assistant. An understanding was arrived at prior to

the interview that a transcription of the conversation would be provided to this agency. Writer and Sgt Shields ascertained the following information: Bob Dirschel Sr. spent a normal day an 12 Mar 77 working in the yard and according to his wife did not appear to be upset, abnormal acting in any way. He is said to have spent the bulk of the day working in the yard. He was supposed to go to the five o'clock mass Saturday but mistakenly put contact lens fluid in his eyes rather than the rinse he normally used, this caused a headache and he arranged for a substitute lector at the church. The night is said to have gone normally with the victim awakening shortly after 0730 hours. Just prior to the shot Dirsherl is said to have asked his wife for iodine. The reason for this request is undetermined, a check was made by the office of the medical examiner for marks of iodine on the body to no avail. Bob Dirschel Jr. said that he called Moss funeral home and requested a check of the body and they replied that there was what appeared to be a discoloration on the left foot. Whether this is iodine or a mark left by the severe recoil of the weapon is undetermined. We further learned that there was no reported domestic difficulties and no financial strain. The gun was kept unloaded and the ammo was normally kept in a separate room. There was ammo in the room where the incident occurred, but it was of a different size. He is said to have attended church dressed similar to what he was found in and further that he planned to attend church at the nine o'clock mass on the morning of the thirteenth. It is further stated that the victim customary church offering was placed on a table preparatory to attending church. The family further states that he had planned to change his will due to several statutory changes and that was the significance of the note found in the bedroom by initial investigators. The Bruce is a reference to the family attorney. This note is alleged to have been written several months prior to the shooting. IO has informed Alice Sharpe of the Medical Examiners office of the above interview. Writer points out that we were told by Attorney Bruce Biehl that they would contest a finding of suicide by the medical examiner's office and the basic reason for doing so was an insurance policy that would have the proceeds diminished by a finding of suicide. Continuing"

We also received copies of property reports that show what evidence was removed from the house by DPD. The gun, the gun case, the phone book, the ammunition, the "will" note pad, and the personal effects Dad had in his pockets, etc. There was also a report showing they sent the gun to gunsmith Jack Koley, to see if there might be some mechanical problem with the shotgun. At least DPD had the weapon inspected to see if there was a possibility it may have accidentally discharged, which might indicate an intentional suicide was not the cause of death. Koley's inspection and report revealed no such defect.

The next report was initiated and typed by Det. Carlson which states the investigation took place on 14 Mar 77, and the report completed on 17 Mar 77. Det. Carlson writes:

"IO reports that IO have conferred with Mr. David Jordan of the Office of the Medical Examiner in reference to the above captioned matter. He stated it would be the preliminary finding of his office that the death of the above captioned subject is due to suicide, by self inflicted gunshot wound. IO reviewed the entire case with him and advised him of steps that IO would take to bring the whole matter to light. These include interviews with the family, the attorney and test of the weapon.

Continuing"

Unfortunately, Detective Carlson's steps to bring the "whole matter to light" were still based on a flawed investigation, incorrect assumptions and impossible theories.

Since we received copies of police reports and the autopsy report in 1993, Dad's death had become a descriptive gaggle of words on old blurry Xerox copies. Some of those words formed pictures that were accurate, while other words and descriptions describe theories and beliefs that paint a false portrait of Bob Dirscherl. The problem is, whether accurate and true or not, those pictures are stuck in many people's minds. They have become the so-called "truth" to them. The words, ideas and descriptions in the police reports provided some misleading information that supported the supposed suicide. The police reports don't reveal that they ever considered a second person being in the room firing the fatal shot…but they must have. Mom and I were home. We had to at least be considered suspects until eliminated. Once they eliminated us as suspects, it seems the idea that another person could have committed the crime is not even considered.

The portrait they were painting was based on flaws, yet a portrait was emerging none the less. The police investigation was closing; the suicide theory was hatched and was convincing some in the community. Perhaps the autopsy and the Medical Examiner would shed some light on the truth and provide some information to make this nightmare end.

The Medical Examiner (ME) tasked with conducting autopsies for this part of Florida was attached to the Sixth Judicial District. The Chief Medical examiner is appointed by the Governor, and as we discovered, has an enormous amount of power when it comes to death certificates.

The following is the current mission statement of the District Six ME's office copied directly from their homepage:

Mission Statement:

"The mission of the Medical Examiner's office is to fulfill the needs outlined in F.S. 406, to be of service to families of the deceased, and local government agencies. In short, our mission is to determine the cause and manner of death under certain circumstances. This mission requires the utmost objectivity irrespective of personal beliefs or emotional attachment to the circumstances of any particular case."

Dad's autopsy was conducted by Pathologist Dr. Joan Wood. She's the expert responsible for determining the cause and manner of death based on her observations and the input provided by law enforcement. As you read the following information, please keep in mind I'm not trying to discourteously chide, or berate her. I'm simply trying to demonstrate there were some problems that affected the outcome of our case. The painful truth at times is necessary.

The ME office is staffed by a Chief ME, Deputy ME, and several Associate MEs. When it comes to the final status concerning cause and manner of death...the Chief ME is the end-all authority. While many MEs are very talented, competent and honest people, they are, simply stated, people... fallible, imperfect people. Unfortunately, due to their power and position in the state's legal chain, once their decision and assertions are made, there is not much a family can do to challenge their pronouncement. There is the opportunity to question their findings and request they overturn a suicide, but in our case we found this to be the ultimate catch-22. The ME is ultimately responsible for the status of the death certificate. However when we brought our questions and concerns to Dr. Wood and challenged her to prove Dad committed suicide, she candidly stated mistakes could have been made, but she was sticking to her decision of suicide unless law enforcement provided other physical evidence to change her mind.

Sixteen years after the crime, Dunedin police investigators weren't really eager about searching for new physical evidence. So besides a silly confession letter, Police found no evidence that would convince them that they got it wrong, and they conveniently pointed back at the ME, stating she was responsible for amending the death certificate. It's a circular game of chase-your-tale; law enforcement won't admit they were wrong, and point to the ME as responsible for amendment. The ME states she can't change the death certificate without more input from law enforcement. This frustrating ordeal has gone on now since we received the police reports in 1993. Our frustration continued to mount and we were getting down right angry that no one was taking our concerns seriously.

The Autopsy

Patrolman MacKenzie's police report states the Medical Examiner's office did not send anyone to the crime scene that day, but instead the DPD provided a brief synopsis of what happened. I can only assume that synopsis included the theory they were following at the time...the victim placed the shotgun against his chest and triggered it with either his big toe or the phonebook. Armed with this bit of information, Pathologist Dr. Joan E. Wood began her autopsy on March 14, 1977, at approximately 10:20 a.m.

The autopsy report is number M-77-156, and the name in the top left corner of page one is typed DISCHERL, Robert. Although the police officers misspelled the Dirscherl name on all their reports by deleting the R from the last half of the name, the ME misspells the last name by deleting the R from the front half of the name. Mistakes happen.

As I take you through this report, it's important to note the comments concerning the wound and path of the shotgun pellets, as they provide information about the angle of the weapon and the distance between the muzzle and Dad's body. The report was typed and is transcribed here as accurately as possible. It reads:

"PROTOCOL

<u>EXTERNAL EXAMINATION:</u> The body is that of a well-developed, well-nourished, white male measuring 70.5 inches and weighing an estimated 195 pounds. The head is covered by grey hair mixed with a small amount of brown. The eyes are blue, the cornea are clear, the sclerae are white. The mouth contains teeth in good condition. The neck reveals no abnormalities. The chest reveals 2.5 inches to the left of middle and .5 inch medial to the medial aspect of the left breast a one inch in diameter, somewhat oval, entrance-type wound. The oval axis is horizontal. This places the lower border of the wound as 54.5 inches from the instep of the left foot with the medial aspect being 31 inches from the tip of the right thumb. The wound's lower border is on a line with the nipples of the left breast. The upper abdomen reveals dried blood. The lower abdomen reveals no abnormalities. Genitalia are adult male. There is an old left lower quadrant surgical incision approximately 3 inches in length over the right iliac crest. Examination of the left neck reveals a 3-inch long vertical incision along the left side of the neck beginning approximately to the left of midline. The extremities reveal moderate hair loss over the lower extremities. The hands have been previously fingerprinted and are bagged. There is blood present over both hands and both forearms. Examination of the back reveals no abnormalities with the exception of a left flank 3 inch long surgical incision the central portion of which is depressed. Lividity is present over the back. The body is cold. Rigor is minimal. Smoke and powder blackening is noted over the superior aspect of the wound of the left chest extending outwards for a distance of up to .5 inch from the superior border of the wound. No powder residue can be grossly identified on either hand. The body is clad in trousers and a T-shirt.

<u>INTERNAL EXAMINATION:</u> The body is opened by means of the usual Y-shaped incision revealing a gaping 5 x 3.5 inch wound in the left chest involving the ribs, intercostal musculature and with portions of the heart. There is bright pink discoloration of the muscle extending outward for a distance of up to 4 inches in the intercostals

musculature about the defect. The left chest cavity contains approximately 1500 cc of liquid blood. The pericardial cavity has been completely destroyed secondary to the gunshot wound. The right chest cavity contains approximately 150 cc of liquid blood.

TRACHEA AND LARYNX: The trachea and larynx are examined in situ. No areas of obstruction are encountered. No hemorrhages are noted in the soft tissue of the neck. The cervical spine is examined and no abnormalities can be detected by palpation.

LUNGS: The right lung weighs 640 and the left lung weighs 360 grams. The external surfaces are pinkinsh-tan to reddish-purple with a minimal amount of carbon pigmentation present. Ther is a hemorrhage secondary to injury along the anterior-inferior surface of the linguls of the left lung with associated dark reddish-purple discoloration of the parenchyma. There is also noted injury to the posterior medial aspect of the right lower lobe of the lung associated with the presence of Birdshot within the parenchyma of the right lung. There is also Birdshot noted in the diaphragm. The bronchi contain a minimal amount of liquid blood. As previously noted, there are marked adhesions of the right lung. The parenchyma is dark reddish-purple with no areas of infarct or conseliation noted. There is hemorrhage noted, most markedly in the parenchyma of the left lower lobe of the lungs, secondary to the previously described injuries.

HEART: The heart has been markedly injured, secondary to passage of shot through the heart. The portion of the heart remaining weighs 370 grams. There is injury to the left and right ventricular myocardium with destruction of the interventricular septum. Coronary arteries reveal mild arteriosclerosis. The endocardium is transparent. The posterior leaflet of the mitral valve has been destroyed secondary to the passage of shot. The aortic valve is intact. Examination of the aorta reveals marked injury to the anterior wall of the abdominal aorta.

SPLEEN: The spleen weighs 150 grams. There is an umbilicated, calcified area noted on the lateral aspect of the spleen measuring approximately 2 inches in diameter and involving the capsule. The spleen itself is dark reddish-purple. The capsule is wrinkled. No areas of injury to the spleen are identified.

PANCREAS: The pancreas has been completely transected secondary to the passage of the shot through this region and there is hemorrhage present in the pancreas and in the paripancreatic tissue.

LIVER: *The liver weighs 1810 grams. The external surface is reddish-brown. The margins are sharp. The gallbladder is present and contains approximately 3 cc of viscid bile. There is a stellate injury in the upper left lobe of the liver involving the complete thickness of the lobe and with associated tearing of the capsule in multiple directions. Cut surface of the liver is pale reddish-brown with no abnormalities noted. The liver fractures without difficulty.*

ADRENAL GLANDS: *No abnormalities are noted.*

INTRA-ABDOMINAL LYMPH NODES: *No abnormalities are noted.*

SKIN, MUSCLES AND BREASTS: *See external examination of body.*

BONES: *See examination under chest.*

GENITOURINARY SYSTEM: *The capsules of the kidneys strip with ease revealing smooth- surfaced, reddish-tan kidneys which together weigh 390 grams. There is hemorrhage present about the left kidney in the perinephric fat. There is however no actual injury noted to the parenchyma of the left kidney. Cortico-modullary junctions are well demarcated. Pelves reveal no abnormalities. The uretars appear patent. The bladder contains approximately 10 cc of cloudy yellow urine. There is hemorrhage and injury to the soft tissues of the upper hilum of the left kidney.*

HEAD: *The scalp is reflected and the calvarium removed in the usual fashion. No areas of ecchymosis are noted in the soft tissue of the scalp. The calvarium reveals no evidence of fracturing. No epidural or subdural collections of blood are seen. The brain weighs 1420 grams. Vessels at the base of the brain reveal minimal arteriosclerosis. No uncal grooving or tonsillar herniation is evident. Cut surfaces of the cerebrum, cerebellum and brain stem reveals no areas of hemorrhage or tumor formation.*

PATH OF THE SHOTGUN PELLETS: *The pellets through the left chest and into the chest cavity causing injury to the lingula of the left lung, the heart and into the medial aspect of the lower lobe of the lung. There is also injury to the diaphragm, the midportion of the stomach, the pancreas and the upper abdominal aorta. The path is therefore from left to right, from anterior posterior at an angle of approximately 60 to 75 degrees to the anterior surface of the chest. And from upward downward with the passage of the shot through the heart and chest organs being downward approximately 10 degrees*

and the shot through the upper abdominal viscera being downward approximately 20 degrees. The bulk of the shot does appear to traverse the 20 degree downward path.
    JEW:jbm

TOXICOLOGY
Alcohol – 0g%

Drug screen on heart contents was negative for drugs.
KH:sa

FINAL ANATOMIC DIAGNOSES
Gunshot wound of chest with injury to heart, right and left lung, stomach, pancreas, aorta and left lobe of liver.

    JEW:jbm
    Joan E. Wood, MD
    Pathologist
    Largo, Florida"

I know it's not a big deal that Dr. Wood left the R out of Dad's last name on the autopsy report. But it makes the point mistakes were made, even small ones. In her opening paragraph of the autopsy, she notes an interesting description…first she states that "*the neck reveals no abnormalities.*" Then further down the page, she writes "*Examination of the left neck reveals a 3-inch long vertical incision along the left side of the neck beginning approximately to the left of midline.*" This three-inch incision scar was caused by Dad's neck surgery, and to most people might be considered an abnormality. In the first page of her report, she begins to contradict herself when documenting her observations.

That may seem trivial at this point, but as you read further, you'll understand why this small, perhaps meaningless error is important. Later in Dr. Wood's professional career, this kind of mistake winds up overturning an infamous Clearwater Scientology case, as well as sending at least two innocent men to prison for murders they didn't commit. Small mistakes can be kind of important, especially in the forensics world.

The final DPD supplementary report was completed by Detective Glenn Carlson on 28 March 1977. It's a hand printed report that simply states…

"The office of the Medical Examiner has officially ruled the death of the above captioned subject as due to self inflicted gunshot wound, i.e. Suicide. This case is exceptionally cleared.
Case Closed Exceptionally Cleared"

And so it was official; based on the County Medical Examiner's ruling… the fate, and legacy of Robert John Dirscherl Sr. was sealed.

Chapter 5

Big Bang Theory

Spring 1993 rolled into summer and I was back at work in Panama City. Kook was living in North Carolina, and George was on the east coast of Florida in Ormond Beach. Kandy's husband Pat had retired from the Air Force and they were living in Dunedin near Mom, while Guy had established roots in Clearwater.

We all had copies of the police reports and spent much of our free time going over them trying to figure out what could have happened that fateful Sunday. We tried to recreate the shot angle and pellet trajectory using the toe method, but were unable to reproduce the angle detailed in the autopsy report. Not to mention this theory seemed to imply Dad sat on the floor at the foot of the bed, leaned against the bed, stuck the muzzle against his chest, lifted the butt of the weapon above his shoulder with his deteriorating left arm, held it there while he awkwardly lifted his left foot and pushed the trigger with his big toe. All this had to happen to achieve the recorded angle of the shot traveling through his chest cavity. The gun would have had to recoil forward instead of rearward, flip over his head and land on the bed still wrapped in the gun case according to their reports. Not only does this theory defy most human abilities and the laws of physics, it fails to explain how those blood droplets got on the bed covers near the south side of the bed.

The handy explanation that he used the phone book must also be dismissed as speculation at best. While it conveniently placed him standing at the south side of the bed near the blood spatter, we know Mom retrieved the phone book from the bedside table after she found him. We were discovering some serious issues with the DPD explanations. This suicide was impossible the way they said it happened.

My family and I were not trained forensic investigators, but we did have simple observation skills and enough common sense to know that there were obvious problems with the investigative procedures and that the case had been closed based on inaccurate facts and untested theories.

There are several critical steps investigators should take when observing, theorizing and solving crimes like this. They are:

- Define the problem/question
- Recognize variables/options/possibilities
- Gather and weigh evidence
  - Investigate
  - Carefully process the crime scene
    - Fingerprint, measure, photograph, etc.
  - Form hypothesis
- Organize data
- Test Predictions
- State Opinion

It appears pretty obvious DPD omitted several of these critical steps, and rearranged the others to produce an investigation process that didn't include recognizing variables/possibilities, weighted evidence, organized data, or tested predictions. Instead it appears they used the investigation model:

- Define the problem
- Form hypothesis
- State Opinion
- Process the crime scene (kind of).

Einstein's quote that *"Things should be made as simple as possible, but not simpler"* seems all too fitting.

Unfortunately, bringing up these issues with the detectives, Medical Examiner and agencies that were responsible for the miscues in the first place, was and still is an uphill battle. Experts are human, and some of them have a hard time swallowing pride and admitting they may have made mistakes.

While we were reading through the reports discovering impossible explanations, Chief McBride and Detective Farrell were having the confession letter checked for finger prints, and were following up on local individuals that may be dying of AIDS. Several days later we received some shocking news that Chief McBride had suffered a massive coronary and was in pretty bad condition. We didn't receive much information on his condition, but it was obvious he was going to be on convalescent leave for a while and would no longer be working our case.

We assumed Detective Farrell was now in charge. He did contact Mom and Kandy with a name of a local kid he had tracked down who was a possible suspect and who was dying of AIDS. But this individual would have been about eleven years old at the time of the shooting, and his health problems seemed to clear him from writing the letter as his right arm was paralyzed.

As weeks rolled on, we heard nothing more from Farrell. When we'd call to see what was going on with our case, the usual response was that he was in the field working another case. We were becoming a bit frustrated as we hadn't heard anything about finger prints on the letter. We were in a paused sort of limbo, just standing by waiting to hear some news. Farrell and McBride were now out of the picture, but a new detective was about to pick up the torch and champion our cause.

Mom received a call from a young female detective named Stephanie Brown who informed us she had taken over our case, and that she would contact us with any new information. The next bit of news she shared was a bit of a shocker that didn't sit very well with the family. It seems there had been some changes at DPD and there was a new Chief of Homicide…a familiar name that had deep ties to the original investigation. The new Chief of Homicide who was the final authority on this new investigation was the officer who determined in his own mind sixteen years ago that Dad had committed suicide. The new Chief of Homicide was one James Allen MacKenzie. Yes… the person assigned to assess potential problems with the case that had been closed years prior based on physical impossibilities, was the very same person who spawned those impossibilities. Amazing! Fate can be kind, and fate can be cruel, but at times it can be downright mind-blowing.

I have to take a moment to share a belief I have concerning fate. I personally believe there is a God who has a purpose for each of us. I don't believe He is a puppet-master who controls every aspect of our life, but I believe there is some purpose behind the things that happen. I don't know how or why, but I believe things happen for a reason...even if we never discover what that reason is. Perhaps God exists and puts us where we're supposed to be for reasons we can't understand. Or perhaps He doesn't exist, and things just happen by coincidence. One of those "coincidences" lead to my twenty-year Air Force career, and experiences with weapons and law enforcement that helped me understand there were problems with this investigation.

When I entered the Air Force in March of 1983, I signed up and didn't ask for a specific job. Instead I told the recruiter I would take any job they had to offer, so my status was what's called "Open General" The first job they needed filled...I was the guy to fill it. I had a chance to write down three areas of interest, and hope I was placed into one of those preferences; no guarantees, just a wish list.

I selected the general topics of Small Arms, Weather, & Photography. I had taken the ASVAB (Armed Forces Vocational Aptitude Battery) tests, and had scored quite highly across the board, which made me eligible for just about any job the Air Force offered enlisted members. My recruiter encouraged me to pursue a career as a Linguist, as there was quite a need for ease droppers who could speak a foreign language. I did a bit of checking and learned this job required a year-long technical school at Lackland Air Force Base learning Russian or Chinese, and Linguists spent much of their careers on aircraft in faraway places ease dropping on enemies and potential enemies. I was a newlywed, and the thought of all that away-time didn't really appeal to me. Prior to entering the Air Force I had just lost a sales job in Texas, and didn't want to spend another year in that state. Texas has some gorgeous places, but I happened to live in an area of southwest Houston, which I affectionately referred to as "The Armpit of America". I told the recruiter no thanks, and kept my dream sheet list as Small Arms, Weather, & Photography.

After graduating from Basic Training in April of 1983, I received my new career appointment. I was told I was going to be a Combat Arms Training & Maintenance (CATM) Instructor. What an ironic blessing. This career path meant for the next twenty years I was going to be able to learn about firearms, teach people how to safely handle weapons, and train thousands of American Soldiers, Sailors, Airmen, Marines, Coast Guard and civilians how to protect themselves and their nation. It turned out to be one of the most rewarding jobs I could imagine. I truly loved leading the classroom environment, and reaping the fruits of my teaching efforts on the firing range. It was simple gratification to see instruction absorbed and a goal accomplished as we transitioned from classroom to firing range. Pretty neat to see a frightened, twenty-five year-old female lieutenant, who had never previously handled a firearm become an expert marksman by absorbing and applying my instruction.

CATM troops were the Air Force experts when it came to firearms, and we were known throughout the Air Force as "Red Hats", due to the bright red baseball caps we wore on the firing range. Not only did we instruct the base populace on shooting skills, we maintained, inspected and repaired the thousands of weapons at each base. This meant I became very familiar with weaponry including revolvers, semi-automatic pistols, rifles, machineguns, grenade launchers and shotguns. It also meant I had the privilege to train with some very incredible folks along the way. At tallies' end, I enjoyed the wonderful experience of training over 65,000 personnel, and had gained a bit of knowledge and respect for weaponry.

CATM worked very closely with the Air Force Security Police. They were our primary customer and we spent hundreds of hours per year teaching, and learning from them. In 1984, CATM personnel were realigned from our previous association with Education and Training units and were administratively aligned under the Security Police units.

In 1997, the Air Force was further downsizing and realigning, and CATM actually merged with Air Force law enforcement and installation security troops to form the new "Security Forces" entity. Prior to the merger there were less than a thousand CATM instructors worldwide. Once merged, we lost our autonomy as Red Hats, and were now one of the tens of thousands of Security Forces who happen to work at firing ranges.

While it was a sad day for the CATM career field, it did allow an opportunity to expand our knowledge base and gain some law enforcement experience. We were no longer just weapons experts; we were now also trained in law enforcement and installation security and became badge carrying police. Since 1984 we had always been law enforcement augmentees, working closely with the Cops, but the merger meant we were able to receive more in depth law enforcement training and experience. I was a Master Sergeant at the time of the merger and moved from the firing range into other security and law enforcement managerial positions where I was able to get a taste of the police world.

I share this history to let you know I had a bit of firearms and law enforcement experience as Dad's case unfolded. I don't claim to be an investigative mastermind, but I did understand how the process was supposed to work. Investigations are supposed to be solved based on evidence, not supposition. And death certificates are supposed to indicate an accurate cause and manner of death.

Us and Them

Since I worked on a firing range I decided to do a little experimenting to see if I could replicate the angles and size of Dad's wound. After seeing watermelons and water jugs explode when hit from several yards away, I was under the impression a shotgun blast would cause a massive entry wound. But I never really considered what size torso wound would be created from very close range.

Discussing shooting techniques, ballistics, weapon stopping power, etc. with thousands of students, I learned pretty early on that most people get the majority of their shooting knowledge and beliefs from television and movies. The special effects used to enhance the shock of a gunshot scene are usually not based in reality but instead Hollywood make-believe.

We've all seen television or cinematic handgun shootouts that lift people off their feet and propel them through plate glass windows...usually in slow motion. You've probably also seen the ever so common Hollywood fantasy shootout where a bad guy fires dozens of rounds from his handgun without reloading, and can't hit the broad side of the barn, but is finally dropped by the cop with a .38 caliber snub-nosed revolver from a hundred yards or so. Anyone remember the old TV show detectives Frank Cannon, Joe Mannix or Barnaby Jones? Seems those guys carried magic revolvers that just couldn't miss.

I became quite amazed at the impact Hollywood and television had on the public surrounding firearms. Besides the Hollywood effect, people have their own theories about shooting I guess they just make up. I had one student, an Air Force Major, who was training with a .38 caliber revolver and was having trouble hitting his man-sized target at 15 yards. He assured me that the fog was deflecting his bullets and causing his poor performance. Other strange shooting theories permeated the firearms classrooms and ranges because many folks believe what they see on TV…at least to some degree.

I too was conditioned to some degree to believe that all shotgun blasts would leave extremely nasty wounds. I had conducted quite a bit of law enforcement shotgun training using 00-Buck rounds, which contained nine lead pellets, each about the size of a large pea. I had seen what they would do to cardboard targets, watermelons, jugs filled with water, and wooden firing range supports. Their destructive force and stopping power is revered throughout the law enforcement community. In 1986 I had an Air Force acquaintance who killed himself by placing the muzzle of a 12-guage shotgun loaded with a 00-Buck round under his chin. The energy basically removed the majority of his head and they had problems identifying the body. In my mind, I expected any shotgun wound to produce a massive entrance wound.

In late October, 1993, I decided to conduct some test firing with the Mauser shotgun that inflicted Dad's fatal wound. I wanted to see at what distance #8 Birdshot produced a wound similar in size to the wound in Dad's chest. I had studied photos and explanations in the book *Gunshot Wounds* which was authored by the nation's foremost authority on gunshot wounds and related forensic techniques; Dr. Vincent J.M. DiMaio. This book provided just what I was looking for…close-up photos of shotgun wounds to the human torso. It contained photos that ranged from hard contact wounds, to light contact wounds, to near contact wounds, to wounds up to several feet away.

The autopsy report never specified if Dad's wound was a contact wound or not. But the third theory that was about to be launched by DPD implied Dad leaned over the bed and onto the muzzle. It seems logical this process would produce a hard contact wound.

I placed some cardboard backers on our dirt backstop at the Tyndall firing range and using a protractor to establish the proper angles, began to fire #8 Birdshot rounds into the target from different ranges. I wasn't trying to reproduce all the wound effects; I was simply trying to see how far away I could reproduce the approximate wound size, which was described as approximately thirty millimeters by forty millimeters.

Dr. DiMaio stated in his book that a shotgun muzzle placed against a torso (contact wound), would usually create a wound nearly the same size as the muzzle diameter. Although neither the police reports nor the autopsy reports state the diameter of the shotgun barrels, I measured them and both muzzle interior measurements were eighteen millimeters in diameter, about the size of a dime. This led to the question…if the double barreled shotgun was leaned upon, shouldn't the wound be approximately eighteen millimeters in diameter, instead of the stated thirty by forty millimeters?

As I tested the #8 Birdshot on the cardboard targets at the Tyndall firing range, I replicated angles and then gradually move further and further from the target. The first shot was contact at a ninety degree angle, straight into the target just for reference. The hole was about eighteen millimeters in diameter and there was an obvious dent and imprint of the second barrel. The rest of the shots were fired at the autopsy angles of sixty-five degrees right to left into the chest and elevated to approximately fifteen degrees. I fired from distances of one inch, three inches, six inches, twelve inches and fifteen inches. Even out to fifteen inches away I was making a hole no larger than twenty-eight millimeters. The closest matches to the autopsy description of the wound were two shots; one fired from three inches away, the other from six inches. Both these shots left a slightly elongated hole approximately twenty-six to twenty-eight millimeters high. The smoke and powder blackening from these shots was also very similar to the autopsy report; showing blackening over the superior aspect of the wound extending outward approximately one half inch. I mailed target photos and test fire results to Detective Brown at the DPD, as she was the new detective looking into our case.

In Nov of 1993, Kim the kids and I were headed to Daytona Beach for the wedding of George's eldest son. We made arrangements to spend some time in Dunedin and Kandy and Mom set up an appointment with Stephanie Brown to discuss the case. The three of us met with Brown at the Dunedin police station to talk face to face with the investigator and see if our questions and concern were being looked into.

Detective Brown was friendly and began the meeting stating she understood that we were upset about the case. Within a few minutes the door opened, and Chief MacKenzie entered. We could feel an immediate power shift in the room as he began to take over the conversation and explain how this case was going to remain closed as a suicide.

I don't want to come across as judgmental here…I understand people have different personalities, values, ethics and opinions. But I must say we had just entered a world where we were treated as dim-witted bumpkins who had no idea what we were talking about, and that we were really wasting the DPD's time.

We all noticed an uncomfortable look on Brown's face as MacKenzie belittled our questions and discussions of possible mistakes. Before he entered the room, we felt our concerns were being taken seriously, and felt Detective Brown was handling this case with an open mind. But once Chief MacKenzie began to speak, it was evident where the investigation was going. It was obvious he was exercising his newly acquired authority and was not about to have his original theories questioned by the trio of emotional civilians seated in front of him. This was the first real sense that we were being viewed as a potential enemy with an agenda, instead of a family who may have been wronged and who simply wanted to discover the truth.

Our family had gone through the reports and had discovered some serious problems. Not only did it appear the mindset of the investigators was to document an alleged suicide, but many of the facts they were dealing with were wrong. We wanted to bring this info to the agency responsible…not to accuse them of erring, but to get to the truth and hopefully justice. We were assured that police solved cases based on the facts; but what do you do when the facts are wrong and the theories are flawed? And what do you do when the investigator who hatched the faulty theories is now in charge of the re-opened case? That old cliché, "The fox guarding the hen house" had metaphorically metamorphosized.

When I mentioned my target tests and results, Detective Brown explained that human tissue would react differently than cardboard, and that the tests didn't validate anything credible concerning the wound. I explained I wasn't trying to replicate the wound, but simply trying to demonstrate that the size of the hole may not confirm a hard contact wound. The attitude we encountered reminded me of an old tongue-in-cheek military phrase I'd heard many times when submitting a recommendation or making a suggestion superiors didn't like. The refuting response was…"Disapproved; resubmit in thirty days for further disapproval." The wall was up and it was obvious our concerns were not being taken seriously.

Another issue we raised with the Chief and Detective concerned the Mauser shotgun, and its location on the bed. Original investigators placed quite a bit of importance on the issue that the shotgun used was Dad's favorite gun, which is obviously why he chose it to kill himself. I'm open-minded enough to consider that a possibility, as nobody except Dad knows what he was thinking that morning. But while the police report stated the shotgun was kept unloaded, the truth of the matter is that the shotgun was kept loaded ever since the recent death of our dog. Mom told them the gun was kept unloaded because that's what she was led to believe. This inaccurate information becomes another critical revelation in the investigation, because the original implication was an intruder would have to enter the house and load the shotgun before shooting Dad. However, an intruder attempting to steal the gun, or wrestling with it when it was already loaded means the shooter didn't have to load it.

If an intruder found this expensive gun, or knew it was there and was surprised by Dad while attempting to steal it, then the shot may not have even been intentional. It could have been, and in my opinion was, likely discharged during a struggle when Dad tried to take it away. But the police were under the impression Dad loaded it that morning before awkwardly holding it to his chest, and magically manipulating the trigger. The investigators didn't seem interested in hearing new information that challenged their closed case.

I had a few more bothersome questions concerning this theory. If Dad did load the shotgun to kill himself, why would he load it with #8 Birdshot? There were two rounds of Birdshot in the weapon when fired, but there was also #2 Buckshot ammunition in a drawer in the bedroom. #8 Birdshot contains hundreds of small, light lead pellets designed to disperse and bring down a bird without destroying the small animal. #2 Buckshot ammunition is definitely more fatal and designed to bring down larger animals. Dad was a hunter and knew this fact. Why would he load the gun with Birdshot to kill himself? The answer is he didn't. A shotgun loaded with Birdshot is an effective home defense weapon since Birdshot is less likely to penetrate doors and walls like the heavier Buckshot, preventing unintended injury in nearby rooms. The Birdshot in the weapon makes sense for home defense, but the Buckshot would have made more sense for a suicide.

And instead of using the awkward shotgun, why not grab the German Luger handgun that was kept nearby and finish things that way? Seems that handy pistol would have been the quickest, simplest method. To the investigators it made more suicide-sense to speculate Dad loaded his favorite gun that morning as he was planning to kill himself.

The other weapon issue discussed was the location of the gun in the sketches. When asked why the gun was drawn lying at the edge of the bed pointing south with the gun case over it; Brown explained on page three of her report that, *"Paramedics and officers went into the house to check on Mr. Dirscherl and, at any time, this weapon could have been moved from its original location for safety reasons. The victim was standing next to the bed and there was a contact wound to his chest."*

So my logical response was…isn't the actual and factual location of the weapon important in a suspicious homicide/suicide case? Doesn't the erroneous description of the gun's placement cause some reason to consider a possible dilemma with their theories? Apparently not; DPD seemed to dismiss our concern that the weapon was originally in the middle of the bed not covered by the case, instead of hanging off the bed with the case *"entwined over and under the gun"* as their reports indicate.

Brown's report continues to record MacKenzie's comments that *"there was nothing suspicious on the outside of the residence to cause him to feel someone had entered the residence while the family was home."* This statement seems to again suggest the Chief was solving the case based on feelings, instead of physical evidence. Did this statement suggest that his "feelings" confirmed an intruder could not have entered the home? The house was unlocked and it was very possible that an intruder could have simply entered the home without breaking in. Of course since they didn't fingerprint the bedroom, residence, or weapon, any possible intruder evidence was lost to history.

Brown also reported, *"Based on the police reports, I could find that they did lift prints but it is unknown if they actually had them compared to anything."* None of the reports state fingerprints were lifted from anything except Dad's hands. Not the weapon, not the room, not the doors or windows…just the dead man's hands.

Our conversation continued even though it seemed we were engaged in a pointless discussion, where every question or possibility we raised was immediately countered and dismissed. It was like one of those discussions you initiate with a boss when you have a serious company concern or problem to bring up, but it's bad news the boss doesn't want to hear it. The boss gets a bit frustrated at you for raising the issue, denies the bad news, and hurries the conversation pretending the problem doesn't exist. This was the atmosphere of the meeting and it was frustrating, but we had to continue to present our factual and justified concerns.

Our inquiry next led to questions about how the gun was held and fired. Brown captured the discussion in her report this way; *"There were a lot of theories noted in the police reports and also told to the family that might have been misconstrued by them. Apparently something was said that the phone book could have been used as a trigger mechanism. There was also inference made that it could have been his toe or finger. Dan Dirscherl does not feel that it could have been his hand because of his father's limited use of his left arm and, in no way could he have supported the gun. Capt MacKenzie advised him that he could have been able to support the gun by using his other arm and leaning the gun up against his chest."*

I just have to clarify; I don't think we were misconstruing police explanations. Nor did the police apparently mention or infer it may have been the phone book or his toe. They were basing the suicide judgment on these facts, and had closed the case based on these imperative theories. These comments were not just investigator sidebar discussions we were concerned with, they were the official manner of death of a closed suicide case. If they were certain it was Dad who pulled the trigger, and not an intruder, we wanted to be convinced based on physical evidence and not impossible supposition...call us hard-headed.

Since Dad's body was found near the foot of the bed along the west bedroom wall and was only wearing one slipper, police initially theorized he sat on the floor near where he was found, leaned against the foot-board of the bead, held the gun against his chest and pushed the trigger with his toe. How else would he wind up in this location? As I've discussed, the blood spatter on the covers indicated the shot took place along the south side of the bed, so their first theory was problematic, not to mention physically impossible. Their second theory placed him standing near the south side of the bed using the phone book to trigger the shotgun. We know that was impossible...but that theory implied he stood at the south side of the bed, fired the fatal shot to the chest, then walked approximately six to eight steps around the bed, and collapsed where his body was found.

Chief MacKenzie began to see that his original toe and phonebook theories were flawed, but apparently he was convinced it was still a suicide. Faced with this conundrum, he proposed a new, third theory that perhaps Dad stood at the south side of the bed near the bathroom, placed the butt of the shotgun out on the bed, leaned forward over the bed resting his chest against the muzzle, and pushed the trigger to the rear with his finger. This theory allowed for blood spatter on the bed, justified the (inaccurate) gun position in their sketch, and it didn't involve the impossible toe manipulation, or the magically appearing phone book. Theory number three was hatched; now we were required to absorb, process, and accept this revelation as their new truth.

Perhaps you've heard the old adage... "Fool me once, shame on you. Fool me twice, shame on me." Knowing we had proven the initial theories wrong, we weren't quite so quick to accept this newest impromptu proposal. Was this method possible? And if it was possible, was it the true depiction of what actually took place or just more guesswork?

This theory implied after Dad leaned over the bed and onto the muzzle and fired the shot that destroyed his heart and traveled through his body at a downward angle, he would have had to lean back up, walk about five feet to the corner of the bed, turn the corner and continue walking forward another six feet or so while upright, before falling backwards and landing on his back. Maybe that's what happened, but I find it a much more plausible that a person involved in a struggle for their life is more likely to move around the room during a struggle or shortly after being shot. I know that's speculation on my part, but I just can't figure out why he would walk that far around the bed after inflicting a suicidal wound.

I know through my law enforcement and firearms training that fatally wounded people can do some pretty amazing things after being shot. I've spoken with several shooting victims, some of whom didn't even realize they had been shot. I realize it may have been a physiological possibility that Dad could have been able to move that distance after the fatal wound was inflicted...but my questions are how and why? I know there is no sure way to know why people do things, but it seems if a person has made up their mind they are going to end their life with a shotgun blast, they might want to make their peace, prepare to die, then do the...ready, set, now! I find it difficult to imagine anyone preparing to shoot themselves, pulling the trigger, then recovering from a leaning position and walking around the bed towards the vacant corner of the room for no apparent reason.

As far as determining the "how"...our concern with this theory was that if Dad had positioned the gun in this fashion and leaned onto it as they speculated, wouldn't he fall forward onto the gun and bed right there as gravity continued to pull his leaning body down and forward? Remember he had to place the butt of the gun on a 31-32 inch high bed, lean onto it and still create a ten to twenty degree downward angle through his chest. Wouldn't there be much more blood on the bed?

In order to achieve this angle and produce the telling tattooing and powder burns inflicted around the top and outer edge of the wound, this would have been a rather unbalanced leaning posture. From this position it seems highly unlikely after shooting himself he could then overcome his lean and gravity, stand up and walk the six to eight steps around the bed to fall and die where he was found. Were they really implying this was the new and accurate suicide scenario? Brown and MacKenzie seemed confident this may have been how he killed himself and it became the third theory provided by DPD. Once again the physical evidence and laws of physics seemed to conflict with dubious theory number three.

We were not so quick to accept their new proposal, but that didn't matter. If we didn't agree with that improbable possibility, there was another one about to be revealed. Brown suggested that since the gun case was entwined over and under the gun (reportedly), perhaps he used the little leather loop attached to the tip of the case, and slipped it over the trigger and pulled. Again, without testing the theory, Brown purported another suicide possibility to defend the standing conclusion the wound had to have been self inflicted. While the idea seemed plausible to Brown who suggested it, it was another physical impossibility. The clearance between the trigger and the trigger guard was very narrow; about one thirty-second of an inch. But the hefty leather loop was over an eighth of an inch thick.

Although it was physically impossible to hook the loop over the trigger, the gun case loop idea became the second expert opinion expressed during our meeting, and their forth suicide theory overall.

Instead of stepping back and objectively considering the possibility another person fired the shot, they seemed to be more intent on providing spontaneous explanations and more impossible ideas. It was becoming obvious they were still guessing at what happened that awful morning, but had still not produced a plausible theory. It seems so simple when you consider a second person pulling the trigger.

We felt the information and concerns we were providing placed some serious doubts on the suicide case. But we were realizing that proving Dad's death was a homicide was not going to be an easy endeavor, especially with the prejudiced resistance we were encountering. MacKenzie would not even entertain the idea that mistakes may have been made or evidence had been overlooked.

We also attempted to explain to MacKenzie and Brown that Dad had not been the depressed hermit described in the reports. This type of discussion tends to come from feelings and subjective observation and is easily argued and dismissed. We understood that to them it was useless information, but we still felt it had to be stated, since their reports leaned so far the other way.

We questioned further about other homicide possibilities. Page five of Brown's report ends with the following paragraph: "*Capt. MacKenzie advised them/him that there was no way for us to really know what happened, but based on the evidence that he saw at the scene, he had no doubt in his mind that this investigation of Robert Dirscherl was done properly and that this was a suicide. There was no evidence leading to the point that he or other detectives would feel this was a homicide.*"

Read that again, slowly and comprehendingly and notice the oxymoronic implication. What the first sentence of this paragraph in Detective Brown's report clearly states is, "*Capt. MacKenzie advised them/him that **there was no way for us to really know what happened**, but based on the evidence that he saw at the scene, he had no doubt in his mind that this investigation of Robert Dirscherl was done properly and that this was a suicide.*" So how does an agency close a case twice as a suicide, instead of undetermined, if they don't really know what happened?

The second sentence in this paragraph states, *"There was **no evidence** leading to the point that he or other detectives would feel this was a homicide."* To this statement I just have to respond… "Seriously?…no evidence? Couldn't possibly be a homicide?" Granted the original evidence at the scene did not include the confession letter, but didn't that letter change the situation a bit? Are they not considering someone just confessed to a murder which kind of puts a new spin on the evidence they collected and failed to collect? So apparently there is no possibility that someone entered the unlocked house, found the loaded shotgun in the bedroom, and was startled by Dad who entered the room to treat his athlete's foot? No possibility Dad leaned forward to grab the shotgun and pulled the muzzle towards his chest? No possibility another individual's finger was on that trigger when the weapon fired? No possibility Dad was shot by another near the side of the bed and stumbled to his final resting place? No possibility an intruder could have caused this accidental death then fled the scene. No possibility that fifteen years later while on their deathbed, the killer penned a confession letter and sent it to the only Dirscherl sibling in the phone book. No possibility someone else was responsible for Dad's death? None of this is plausible? Did these officers really believe there was no evidence to support a possible homicide? Are the unproven, impossible police theories the end of the story? This can't be.

During our meeting, Detective Brown at times seemed a bit sympathetic to our situation, but it became obvious she wasn't in a position to further the investigation. She had done her part and her boss was in the room letting everyone know this case was closed. She gave us back the original confession letter, and informed us they could find no good fingerprints on it. She let us know with a consoling smile, she was done with the investigation.

Chief MacKenzie was also wrapping up the meeting. He reiterated that now, and at the time of the shooting, there was consensus that this was a suicide. They had no suspects to prove otherwise and they could not afford to spend any more time on the case. Kandy asked Chief MacKenzie if he thought the confession letter was authentic. He said he didn't know for sure, but he doubted it was genuine. She then asked him what it would take to convince them Dad was killed by someone else. MacKenzie said that if the killer walked into the police station, admitted he was the killer, and brought a witness who would swear he saw him do it, the police might change their minds. He then actually suggested we forget about this issue, or "Come up with the little green men from Venus who committed the murder". That comment seemed to be the straw that broke the camel's back. Mom took that little jab as a serious insult to our questions and concerns and seemed angry enough to spit. It was obvious there was no use in spending any more time with this agency. We took the confession letter and left.

If we were going to clear Dad's name, were going to have a serious challenge. But we felt we didn't necessarily have to prove homicide. Florida death certificates have several important blocks for recording information. One asks for the cause of death. On Dad's certificate it states: *"Gunshot wound of chest"*. The next block asks for the manner of death. The options are: Accident, Suicide, Homicide, or Undetermined. Dad's certificate says *"Suicide"*. The third block asks how the injury occurred. Dad's certificate states *"Shot self"*. One would think these statements should be factual or at least possible. If not, the ME has the opportunity to choose the option "Undetermined".

As we reviewed the reports and replaced the inaccurate information and mistruths with factual evidence, we assumed the experts would see the obvious problems with their suicide determination and would be convinced the manner of death should be changed…at least to Undetermined. Never assume anything.

We were angry, frustrated and stuck. We knew the case had been solved on inaccurate facts and guess work, yet the new investigation was going nowhere. Instead of trying to prove Dad's death was a homicide, our goal now was to provide enough evidence to counter their suicide finding, raise enough doubt that suicide was proven, and hope the ME would change the death certificate manner of death block to Undetermined. But our dilemma was this: Since DPD and the ME were in agreement, both of them had to be wrong, and we were right. Or conversely, they were correct and we were just that emotional nagging family that had our facts all mixed up and simply could not accept the truth concerning that elephant in the room.

Later that week Detective Brown did call Mom to let her know that the ME had a few autopsy photos, and that she would provide us copies once she received them. After several calls and two more months passed, Mom, Guy and Kandy did finally receive the autopsy photos; they were about to experience a photographic flash-back that returned them to that Sunday morning so many years ago.

The Photos

In January of 1994, Mom forwarded what would become my set of autopsy photos. Four awkwardly horrible, yet simultaneously calming photos I would come to know well. I hadn't seen Dad in nearly seventeen years, and there weren't a lot of photos of him around since he was always the one taking the pictures. I psychologically prepared myself before viewing them and attempted to mentally distance myself from the fatherly connection before I opened the envelope and took my first look. The memories and reality of that unthinkable Sunday returned in an instant.

But...supposedly time heals all wounds. After the initial anguish of seeing the photos, I eventually was able to view them with an impersonal, somewhat remote mindset. As I repeatedly studied the photos and postulated the possible causes of the wound, the recurring viewing desensitized the goriness, kind of like a teenager repeatedly playing violent video games.

Over the ensuing weeks, months and years I would look at the photos and daydream; trying to get into Dad's mind and imagine what he was thinking and experiencing in his last few moments of life. The last time I saw him in the house, he was lying on the floor in a pool of blood, staring at the ceiling with a look of shock and horror on his face. Three of these autopsy photos showed his face, and while there was a lot of blood that immediately caught the viewer's eye, I was drawn to the expression on his face. His eyes were now closed, his mouth was shut, and there was a look of peace on his face...it almost looked as if there was a hint of a smile.

I know it may sound weird, but over time these photos in some ways provided me a strange and awkward sense of peace. Although the photos are simply two dimensional chemically produced images printed on some shiny paper, they take me back to times and places that recount stories, memories, and a day when I had a father alive in my life.

Besides the emotional connection, the photos also provided us our first real look at some physical crime scene evidence. The wound to Dad's chest was a bit surprising as it didn't replicate the entrance wound damage I was expecting. No jagged shredding of tissue; instead a fairly smooth-edged hole a little bigger than a bottle cap, only a bit more oval shaped with the long axis running horizontally. The edges appeared mostly smooth, but it appears there was a hint of scalloping present. And to quote Dr. Wood's autopsy report, *"Smoke and powder blackening is noted over the superior aspect of the wound of the left chest extending outwards for a distance of up to one half inch from the superior border of the wound."*

Although the shotgun's relative position, attitude and distance from the body when fired are not specifically addressed in the report, the autopsy and police reports implied the shotgun had been held against Dad's chest and produced a pellet trajectory that entered his body from anterior to posterior at approximately 60-75 degrees, and from upward to downward through his chest cavity at approximately 10 degrees, then through the abdominal viscera at approximately 20 degrees. Observing the forensic evidence of the pellet trajectory, color of the muscle tissue, blood spatter, smoke and powder blackening, condition of the shirt he was wearing, and the wound's visual characteristics should provide an accurate picture of how the weapon was positioned when the shot was fired.

Another physiological influence that may have played a part in the wound's size and shape are what's called Langer lines, or cleavage lines. Langer Lines have to do with the natural elasticity of the skin, and can be visualized if you imagine which direction human skin will split when it is cut or punctured. This stretching effect can cause wounds to appear more ellipsoidal due to the natural tension in the skin. While the relatively small wound seemed to indicate a close-range or contact wound, there was a notable characteristic that seemed to be missing. There was no mention of, or any obvious imprint of the second shotgun barrel.

In his book Dr. DiMaio states that with a contact wound, a shotgun's massive blast of gasses into the human torso causes the chest cavity to expand rapidly, which many times will leave a definite and detailed imprint and/or bruising from anything very close to the skin's surface; especially something as prominent as the second barrel of a double barreled shotgun. His book contains autopsy photos that show a self-inflicted suicide wound where the person grabbed the barrel near the muzzle to support it and rested their closed fist and wrist against their body when they pulled the trigger. The ensuing blast and torso expansion left a very clear bruising of the closed fist and a perfect imprint of the person's wrist watch. If Dad had leaned onto the muzzle as suggested in 1993, surely there would have been obvious markings left behind that a medical examiner should note. So why no mention of any second barrel markings or of anything similar by Joan Wood in her 1977 autopsy report? Probably because the "leaning" theory had not yet been hatched and she was still operating on the assumption suggested by police that the weapon was discharged by a toe or phonebook.

The main question I had was, did the preponderance of the physical and forensic evidence indicate the shot was self-inflicted, or was there the likelihood it could have been inflicted by a second person in the room? The autopsy really didn't seem to clearly answer that question. And while Dr. Wood, Chief MacKenzie, and the DPD are comfortable with their official explanations, my family and two independent forensic experts aren't quite so sure. (More on the two forensic experts later.)

Eight months after our meeting with Detective Brown and Chief MacKenzie, Detective Brown provided us a copy of her final report which summarized their investigation and discussed our meeting with them in November. The first issue Det. Brown mentioned in her report was that of the "will" note. Amazingly her report inaccurately states the note was "found on the bed", when in reality the note was found in Dad's office and had been written months prior. Another little mistake that carries huge weight and erroneously supports a suicide motive. Anyone reading her official report and absorbing the false statement that Dad had written the word "will" on a notepad which was found on the bed with him on the floor dead next to it, just might understandably consider it a serious indication of intent.

Perhaps this erroneous evidence concerning the note had been read or regurgitated enough times that it took hold in their minds and became a belief they couldn't shake. Perhaps they subconsciously and repeatedly overlooked the truth that the note was found in Dad's office and accepted the false suicidal evidence that made sense to them, and supported their desired outcome. Or perhaps it was just an honest mistake that revealed another bit of sloppiness with this case. Whatever the reason, the truth was blurred, facts were fiction, and the case was unexplainably closed as a suicide for the second time.

A wall had been erected and the frustration of not being heard morphed into anger towards the experts. The darkness of anger and resentment had begun to take a foothold in some of our hearts and our attempts at justice had turned into an unwanted battle. At times I began to focus on that battle and what appeared to be a prideful, cynical power-play by the police, and I was beginning to feel overwhelmed by our lack of success.

We were into 1994 and our journey mimicked an unpleasant rollercoaster ride. There were ups and downs, peaks and valleys and stomach-flipping turns that increased our nauseating symptoms. We were feeling quite ill at times...perhaps a visit to the doctor would help.

Chapter 6

The Doctor Will See You Now

Frustration, aggravation, and disappointment; combine all three, but add a dash of hope; this is the place we'd come to know well. Beating our heads against the wall dealing with DPD had us annoyed, yet we all felt a deeply veiled, yet very real sense of optimism and hope deep down inside that kept us moving forward. We knew we were on to something more than just wishful thinking.

In February of 1994, Guy, Kandy and Mom met with Dr. Wood at her office to discuss the details of her autopsy report. They had legitimate questions and concerns and wanted to hear the Doctor explain how she came to the conclusions she did. Eventually this autopsy report would become even more significant because it was performed by Dr. Wood, the soon-to-be Chief Medical Examiner who ran into a few problems later in her career.

We were in a quandary because we felt the police had gotten things wrong, yet the ME was agreeing with their suggestions concerning the suicide. Although nobody from the ME's office responded to the scene, Dr. Wood received a "brief synopsis" from police and determined suicide was the cause of death. Although it had been nearly seventeen years since she conducted the autopsy, she was certain her findings were accurate...at least at the beginning of the meeting.

Dr. Wood remembered our case and assured the three family representatives that everything about the investigation seemed to be on the up-and-up, and that her forensic examination supported the police description. She didn't go into a lot of detail, just seemed to support the validity of her original data and conclusion. When Mom, Guy and Kandy explained that the trigger manipulation methods stated in the police reports were not possible, she seemed to silently acknowledge that the evidence didn't support the investigator's theories…but she held firm to her official position.

When they explained the physical evidence didn't seem to confirm or even indicate suicide, she confidently clarified the self-inflicted wound was still a probability. When Kandy provided her a photocopy from Dr. DiMaio's book that showed a wound caused by a shotgun blast to the chest, she pointed at it and confidently exclaimed,

"Yes, that's your father's wound."

She had just identified a photo of a shotgun wound that had been caused by a weapon with a muzzle approximately three feet from the victim.

Mom finally tried to explain that Dad was not suicidal, did not show any signs of depression or hopelessness, and would not have killed himself at home in his bedroom. The doctor's facial expression changed slightly and her voice became more emboldened. She looked Mom in the eyes and declared with an emotional decree,

"If my husband can commit suicide, anyone can."

This distressing revelation seemed to immediately change the sentiment in the room. It was a discussion climax that brought on that uncomfortable feeling when an unexpected or shocking statement is blurted out. Not really sure how to respond, or question why that was relative to our loved one's case, the family realized there was an emotional attachment deeply buried in the good doctor that shouldn't be weighing on the case we'd brought her; yet it was.

As she gathered her emotions and glanced at the photos of Dad, she softly proclaimed,

"There may have been mistakes made at the time, but I base my findings on the evidence provided by the police and the forensic evidence I observe."

She explained it's the police's job to investigate the physical evidence. They were the ones that needed to provide more evidence in order to change the death certificate.

There it was again; that maddening Catch-22. DPD was stating the ME was the authority responsible for amending the death certificate, and the ME was pointing back at DPD to provide new evidence to amend the certificate. We were once again caught in that endless trap of circular reasoning, and the frustration of mirrored finger pointing. As the meeting ended, she quipped we might want to get with the TV show Unsolved Mysteries to help solve our case. That was the family's final discussion with Dr. Wood.

We knew we were not likely to convince MacKenzie and Brown of our beliefs, when the ME who was held in high esteem by local law enforcement authorities agreed with them. Brown captured our situation quite succinctly on the bottom of page nine of her report when she stated:

"I am taking the opinion of Dr. Wood in reference to this case of the shotgun blast into Mr. Dirscherl's chest was a contact wound. She is very knowledgeable and has a lot of training in respect to gunshot wounds."

We were again on the roller coaster which was headed downwards taking us into one of the valleys we were beginning to know well. Disappointed that we had no credibility with the police, then hopeful the ME would understand the new evidence, then hopes dashed again as she too dismissed our facts and concerns. Frustration seemed to be our constant companion; but then a bit of positive news or information would appear at the right time to raise our hopes and keep us plodding forward.

We had convinced ourselves that when the errors and inaccuracies were corrected, and factual evidence replaced supposition, the reality of what happened that morning distinctly revealed a frightening truth…an uninvited visitor met my father in his bedroom, and literally got away with murder.

Although we were zeroed in on facts, physics and tangible evidence, the next revelation would take us all by surprise and seriously challenge sound minds and mortal beliefs. While the first shocking piece of the puzzle was delivered to my brother's mailbox by the postman, the next puzzle piece would arrive by train.

Chapter 7

Locomotive Breath

As 1994 rolled on, Kim and I were discussing the possibility of seeing a bit more of the world. We'd been stationed at Tyndall Air Force Base for almost eight years, and although I loved the job and the Florida Panhandle, the Air Force was a vehicle that allowed for travel and new experiences.

Friends and acquaintances who'd been stationed in Alaska shared amazing stories of beauty and grandeur. We had seen pictures and heard descriptions of incredible mountains, glaciers, fauna and flora that boggled our imaginations. We decided to list Alaska at the top of our dream sheet, and pursue a possible move.

I'd been stateside my whole career and was getting hot for an overseas assignment. What made it the perfect move was that in the eyes of the military, Alaska was considered an overseas assignment. In the spring of 1994, Air Force orders appeared directing us to head north to the 49th state. That June Shelbi, DeeDee, Kim and I said goodbye to family and friends in Florida, loaded up the Lumina minivan and drove fifty-five hundred miles from Dunedin to Anchorage…and experienced a stunning chunk of North America along the way.

The beauty we experienced did not disappoint; we were surrounded by it and were able to rent our first home in Eagle River, Alaska, a gorgeous community in a river valley about ten miles north of Anchorage. Our Alaska dream had begun and we were loving life. But in March 1995, we were about to discover that the third month meant more than just the beginning of spring, the month of Mom's birth, and a time period on a calendar. It was becoming a marker in our lives that brought with it unexpected events. March 1977 marked Dad's untimely death. March of 1991 involved my not-so-fun skirmish in the stairwell of a coworker. March 1993, brought the strange confession letter from an unknown killer confessing to Dad's murder. While those things made March a month whose presence concerned me, March 1995 brought with it the most incredible and unexplainable phenomenon, event, occurrence... I'm not really sure what to call it, so we'll just go with "The Train Incident." It's one of the most amazing stories I've ever heard and it boldly challenged my beliefs, altered my perception of life and reality, and it still gives me goose bumps when I begin to share the tale. First, a brief explanation...

In 1971 the English Rock Band Jethro Tull released their album *Aqualung*. The album contained several great musical creations including the song *Locomotive Breath*. It was a rocking bluesy ballad with some incredible flute, guitar and piano riffs that always had me singing along. The lyrics portray the imagery of an impending train wreck as an allegory of a man's life falling apart. Ian Anderson, Tull's lead singer/song writer explained the song was a metaphor for life's journey, and how bad things don't stop you; they keep coming and you just have to survive them until the journey ends.

Another more literal meaning of "Locomotive Breath" is the visual imagery of steam billowing from the stack of a steam-powered locomotive as it muscles down the track, or the eerie image of a train engine's heavy breathing as it rests in a steam-filled train station from centuries past. Those are the most common meanings of the term.

In our case "Locomotive Breath" was about to take on a whole new meaning...an ethereal whisper, a breath, or a voice that came from the other side of the grave which was delivered through a stranger on a train. This Locomotive Breath introduced us to a strange new realm of existence we'd never before experienced, and it lead us down the tracks to new leads, new questions, and an amazing revelation that God was involved in this extraordinary chapter of our lives.

The Train Incident began with a phone call from Mom's youngest sister, Mary. She was married to and divorced from Bruce Beihl, previously mentioned in police reports as our family attorney. Mary called my sister Kandy and explained she had received a cassette tape from her ex-husband Bruce. Mary explained the tape had been recorded by my Aunt Fran Bruning and her son Bob. With a flustered voice Mary told Kandy the tape was bizarre and it needed to get to Mom right away. Mary was a bit leery of springing this tape on Mom due to its content, but the next day she met Kandy at Mom's house so the three of them could listen to the tape.

My Aunt Fran Bruning was Mom's and Mary's eldest sister who was still living in Batesville, Indiana; the town in which my mom's and dad's families grew up. Aunt Fran was one of the sweetest, kindest ladies I've ever met; soft spoken, always pleasant, and as honest as the day is long. She was the matriarch of a musical family, a mother of three talented musicians, and wife of Earl Bruning...also a musician and a good man. I remember Aunt Fran and Uncle Earl as the near perfect knock offs for parents in old television shows like Father Knows Best, Leave It To Beaver, and Ozzie and Harriet. You get the drift; kind, loving, wholesome Midwesterners who didn't stray far from the straight and narrow. Uncle Earl passed away some years earlier and Aunt Fran purchased a senior citizen Amtrak travel pass which allowed her to travel the country by rail.

In February 1995, Aunt Fran from Indiana visited with my mom in Florida. She spent a few days in the Sunshine State before heading to California to see her youngest son Bob. When Fran arrived in California and departed the train, she shared with Bob an amazing account of this outlandish encounter she had just been a part of. Bob was so astounded he immediately took her to his home recording studio to record the eerie tale that chronicled Fran's strange train ride which began shortly after she departed the New Orleans station.

I'd like to take a moment here to preface what you're about to read. I'll be the first to admit it sounds quite incredible and unbelievable. So much so, that shortly after it happened my family and I were hesitant about revealing this event. We were already viewed by some of the case investigators as emotional family members of a suicide victim who couldn't deal with reality. This incident was certain to enhance that position for some. That being said, it's a true story that sparked that moniker "The most bizarre unsolved murder mystery in Tampa Bay history"...so here we go.

When Fran's visit with Mom ended in February 1995, she left Florida on her Amtrak adventure, headed for California to see her son Bob. The train made a few stops along the way, but shortly after departing the New Orleans station, Fran noticed a young woman who kept staring at her. Fran didn't recognize the lady; she seemed to be in her late twenties, and was wearing blue jeans, a T-shirt and a baseball cap. After several minutes of staring, she moved to the seat in front of Fran, peered over the top and reluctantly addressed Fran with a one word question...

"Fran?"

Since the young lady knew her name, Fran thought perhaps they had met before. Fran replied "Yes" to the questioning tone and the young lady continued. She introduced herself as Nancy Durham, and explained they had never met, but then quickly uttered the query,

"Was your husband a doctor, and was his name John?"

Fran said "No, my *father* was a doctor and his name was John."

Nancy clarified, "Then your husband's name was Earl."

Fran confirmed the inference, and Nancy continued...

"Well, they're here... with Bob."

Fran was confused because she was on her way to California to see her son Bob. She questioned with a worried tone,

"Bob?"

Nancy replied, "Yes, your sister's husband Bob...and he was murdered about fifteen years ago." Nancy continued, "There are several other people with them, and my father is their spokesman. I've had several experiences like this."

Nancy continued speaking, trying to calm Fran who was now showing obvious signs of confusion and anxiety.

"Please don't be frightened; I'm not a mystic or anything of that kind. I was raised in a very strict Catholic family and that's against our religion...but I've had these strange encounters several times where my father helps me to help somebody else. He has told me that he can't help me, but he can help me help other people. Can we go somewhere where we can talk?"

The two ladies headed to the Club Car and sat across from each other at a table. The young blonde quickly picked up where she had left off.

"My father is going to give me a message for your sister... he is the leader in this group because he has lived through more life times than any of the rest...I think I better write this as he gives me the message."

She grabbed a large Amtrak napkin from the table, unfolded the makeshift notepad and asked Fran for a pen. She then began to channel and put in writing a strange message to Fran's sister...my mom.

Keep in mind this bizarre message was penned by a stranger from Hawaii on a train leaving New Orleans heading for California. It was given to my Aunt from Indiana who was supposed to pass it on to my mother in Florida. And, oh yeah…it was supposedly being channeled through this stranger in real-time by her father who had passed away, and was now hanging out with my deceased father and uncle.

I told you it was going to get pretty weird. The grammar and punctuation are transcribed as closely as possible to Nancy's perplexing written message.

"As I sit on the Amtrak train conversing with Fran I saw a picture in my mind: The Murder of your Husband, Bob. I saw a narrow door opening with a gun case showing. As your husband went to the cabinet near the reflector to get (Dr. Schoals?) foot treatment for athletes feet - He looked up (out) and your husband saw a stranger in the adjoining room - Alarmed the robber fought to keep your husband from taking the gun out of the gun case and the robber shot him at close range - also I believe the robber may have been under the influence of drugs and dangerous. You should get hold of a competent psychic who already does police work whether in United States or overseas does not matter. Then the District Attorney of your state not local should be involved with the new findings to reverse the suicide. It was not suicide and you Ginny, were kept out (by God) to protect you as it was not your time to die. Contact your Insurance carrier with the proper authentic paperwork. The Insurance Co. will reinstate the coverage (over) due to you & your family (loved ones) who have needlessly suffered all these years. I believe your husband Bob (in Spirit) spoke to me as I was conversing on the Amtrak train with your sister Fran. Please contact a competent psychic as soon as humanly possible. You Ginny are not at fault - you could not have saved your husband. It was his time to go home to God. It was not your turn. If you walked into the kitchen at that time (you in spirit were held back by angels - you were not to go into the kitchen for you would have been murdered also.)

"Do not blame yourself" your husband is telling me to tell you. The police wanted to solve too quickly and were wrong. It happens! But the new police will correct. Let go of all guilt It is unfounded & unnecessary. Let go so I can let go where I am. Your depression holds

me back from going to a higher dimension of work. I love you - Be happy - learn to laugh again - see funny movies etc. Force yourself only to think of the happy loving pleasant times. Go in peace & love, Your Husband Bob I love you & Dan & Children and I love All."

After transcribing the clairvoyant episode she'd just experienced, Nancy explained she didn't really know why or how she had this ability. She didn't pursue it or try to contact spirits, it just happened; sometimes when she least expected it. She shared a story with Fran about the first time it happened, and explained it really freaked her out.

She told Fran one night she was in a restaurant having dinner, when she clearly heard a familiar voice, yet no one physically near her was speaking. A voice that sounded like her father's popped into her head and repeated the simple phrase,

"Ice and Water, Ice and Water".

This mystical yet familiar voice startled her and she looked around to see where it was coming from. As she sat there pondering the voice and the message, a young boy darted past her table and collided with a waiter carrying a tray containing a decanter of hot coffee. The scalding coffee sloshed from the tumbling vessel and doused the boy's hand, causing immediate pain and wailing. At nearly the same moment Nancy intuitively reached for the pitcher of ice water that was conveniently sitting on the table directly in front of her. As the boy began to cry from the pain, she grabbed his hand and stuck it in the pitcher of ice water, reducing the pain and calming the young lad. A few moments later the incident was over, normalcy returned to her table, but she was in a state of shock as she tried to comprehend what had just happened.

Fran sat there and listened to the story, probably with her jaw hanging, and her mouth wide open. How? Why? What was going on? These thoughts ran through Fran's mind as she sat there stumped. She had never encountered anything like this and didn't know what to think.

The more time Fran spent with Nancy, the more she realized the young blonde in the ball cap was as normal as they come. Not bizarre, not "out there" just a regular girl who seemed to have an amazing ability she never asked for.

Nancy signed and dated the napkin, and gave a forwarding address. She told Fran she worked for a realtor named Moses in

Maui, and she was going to Hawaii to be married the following fall and invited Fran to the wedding.

The strange encounter neared its end as the train pulled in to the Los Angeles Union Station. Upon its arrival, Fran quickly disembarked and made a beeline towards her son Bob, who was expecting a calm greeting and warm hug from his tired mother. He saw her hustling towards him at a more lively clip and she was excited, speaking uncharacteristically quickly, postponing her traditional mushy greeting as she wanted to get as much of her tale out before Nancy caught up with her.

She wasn't able to share much before the blonde met the two of them at the baggage claim area. Fran introduced her new friend and the threesome made small talk; mostly about Nancy's wedding and how she wanted Fran to attend. Bob hadn't had a chance to unravel or digest what his mother had been trying to quickly tell him. After bags were collected and parting hugs were shared, Nancy went on her way; leaving a confused and psychologically drained retired school teacher standing at the Union Station. Fran shared her chronicle with Bob during their hour-long drive to his home in the San Fernando Valley.

Bob's passion for, and involvement in the music world meant there was a tricked out computer recording station set up at his house. Once they arrived home and settled in, Bob loaded a fresh tape into the cassette recorder and began an impromptu interview with his mother to capture this most bizarre tale before facts blurred and memories faded.

I know this whole encounter sounds like a really bad "B" movie. If I had not seen the letter and heard the story from those personally involved I would have thought, "What a crock!" We still can't explain this weird and wonderful encounter; and no, we did not just fall off the turnip truck. If you think you're skeptical, you should spend some time with my family. However there were some things revealed in that letter that only Mom and Dad knew; some very personal references that my mom had held close.

For instance, towards the end of the writing when Nancy is supposedly channeling my father's words to my mom, she wrote, "*Be happy - learn to laugh again - see funny movies etc.*" This short comment really floored my mom because that reference was a personal memory she and Dad shared years before. When Mom was going through menopause, she had the typical mood swings, so Dad would take her to see funny movies. It became an inside joke between the two of them that nobody knew about until Mom shared it after reading the note.

Another strange statement Nancy passed on was that *"The police wanted to solve too quickly and were wrong. It happens! But the new police will correct."* The new police? This reference seems to apply to something that would happen eight months in the future. The Dunedin Police Department would shut down the following October, and the Pinellas County Sheriff's Office (PCSO) would take over law enforcement responsibilities for the city of Dunedin. It seems the mention of the "New Police" was more than just a meaningless enigma in Nancy's psychic rambling...it seemed to be a reference to a coming future event that had not yet taken place.

As my family and I tried to process this whole train incident, we had some trouble wrapping our minds around it. We all were quite skeptical about psychic phenomena and uncomfortable with its reputation. Remember this encounter took place in 1995 during the heyday of the Psychic Friends Network, where for only $3.99 per minute Dionne Warwick promised anyone could call and receive valuable psychic advice from the network's real psychics.

Then there was Ms. Cleo and the Psychic Readers Network, who were accused of fraud for providing supposed personalized psychic readings which were actually generated from generic scripts. There were psychic reading scams appearing everywhere. Of course many believed the phone psychic's abilities were real, and continued to shell out their $3.99 per minute to hear the scripted messages.

This type of scam and rip-off culture certainly didn't help bolster faith in anyone claiming to have psychic abilities. And here we were, perhaps being swindled by the same type of charlatan.

For days, weeks, and months, questions and doubts filled our heads. Were we being played, or were there really folks out there with psychic abilities? Was Nancy's message for real, or was this some type of ploy for money? Our radar was up, but the request for monetary compensation never came.

We figured there were three possibilities concerning this incident. Option one: Nancy was a phony who had no psychic abilities. Somehow she knew my aunts travel plans, her family background, the story of my father's death, and all the details surrounding it. Then she made up the entire fairy-tale, and arranged the complicated chance meeting.

Why would Nancy go to all that trouble and expense? Why board a train in New Orleans, tell my aunt a crazy, detailed account about the supposed murder of my dad, then depart the train in California, never to contact us again? Was this a failed attempt to extort money from the family? If this was the answer then she did a really good job on the research end of her plan; but she sure wasn't the successful closer of the deal, as there was no attempt to gain in any fashion. Was she plotting a future rip-off, and would soon set the hook; perhaps contacting us for payment later by convincing us she had more critical information that we needed…at a steep cost? No such contact or request was ever made. This answer may be a possibility, but it's highly implausible.

The second option was that Nancy didn't even exist, and Fran made up the whole story with good intentions to help Mom cope with her loss. Perhaps Fran hoped the details about a killer, the mistakes of the police, and the warm fuzzy message from Dad might provide Mom a sense of closure, and relieve any survivor's guilt she might be experiencing. If Fran concocted the whole yarn, she did a darn good job of it, and got her son Bob to go along with it, as Bob also provided details about meeting Nancy at the train station.

This theory is also busted because after I heard the story, I located a Robert Moses Realty in Maui, and on March 13, 1995 (yes…the eighteenth anniversary of Dad's death) I called and spoke to Moses, who said Nancy was out for a few weeks, but he would leave her a message. I didn't hear anything for months, so on July 21st, I called Moses again. He said he passed on several messages to her; he then gave me a phone number and name of apartments where she once lived. I called the PoinCiana apartments but got an answering machine at the front desk, not her personal apartment.

Three days later I mailed letters asking Nancy to please contact me. I mailed one to her last apartment address and one to Mr. Moses asking him to forward it to her. On August 10th I received an envelope from Honolulu addressed to me. It had no return address, and the only thing inside was a half page torn from the MAUI'ANA magazine, August 1995 edition. It was an advertisement for a psychic spiritual healer named Dawn Christie. Nancy Durham really existed, but apparently she was quite busy with her life and wedding plans, and didn't want to be involved any further with our case, or her uncomfortable ability. So Fran and Bob had not created this mystery person, or lied about the meeting…she was real, as was their story.

The third option was beginning to make the most sense, even though it was one of the toughest to believe. It was the possibility this psychic incident actually happened as described. It meant believing this young blonde stranger on the train really did receive a message from her father on the other side, and was passing that info on to a retired Midwestern school teacher with the intent to help complete strangers. Perhaps there were people who really did have extraordinary gifts and could do the things they claimed…people like Nancy Durham.

If her story was true, and the strange vision she shared was a genuine recall of what happened March 13, 1977, then her gift and abilities were real, and her placement on the train with my aunt was not just coincidence. What makes this whole issue even more marvelous and astounding, is the greater issue this incident brings to light.

A few key sentences of her message provide answers to one of the most important question humans struggle with…Is there a God?

"It was not suicide and you Ginny, were kept out (by God) to protect you as it was not your time to die." And…

"It was his time to go home to God. It was not your turn. If you walked into the kitchen at that time (you in spirit were held back by angels - you were not to go into the kitchen for you would have been murdered also.)"

These words she wrote were supposedly not her own, and at some point she stopped channeling her father and began passing on information directly from my dad to my mother. But this strange message was coming from two men who had left this world and were in a different place, or a different life, a different dimension, or perhaps a heaven. The words and message Nancy passed on clearly imply there is a God. Not only do her words buttress the reality of God, but they imply a personal involvement by this God and suggest He is engaged in our individual lives…and apparently has plans for our future.

So were Dad's death, the botched police investigation, the lady on a train, and all the other peripheral details just random and meaningless; perhaps caused by the chaos of an accidental universe…or was there design and planning behind the scene?

This matter leads me back to that Sunday morning and the questions about why I didn't hear the shotgun go off. If Nancy's details were accurate, perhaps I had experienced a God-thing that morning, and I wasn't supposed to hear the gun go off. Perhaps there was some ethereal plan at work. Perhaps God-things can happen anytime, anyplace, to anyone?

Does the fact that many people don't believe this possibility make it false? If it's true, then those who don't believe are by definition, wrong. We believe what we want to believe, but the truth is the truth no matter what. And our beliefs may make us who we are; but they don't make us right.

It seemed paranormal and supernatural involvement had entered and enveloped parts of our story. March 1995 came and went; but it left us with a memory and an experience that would challenge our beliefs and cause us to question life as we knew it. We knew the police were going to love this new evidence.

Chapter 8

Beliefs...

"They make us who we are, but they don't make us right."

Dad died when I was fourteen, and for years I never really psychoanalyzed the deep affects this proclaimed suicide was having on everyone. But over the years of investigating details, as well as stepping back and gazing at the big picture; trying to figure out what happened, and what didn't, I began to look a little deeper into my own psyche, and began to discover how Dad's life and death had impacted my own life, actions, decisions, values, and beliefs.

Not only was I able to realize how my life had been impacted, I was also able in some ways to understand a bit more about how Dad's death affected Mom and my siblings as well. I'm not claiming I understand everything my family is feeling or has felt over the years. But it's kind of enlightening to step back and try to understand how my brothers and sister dealt with, and are currently dealing with the situation.

In recent years, I've dug down deep into my memory and my soul and I've discovered some truths about myself. I realize that even though I felt compassion and sorrow for Dad, I realized at some point years ago I probably touched on anger towards him as well. Even though I didn't believe it was suicide from the get-go, I had to at times accept that the experts were right; or at least admit the slim possibility Dad could have committed suicide.

When trying to recreate theories and possibilities of how he may have killed himself, I had to consider the idea that he shot himself. That was a difficult premise to wrap my mind around, and it made me angry inside…thinking he may have decided suicide was the easy way out of a situation and that our family would be left behind to deal with the issue, the stigma, the elephant. Even though those thoughts were short lived and not based in truth, they were there, at least subconsciously. The elephant had unexpectedly entered our lives and for years lurked in the background, just noticeable enough to remind us of the suicide stigma and Dad's possible sin.

One of the most recurrent effects the stigma had on me was when I would meet new friends. Being in the military and moving around quite a bit, I was always meeting new friends, coworkers, bosses, etc. Getting close to people and discussing family backgrounds, upbringing and childhoods was always a bit uncomfortable. Whenever a new friend would ask about my mom and dad, my answer would always include a clarifying explanation. I felt I had to try to explain the situation in a one minute spiel.

"My mom lives in Florida, my dad was killed in 77"...do I continue with, "the police called it a suicide, but it's a really strange story and...." How far do I go with this story? Do I just leave it at, "Dad was killed?" Do I go into the whole Unsolved Mysteries episode? Is this simple question about my family going to result in a baffling twenty-minute chronicle?

I wanted people to know the truth instead of walking away thinking my father had killed himself, so some of my close friends got the 20-minute version, while others just got a snippet.

This experience hasn't ended. To this day my explanation still takes some time, but the personal stigma of suicide is much farther removed, and has been replaced with a bit of comfort knowing the truth Dad was killed by another. How's that for a bit of irony; gaining comfort knowing your father was murdered?

As facts began to clear his name that guilty shameful feeling began to subside, and I think all of us were able to breathe a little easier knowing this claim of suicide was false. That familiar, self-imposed pachyderm was on its way out...we were no longer the children whose father committed suicide.

As I mentioned at the beginning of this book, beliefs are extraordinarily powerful shaping entities, responsible in some ways for every human event and decision throughout history. What is so interesting is that we can choose to believe anything...and we do. If you can think it, there is probably someone out there who will believe it.

Some beliefs we may doubt a bit, some beliefs we may consider to be true, and other beliefs we may bet our lives on. While we wish believing something would make it true, that's not necessarily the case. The reality of the matter is, no matter how strongly you or I believe something, we may be wrong. I point out this obvious statement because some folks have a problem admitting it, especially if they've placed a great deal of time, energy and faith in their belief and attempted to convince their peers they're right. For some it's painful to admit the error of their ways, but the reality is at some point in our lives we all choose to believe a lie. In these times we live, this truism seems to be dimming in the minds of many. To some there is no such thing as being wrong; empirical truths have blurred, and relative truths seem to be the accepted rule.

Years ago I began writing another book; at least I began writing it in my mind. It was a book about beliefs, and how they affect, impact and shape our lives. The problem was I knew I had to tell the story of my father's death from a family perspective so the world would know the truth about what happened. I realized I probably wasn't going to be able to complete two quality books anytime soon, and the truth about Dad's death was a much more important story that needed to be told.

As I decided to shelve *The Belief Project* and begin penning this book, I realized the two naturally converged. It became apparent this whole police case, lack of justice, and our frustrations were, and still are based on beliefs. The police believed Dad committed suicide. They established those beliefs in the first 30 minutes of their investigation. The Medical Examiner believed their "brief synopsis" which may have skewed her observations. The nurse who hadn't seen Dad in two years believed he was depressed enough to kill himself. We believed otherwise.

Unfortunately their beliefs were formed around the original ideas and reports offered by those police officers shortly after the shooting. That Sunday morning, their hurried conclusion that my father committed suicide initiated a cognitive process, and convincing reasoning that extended through lives, the community, and now through history.

How do beliefs morph from an abstract idea into a potential life shaping conviction? What makes a person believe something? What makes you believe the things you believe right now? I don't pretend to know the whole complicated answer to that question, but I do believe I know some of the influences on the list: Memories, emotions, values, morals, religion, observations, experiences, conscience, imagination, and suggestions. These are a few terms that come to mind when I think about what might influence personal beliefs. The remarkable thing is that once you believe something, it's likely to influence your actions and behavior which leads to inevitable consequences.

While the police had based their beliefs on faulty observations and skewed data, once they announced their convictions as truth, the toothpaste was pretty much out of the tube, and their reputations were on the line. If through further investigation new facts and evidence were revealed that challenged or even disproved their beliefs, some weren't likely to alter their viewpoint. I believe pride captured some of their hearts and wouldn't let them admit the truth, even though they knew deep down inside they may have made mistakes. Pride is a bully that coerces humble beings into believing their lies.

As I write about this topic, I know there are psychologists, scientists, scholars and theologians who may disagree with my concepts. But I'm sharing these beliefs about beliefs to reveal their importance in the life-altering events surrounding Dad's death. Pondering these questions and searching for the answers gave me a new perspective on this whole story of Dad's life, death, and beyond. It also revealed to me why the police were sticking to their beliefs, and why we were sticking to ours. And it led to a deeper connection in my life that's greater than all these details. That deeper connection was a simple life changing recognition; the recognition of the reality of God, and the uncomplicated act of receiving His Son as my Savior.

We had all been angry with the Police, angry with the Medical Examiner and angry with the State's Attorney. My anger and quest for revenge began to subside as I grew in my new relationship. Through the early 1990s, I had been developing a different relationship with God. My personal religious experience with Catholicism had provided me information, doctrine, and ceremony…a religious system if you will; but it left me with a void I wasn't sure how to fill, and doubts I wasn't sure how to address.

While stationed at Tyndall we regularly attended Catholic Mass. I also would provide Gospel readings as the lector and was teaching second graders the Church's doctrine through the Confraternity of

Christian Doctrine (CCD). I would occasionally get into interesting discussions about the Church with the young Air Force Chaplain Priest. Unfortunately the more I spoke with him, the more I realized he didn't believe what he was preaching, didn't believe scripture was the Word of God, and implied the Bible was mostly fiction designed to help people feel good; yet here he was leading his sheep…somewhere.

All I knew was Catholicism, and here was this Catholic principal pointing me somewhere I knew in my heart was the wrong direction. I realized I personally had been learning how to be a good Catholic, but I knew there was more to it than that. There was a void that wasn't being filled, and a question that hadn't been answered. I was slowly and steadily being drawn to the Truth before I even knew I was searching for it.

Even though my priest seemed to be denying the reality of God, I still believed in the God of the Bible and I began to search for evidence to support my belief…if it was out there. What was this passionate draw…this captivating sensation that there was something more to learn…what was the Good News?

I began to study and became extremely intrigued with the Creation-Evolution debate, and prophesy and eschatology. Since I was in the bible studying Genesis and Revelation…I figured the information between the first and last books might contain some interesting information as well. (Amazing how God works)

After looking at the secular world and its explanations, I had to decide…based on the evidence; was this Bible true or was it a myth…a nice story and all, but perhaps not worth betting my eternal life on.

As my weekly Catholic traditions were no longer feeding my soul, a friend invited me to a Protestant church service where I encountered an experience and a message of salvation that was based solely on God's Grace. I finally understood the Good News and realized how simple it all was...for some, too simple.

The void I had been experiencing was filled to capacity; I began my personal relationship with Christ, which I believe is what He wants with all of us. God's promise was kept and the Holy Spirit entered my life. Those who haven't experienced the Holy Spirit in this way won't understand it…but it happens just like scripture promises.

As I began to travel down this new fork in the road, I also coincidentally began to listen to new music. My teen years and early adult life had been filled primarily with classic rock, from AC/DC to

Zeppelin, which I still enjoy today. But as I matured a bit, I got tired of listening to the "in your face" disc jockeys whose sense of humor pushed comfortable limits and influenced listeners with negative, discouraging and smutty attitudes. If you listen to Pop or Rock radio stations today, you know what I'm talking about.

I occasionally found myself tuning my car radio to a local Christian station and discovered a world of great music that contained a positive message. It seemed I was still hearing the rock music I learned to love, but the messages of the disc jockeys and the Godly lyrics brought a welcomed positive glow to the mix. I was experiencing fantastic rock love songs and even some heavy metal anthems that were praising and glorifying God. It seemed I had stumbled on to the best of both worlds.

Today there is a phenomenal radio and web-based nonprofit music ministry called K-LOVE, and it's filling this country and the world with positive encouraging music performed by some of the most talented artist out there. If you think you have to give up great rock 'n roll to experience a Godly message, I challenge you to listen to K-LOVE for a week. If you can't find them on your dial, try their free smart phone application or check them out on the web at www.klove.com. Give it a day or two, not just one song; and listen with an open mind and heart.

When I began to understand the Good News through less religious worship, and more through personal relationship, I wanted to share it with others, especially my family. Trying to explain supernatural phenomenon is not always easy (as we involved in this story are all well aware). I equate trying to explain the mystery of the Holy Spirit entering my heart, to that of a new mother trying to explain the unequalled experience and bond of carrying and delivering a new life. If someone has never experienced that amazing blessing, they really can't fully understand or appreciate it. And though scoffers may try to tell the new mother it's a remarkable biological process...but there's really nothing *that* special about it, I don't think most moms would agree. Trying to explain the experience is a bit like trying to describe the most beautiful sight you've ever seen, by showing someone a photo. It doesn't do justice, or capture the real essence.

When I accepted Christ in my life, there was no momentary revelation, no flash of lightning, nor a date I can pinpoint. It was simply a growing knowledge He was real, and He wanted me to know Him better. All it took was softening my heart towards the possibility and accepting the truth He wanted to share.

I know to some this Holy Spirit stuff sounds as crazy as the psychic on the train…but apparently she too was real. And this new acceptance in my life brought with it a wisdom and knowledge, just as promised. I had accepted Christ in my life and through the Holy Spirit I was being introduced to things I had not experienced before; one of the most important…a softened heart and the ability to forgive. The other, equally as important…the ability to cast my worries upon the Lord, and turn over this whole redemptive quest to God, because I now understood He was in charge and had a plan.

I began to reflect on the strange happenings throughout the case from the standpoint God had been involved. The moment Dad was shot; was this a moment in time when there was a protection placed over me…the hand of God, or an Angel? Perhaps it was a comforting protecting hand that kept me from rushing into the middle of a murder in progress; a hedge of protection that ultimately saved my life for a reason; a reason I couldn't understand, but for a purpose none the less. Was this a God-thing I'd experienced? At that time I reasoned it must have just been the unconscious brain of a sleeping teenager that numbly muffled the blast and concussion at the other side of the house. Perhaps…perhaps not.

Dad's death, which initiated this incredible thirty-plus year journey, has been a life-changing tragedy…but it was also a fork in the road that changed the Dirscherls, plus hundreds, if not thousands of people's lives. When that shotgun discharged and Dad left this world, the butterfly-effect engaged and one thing began to affect another. Mom and I eventually moved, met new people, changed habits, and went about lives in ways that would have been different if Dad were around. Siblings moved, formed new lives, encountered new people and relationships. I often wonder how our lives would be different if Dad were still with us. Would he be sitting in Alaska enjoying his grandkids? Would I even have these kids? Would I have met my wife? Would I have joined the military?

I felt it necessary to explain my life with Christ and how Catholicism played a very important part in that relationship. I believe everything happens for a reason, and apparently this was God's plan for my family and me. I hope and pray He also plans to clear up very soon, the mystery surrounding our story.

Chapter 9

Unsolved Mysteries

In March (of course) of 1995, I was watching an episode of the very popular television show Unsolved Mysteries. It included a story about a Psychic named Noreen Renier who had worked with, and supposedly helped a police department in Marathon Key, Florida. While I was skeptical of the whole psychic angle, watching the calm, cool and apparently level headed detective discuss using the psychic to assist them made me feel a bit more comfortable considering it. Noreen didn't seem like the psychics from the Psychic Hotline, who promised she could read the future. She seemed to be able to present case details and provide enough new information that assisted the police in closing some cold cases. The fact that the police were using this woman's services seemed to legitimize my interest, so I decided to follow up.

On March 14th, 1995, I phoned the Marathon Key Sheriff's Department, Special Operations section, and spoke with a Detective Glover. We chatted a bit about their use of Noreen to assist with a cold case, and I briefly explained our situation to him. Glover told me he was a skeptic and didn't know how she was able to do what she did. But he said her help was real and recommended we give her a try.

On March 20th I phoned and spoke with Noreen, asking questions and tip-toeing around our story trying to find out how she may be able to help. I was careful to mask the story by not providing any names, dates or locations in case she was an imposter who would study the case details and perhaps try to wow us with nothing new.

I explained that I had seen her on Unsolved Mysteries, and told her I had a very strange story and asked if she was still involved in police work; she stated that's all she did. I explained we had a seventeen year-old homicide, and that some new evidence had come to light. I asked her what she did and how she did it. She stated she needed to be involved with the police because she needed to touch something that was on the body when the person was killed.

She said, "I basically relive what they saw, I'm a Psychometrist".

She explained she could draw a face of the killer by holding an article of clothing the victim was wearing at the time of the killing. She said she thought it would look like the killer looked seventeen years ago. She recommended using a ring or pair of glasses worn by the victim. I asked if it would work if she held the weapon.

She gasped and said, "Oh my God, then we would have the bad guy as well! That would be so easy"!

I explained the weapon had been returned to us and she inquired if police were calling it a suicide. I told her that's what they were claiming. She said she would hold the weapon and her artist would draw a picture of the person it fit last. She said hopefully we would pick up the last person who touched it.

I asked what she charged for her services; she said $650 for a session that usually lasts about one and a half to two hours. If we needed a follow-up session it would be an additional $150. She stated if the police requested her service, they would pay her fee; if the family requested her service, they paid her fee. She offered to mail some info about her services, so I gave her two mailing addresses using my wife's and Guys wife's maiden names...just to prevent using the name Dirscherl, which in my skeptical mind might be just what she needed for research.

After hanging up the phone it dawned on me that there could be a problem with her process and results. She said her artist could draw a picture of the person who the gun fit, or who had last touched it.

Kandy had been in possession of the Mauser for the last year or so, since the DPD began their new investigation. And I had the gun for the previous eleven or twelve years. I had hunted with it in North Dakota, and had done some skeet shooting with it at Tyndall, as well as target test fires, etc. The shotgun was one of only a few items of Dad's that I inherited after his death, and I had used it quite a bit. Was all this handling of the weapon going to be a problem? I discussed it with the family and we figured it was worth a try as we had no other hot leads to follow.

In April or May 1995, Mom decided to write the Florida State's attorney's office to share our concerns that there may have been some problems with the DPD's investigation. In August 1995, after a few months of not hearing anything, I called the State's Attorney hoping to speak with the Honorable Bernie McCabe.

My call was transferred to Dick Yerby, the investigator who had been placed on the case. Mr. Yerby said he was preparing a response to Mom's letter. He said he spoke with those police officials involved with Dad's case in 1977 and 1993 and that they convinced him the case was properly closed and there were no new facts to warrant any reinvestigation. He stated he personally believed the confession letter was a hoax, and implied I could have authored the note.

Our conversation became a little heated at times and I was getting frustrated that nobody seemed to be looking at the facts or the possibility of a second person in the room. He said the agencies we needed to convince were DPD and the ME, and his office would take no further action unless there was a problem with the original investigation. He said he placed no merit in police psychics, but didn't condemn trying one.

It was pretty obvious that the State's Attorney's Office was not interested in hearing more concerns about the poor investigation. It was that same recurrent theme playing out through a different agency: They were the experts, we were the distraught family tilting at windmills, and we just needed to deal with it. Once again we received the consoling pat on the head and the masked ridiculing attitude that they were the experts and they had it right.

The little hope we had was fading again. Law enforcement had made up their collective minds the suicide finding would stand. Our hopes were now pinned on the supposed psychic abilities of an eccentric senior citizen in Gainesville, Florida. Maybe Noreen Reneir's psychometry session would open new leads; it was all we had going.

October 1995 brought with it the "New Police" so precisely prophesized on that train napkin. The DPD was being disbanded and law enforcement services for Dunedin were going to be provided by the Pinellas County Sheriff's Department (PCSD). Some of the departing Dunedin police signed on with the PCSD, some didn't. Apparently Captain MacKenzie would not be joining the Sheriff's department, but instead began working with the nearby Tarpon Springs' Police Department.

Although he and Detective Brown considered our case closed, we didn't. Unfortunately the Dunedin Police Department closure meant there was no active law enforcement agency investigating our case. If we were going to continue investigating with the help of law enforcement, we were going to have to start from the beginning, providing all the facts and reestablishing our data, theories and evidence.

It was kind of like the dilemma of visiting a new doctor for the first time. We weren't very happy with our old doctor, but he had a lot of important records and information. While we weren't very confident in the old doc's abilities, there was a small sense of familiarity and history that we hoped would cure our ills. Unfortunately the doctor we were seeing was on the downhill slide, and it was time he retired. The patient was not doing well and the prognosis wasn't good. Perhaps fate, or destiny, or God would find us a new doctor who could work his magic, and find the cure we were desperately searching for.

The family needed to decide what to do next. Time was rolling on; friends, family and people involved with the case were aging, and any leads we had were cooling off and had been shelved by the last doctor. We needed a new path, a new lead, something that would bring us the help we prayed for.

After the police department conversion, our efforts and actions cooled. Reinitiating the whole process with the new department seemed a bit daunting. Cyclical emotional peaks and valleys were becoming the norm. We all seemed to have rolled into one of those emotional valleys where we paused, placed our case and our quest at the back of our minds and got on with the normalcy of our lives.

Although the news about the case had not been that positive, life for the Dirscherls in Alaska was amazing; Kim was pregnant and we were expecting a boy. While none of our kids were "planned additions" God had blessed us with two gorgeous little girls, DeeDee and Shelbi, and now there was a boy on the way to round out our family.

We were discussing boys' names and of course my ego demanded there be a Daniel in the mix, but I also wanted to include some greater family heritage in my son's name. We eventually decided on a name that would include Daniel, and a middle name that would also honor his two grandfathers; one of which he would never meet.

My Dad's first and middle names were Robert John, and Kim's Dad's names were Roy James. We incorporated the common first initials and came up with Daniel R.J. Dirscherl. To this day he goes by R.J. Just to make the whole thing sweeter, he entered the world on December 2nd 1996, which happened to be my 34th birthday. His arrival was a magnificent birthday present, and his name a legacy to honor his grandfathers.

Backing up a few months to August 1996: I was again getting restless about the case and felt like something needed to be done. I decided that I would write a letter to Reader's Digest explaining our situation, with the hopes the right person; a detective, attorney, or forensic expert might pick up the Digest while waiting in their doctor's or dentist's office, read our plea for help and rush to our aid. I knew it was a long shot, but we had been taking the close shots for a few years with no real results to show for it.

I wasn't really keen about the idea of publicly sharing this story because it was such a personal and crazy yarn. I was concerned that going public with our story meant we could be made to look like morons. As I debated pros and cons of sending the letter, I came to the realization that the public had been helping other families find answers and solve cases through new television shows like Dateline, 20/20, Prime Time Live, 48 Hours, and the very popular show Unsolved Mysteries. Dr. Joan Wood had even suggested using Unsolved Mysteries to help find answers, so I decided to write them as well.

The family supported the idea, so on August 15, 1996, I sent an eight page letter to Unsolved Mysteries, Reader's Digest, and a few of the other national television news shows. Two weeks later I received a call at work from Judy Storch with Cosgrove-Meurer Productions. She said Unsolved Mysteries producers were very interested in the story and asked us to provide her copies of the police reports, and the tape of Fran's train incident. Judy began to gather info and coordinate things through my family in Florida and with me in Alaska.

On September 16th, she called me and explained the whole process; she was in the process of writing a research report which would go to the executive producers. If they Okayed it, they would send out a team to scout the area and the story. After a final blessing by the producers, writers would prepare an outline, then they would develop a schedule to film the episode; normally a two to five day process.

I asked Judy if they planned on involving a forensic pathologist. Unfortunately she stated they didn't bring new experts into cases. Instead they planned to show the things we'd discovered, and talk to a few of the people involved; probably Joan Wood, Det. Farrell, and perhaps someone at the Sheriff's Dept. They did also plan to track down Nancy Durham if they could find her.

While I was hoping they might expand the investigation, the reality was they were going to simply tell the story as we knew it. This wasn't the perfect scenario I'd hoped for, but it was something positive, and we were again leaving a valley and heading upwards on our emotional coaster ride.

Mom, Guy and Kandy were also communicating with the "New Police"; the Pinellas County Sheriff's Department. They met with Detective Rob Snipes who had been assigned to our case and was following up on cold leads and seemed to be seriously investigating the case and our concerns. They even went back to the house on Lotus and searched for etched fingerprints and blood spatter evidence from the bedroom some seventeen years after the crime. As one might expect, no incriminating physical evidence was found.

The Unsolved Mysteries project was taking shape; television producers and directors were calling and interviewing the family. We reviewed scripts and shuttled documents back and forth for weeks. In mid October I received my plane ticket from the production folks, and on Tuesday, November 19, 1996, I departed Anchorage, headed for Tampa International Airport, and home to see family.

My connecting flight was through Minneapolis, and when I departed that airport my seat was next to the window directly over the left wing. As the flight continued the Captain's voice came over the speaker system notifying us that the plane had developed a hydraulic fluid leak, but that it shouldn't be a problem. Personally I believed that a hydraulic leak at 36,000 feet was a problem, especially since I was looking out my window watching the fluid leak down the wing.

I knew I shouldn't have gotten on that plane. I had questioned whether or not I should leave for Florida; the baby was due in a couple weeks and the doubts and what-ifs kept popping into my mind. Now the possibility of a horrific plan crash played through my mind's eye, and the negative vibes gave me the willies. I'm pretty sure I wasn't the only person praying on that plane.

Our prayers were answered and we made it to Tampa without a scratch. Once again, all seemed right with the world.

That night I stayed at Guy and Barb's house in Clearwater. Kook flew in from North Carolina, George drove in from Ormond Beach, and Kandy was already nearby as she lived in Dunedin. On

Thursday, the five of us kids had breakfast with Mom at Dunedin Lanes bowling alley; Mom and Dad's old stomping grounds. During their heyday, they were a fixture at those lanes. Their house was full of trophies and bowling memorabilia, so it was a nice place to have breakfast with the family and reminisce a bit.

After Breakfast we headed to a beautiful mansion located on a bayou in Tarpon Springs that the producers had rented for filming. The place was gorgeous, built in 1885, and was filled with personal photos of the owners with Presidents Reagan and Bush 41. This is where we filmed our individual interviews for the show. The next day we filmed at the cemetery where Dad was buried, then more filming back at Mom's house.

We helped crew members locate some classic automobiles which they modified to look like old Dunedin police cars. Another part of the crew rented an actual Amtrak train, and hired two actresses to plan Nancy Durham and Aunt Fran. The train scene alone cost about $100,000 to film.

The filming coordination was impressive; there were so many people running around the house while caterers set up a lunch buffet in Mom's garage. There were grouchy old neighbors complaining about all the vehicles in the neighborhood, but the filming process clicked along like structured chaos.

Another facet of the filming which kind of surprised us all was where they planned to film the murder scene. Producers had coordinated with the current owners of our old house at 1111 East Lotus Drive, and were planning to film the murder scene in Mom and Dad's old bedroom; the actual location where Dad had been killed two decades earlier.

The fact that Unsolved Mysteries chose to film at the actual house where the death occurred played a pivotal role in our ongoing investigation…perhaps more coincidence. While the goal of using Unsolved Mysteries was to get the word out about Dad's death and request help from viewers of the show, the leads we were hoping for began to appear even before the filming had been completed.

It was Friday and producers told us they were handing out flyers in the old Lotus neighborhood explaining to homeowners that the following day, Unsolved Mysteries would be closing off a few roads in the neighborhood so they could film the story of the mysterious 1977 death of Robert Dirscherl. Producers allowed Kandy, Mom,

Kook and I to visit the house as they prepared it for filming. It had been about fifteen years since I'd been in the house, and while it had been repainted, remodeled and filled with stranger's belongings, there was a sense of familiarity. The house looked quite different; smaller and more modern, but there was a familiar smell that brought back distant memories from years gone by.

Producers didn't just rent the house, they asked us to provide personal items that would have been present back in 1977. I remember Mom giving them a watercolor painting of the house I painted in ninth grade art class, which they hung on the wall of the bedroom. We continued to walk the house, as though we were on a tour through a museum; it was foreign yet familiar.

We met the actors who were going to portray Mom and Dad, and got to take one last look through the house before we had to leave. The energy of the producers and film crew was high. They were on a schedule; time is money in the film industry. We had to get out of the way so filming could continue.

As we departed we saw dozens of cars, equipment trucks and police vehicles parked all over the neighborhood. It was an eerily familiar scene that closely mirrored that awful day in 1977. As we left the house and walked the several hundred feet to our car, I kept turning around to view the craziness that was taking place on the corner lot at 1111 East Lotus drive. It was amazing to realize all this was happening so these strangers could film the story of Dad's death to share with the television viewing world. We were filming the story with the hopes that at least one of those TV viewers might come forward with some information that would help us solve our mystery.

The experience was quite surreal and a little overwhelming for us all. Mom was getting a bit tired so after a meal at Country Boys' restaurant, we headed back to her house to relax and watch, what else?...Unsolved Mysteries.

As I've done previously in this book, I'd like to pause and preface what you are about to read. The following pages discuss some beliefs, theories and investigations that involve some family friends. While I'm a little uncomfortable mentioning names, I hope folks understand there is no malice or intent to embarrass anyone. There is already another book out there that includes much of what I'm about to share. My hope is that people understand why I'm including them in this story. As I explained in the preface, one of my goals was to tell this whole mysterious tale so people could hear the complete true story.

When we returned to Mom's house we sat down and turned on Unsolved Mysteries. Just a few minutes into the show, the phone rang and I answered. A familiar female voice on the other end blurted out a phrase that took me by surprise and about knocked me to my knees. The voice belonged to one of my closest childhood friends, Ingrid French. Ingrid's abrupt statement was filled with a confident emotion I could pick up through the phone line. She simply blurted out, "Danny, I think I know who killed your dad."

She explained she had heard about the filming, and had gotten a copy of the confession letter. She asked if we could get together to talk; we agreed to meet at Slider's Pub which was about half way between our old Lotus home, and her parents house. I hung up and told Kook what Ingrid shared, and that she wanted to talk. Mom was tired so I explained Ingrid just wanted to see us while we were in town, so Kook and I were going to meet her at the pub for a beer. We met Ingrid at Slider's and she immediately provided a name.

Ingrid said "I think Matt M. killed your dad."

It was a name I was shocked to hear. Matt and I were in the same class through eight years of elementary and middle school at Our Lady of Lourdes (OLL) Catholic School. His mom was a third grade teacher at OLL, and we were good friends up through about eighth grade. We'd had sleep-overs and had gone to camp together in 1973 and 1974. We both went to Dunedin Sr. High, but our friendship dimmed as we began hanging around different clicks.

Unfortunately, Matt's road forked down a path that lead to a lifestyle that he and his family would regret years later. His rap sheet was long, and included drug charges, breaking-and-entering, burglaries and associated crimes. There were also rumors he was involved somehow in a vampire cult, and had also admitted to a girlfriend he had been present at a murder.

Ingrid was a year younger than Matt and me, but they were boyfriend and girlfriend for a while back in middle school. Ingrid had kept tabs on a lot of old friends and she knew the whereabouts of a bunch of the old OLL gang. She had a memory like a steel trap, and could recall details from the past which I couldn't begin to remember. Ingrid conveyed a serious sense of confidence about her claim. She said she had a letter at her house that would help make sense of her belief that Matt may be involved.

At about 10:00 that night we left Slider's and headed to the French's house to read this eerie letter she mentioned. Ingrid's dad John and her mom Sandy sat with us and explained they all had this creepy feeling they were realizing Matt was likely the writer of the confession letter we had received.

They explained Matt had recently died of complications associated with AIDS and that they too had received a letter; but this letter was from his parents. When they saw a copy of the confession letter we had received, they were seriously creeped out. They searched for the letter they had received but couldn't track it down that night. They asked us to come back the next day so they could have some time to find it.

The next morning, was a Saturday. Guy, Kook, Kandy and I showed up at French's house and sat down to pick up where we had left off. Sandy had the letter they had received from Matt's parents. It was a four page, hand printed letter apparently penned by Matt's dad. The letter was a touching correspondence that explained the family's situation in dealing with Matt's severe illness. They thanked their friends for their thoughts and prayers and discussed Matt's mental and physical states.

This letter may have a lot to do with our suicide/murder investigation, and it reveals a bit of circumstantial evidence showing Matt may have been the one responsible for my dad's death. I'm tempted to share the whole letter here with you, but something inside me keeps me from doing so. While the words reveal much about Matt the possible suspect, they are also a personal communication from the parents of a dying child to friends they wanted to thank and share with. I just don't feel comfortable reprinting the whole personal letter, but I feel I need to share some of the critical evidence.

The reason Ingrid freaked when she read the confession letter we'd received on March 16, 1993, was that it was eerily similar to parts of the letter they had received. Their letter was postmarked through Tampa, and was dated March 16, 1992. Our letter was postmarked through Tampa, but was dated March 13, 1993. Take a close look at the letter we received, and do the math on the dates...

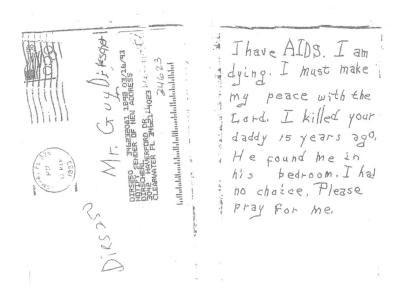

We received the confession letter in March of 1993, but it says "I killed your Daddy 15 years ago…" which implied the letter was actually written in March of 1992, or the math was wrong. The letter the French's received from Matt's family was postmarked March 16th, 1992; almost exactly **fifteen** years after the date of Dad's death. This quirky fluke left an uneasy feeling about the possible relationship between the two letters. The verbiage of the letters showed a strange similarity as well. The French's letter discussed Matt's fatal condition, and contained the phrases, "*Matt is very much at peace-even though he can't be healed. He has asked his uncle, Father Ernie to come give him the Last Rites, the sacrament of the sick, and to be the celebrant at his funeral Mass.*" It goes on to say, "*The top cavity of both lungs are full of abscesses and x-rays show they are continuing to grow. The cultures have been in the lab for 6 weeks and still no diagnosis. Cancer and T.B. have been ruled out. Matt's blood count is around 50 (1000 being the norm) and his immune system is weak.*"

The letter doesn't specifically mention AIDS, but instead almost intentionally avoids the term, perhaps due to its unclean reputation at the time.

Was the confession letter sent to my brother actually written by Matt, or a family member in 1992, at the same time as the explanatory letters mailed by his parents? We began to brainstorm and came up with the believable possibility that the letters may have been written at the same time, but were perhaps mailed a year apart. It seemed possible that if he were dying, and making his peace with the Lord, he may want to purge his sins through a private written confession.

If Matt was responsible, did his parent even know? If they did, perhaps the emotional overload of telling friends Matt was dying, and also sending a confession letter of murder was just too much to handle. Perhaps the confession letter was held until the next anniversary of Dad's death, and was then mailed to Guy's address. He had moved since the letter had been addressed, which is why it took some rerouting to find him. This possibility made sense logically and mathematically, but it was just a theory that we couldn't prove...circumstantial evidence at best.

The more we heard that day about Matt, the more we tended to believe the possibility he was involved. Ingrid's dad shared Matt had worked at a service station in town in the 1980s, but was stealing tools. The owner was a good friend of the family and Matt's dad even worked out a plan where he would compensate the station owner for Matt's wages, just to keep him working and hopefully keep him away from the other influences he'd surrounded himself with.

Ingrid knew one of Matt's old girlfriends who may have some helpful information. Her name was Lori and we decided to phone her that afternoon. We wanted to get something that had been written by Matt so we could provide it to the police for a handwriting comparison. Lori had an old letter Matt had written to her while he was incarcerated in New York, and she agreed to fax it to Ingrid. Ingrid and I jumped in the car and headed to her family's carpet business at the corner of Pinehurst and Main Street to receive the letter now being sent over the phone lines. It was a short drive that was filled with emotion and anticipation. We both had a large swarm of butterflies in our stomach as we pondered this whole crazy possibility.

We turned the faxed letter over to Detective Snipes so the Sheriff's Department could send it to the Florida Department of Law Enforcement for handwriting analysis. We were hopeful that the handwriting samples might be a useful piece of physical evidence, and that the experts would have something tangible to investigate.

While I was still pondering the fresh and uncomfortable lead that Matt may have killed my father, I was happy there was a potential lead being developed, but not so thrilled that it may involve an old friend.

While there was some circumstantial evidence that Matt may have been involved, Ingrid was not the only one who thought it was him. Two other friends and old OLL school chums who read the confession letter shared with us that they immediately thought of Matt.

To this day, there is question and suspicion about Matt's involvement. Knowing the pain Matt's parents had suffered, I was concerned for their feelings that this painful investigation might further wound their already injured hearts. I feel badly that he and his family have been drawn into this mess, especially if he's innocent. I've written his parents and shared these thoughts, and even if he is guilty of the crime, the peripheral damage of the investigation is a sad thing to think about, especially since they lost their only son along the way.

While I can't undo the investigation of their son, I let them know my thoughts and prayers were with them, and hoped they understood our situation. That being said, if we were going to try to find the truth we knew we had to pursue the leads, even if that pursuit was painful.

The next morning, things didn't start off well. Mom was feeling ill and her symptoms weren't going away. Her heart went into tachycardia and she began to feel worse. We loaded her up in the Lincoln and headed to the emergency room where they took x-rays and thought there was a mass in her stomach. They moved her to intensive care and later took more x-rays which revealed no mass was present. They then moved her to cardio intensive care to monitor her racing heart. Eventually her symptoms subsided and she was released from the hospital with no life-threatening problems.

I had to get back to Alaska, the police had handwriting samples and a possible suspect to investigate, and the filming of the Unsolved Mysteries episode was complete. We could finally take a breather and see what the experts could come up with. I was finally heading home to be with my very pregnant wife, and on December 2nd 1996, I received the best birthday present possible…a bouncing baby boy. Life was good.

Over the next few months we inquired once or twice about the handwriting results, and were informed these things take time. We were told we needed to be patient as this was an old case and not at the top of the priority list. Five months later we discovered that the handwriting samples had been "misplaced" at the Sheriff's department and had never even been sent to the lab for analysis.

When a news reporter shared this info with the Sheriff's spokesperson Marianne Pasha, she became angry and accused him of making up the claim about the misplaced handwriting samples.

Once she realized they had dropped the ball and we were correct, she humbly apologized for her angry accusation. Finally, at least a bit of humility presented itself. Detective Snipes and the PCSD had been helpful, but this screw up brought back that growing belief that the experts may not be as infallible and dependable as one might hope. The handwriting results eventually came back as inconclusive.

In January 1997 we received word that the Unsolved Mysteries episode was going to air on February 14th, Valentine's Day. I printed about 100 post cards with a brief explanation about the show and mailed them to friends and family. The two weeks prior to the airing date were filled with nervousness and hopeful anticipation. Friends and family who had received the postcards were calling. Local Tampa Bay area news stations were filming stories and interviewing Mom, Kandy and Guy in Dunedin. Unsolved Mysteries was phoning to ensure they had good contact numbers and addresses for us so they could pass on transcripts of any tips that might be phoned in by viewers. Would the show tell the story we wanted to be told? Would this be a fact-filled version of our ordeal, or would the show expound on more weirdness?

A few days before the UM episode aired, all three Tampa Bay area network news channels began airing their stories about the mysterious Dunedin death. The Unsolved Mysteries air date was nearly upon us. Valentine's Day rolled around and the show finally aired. We all thought it was well done, considering they were trying to tell a complex, twenty year-old story in about 10 minutes.

We received several calls from family and friends who had seen the story and were amazed at the supernatural and psychic aspects. Others called just to share their solace and provide hopeful wishes. The UM phone center received dozens of interesting calls the night the show aired. A few days later they sent me transcripts of thirty-three calls, which I forwarded to family in Dunedin, who forwarded copies to the Sheriff's department.

Unfortunately the callers were not much help. Most of them were from viewers who seemed to be trying to blame their ex-husband, ex-boyfriend or brother-in-law for the murder. Many claimed to recognize the handwriting as belonging to someone they knew who lived in

Florida, so of course they were the murderer. There were a few others that sounded psychotic; callers perhaps off their meds. One stated his friend showed up at the Dirscherl house to shoot chickens and was hiding in the closet and fired the fatal shot. There were a few calls from claimed handwriting experts, coroners, and self described psychics who firmly believed the death was not a suicide.

While Most of the caller's tips were useless, a few were interesting and sounded somewhat believable. One of the eeriest transcripts was from a caller in Ohio who claimed to be slightly psychic, and advised the killing was done by a police officer or someone connected with the police department. She sensed it was someone related to the lead investigator, and that it was not premeditated, but just happened when the suspect was caught stealing something. Our case was strange enough, but what could make it stranger…why of course, a good conspiracy theory.

Was there any truth to this alleged conspiracy? Considering the possibility was an unpleasant experience based on nothing more than a phone call from a self proclaimed psychic. For one, I'm not a conspiracy theorist at heart. Secondly, if there were any truth to the theory, it would not be any fun trying to prove it. Thirdly, without evidence to back up a claim of conspiracy, we were going to appear to be desperately grasping at more psychic straws, and that's not what we wanted our case to be about…we wanted the case solved based on facts, not guesswork.

Some people are drawn to conspiracy theories and soon their paranoid emotions rule their thoughts. Heading down that path can lead to a slippery slope where sensibility and reason are thrown out the window and the facts no longer matter. Although we had to consider all possibilities, we were after facts. Once labeled a conspiracy theorist, one's credibility remains in question no matter how much fact you interject…it's a hard label to shake. We didn't want to go there.

The phone tips after the show were mostly nonsensical ramblings from viewers across the country. Nothing helpful or fact-based was gained by the airing. At least family and friends were able to hear more about Dad's death, and understand the suicide case that was closed by the Dunedin Police was open, and in question.

By the way, did you hear about the two fervent conspiracy theorists who died and went to heaven? They met God at the pearly gates, and He said to them, "Gentlemen, welcome to heaven…but I need to clear up three of your doubts before you enter. First, Lee Harvey Oswald really did act alone. Second, Neil Armstrong really did walk on the moon. And third, radical Islamic terrorists really did fly a jet airliner into the Pentagon." One guy looks at the other and says "See…it really does go all the way to the top!"

Chapter 10

Uncomfortably Numb

In June of 1998, my four-year hitch in Alaska was coming to an end. Kim and I knew this was now home and where we wanted to spend the rest of our lives, but the Air Force had other plans. I requested to extend my hitch in Alaska, but my military rank pretty much guaranteed I would be leaving. I was a Master Sergeant and since we had recently merged with Security Police, I was thrown into the mix with all the other Security Policemen. Our unit's Master Sergeant manning was at nearly three hundred percent; my request to stay was denied so we were definitely heading to a new base.

I received orders to balmy Maxwell Air Force Base in Alabama which I wasn't super thrilled about; but it could have been worse. Then a notice circulated through my squadron that stated Air Force bases with nuclear missions were beefing up Security Forces manpower. I looked over the list, made some calls to several base firing ranges and spoke with the base Red Hats. I got a good vibe from the folks at Offutt Air Force Base, just outside Omaha Nebraska. Hopes turned into military orders to Offutt AFB. July rolled around; we packed up the three kids and hit the Alaska Highway, this time headed south.

There wasn't much progress on dad's case for the next few years. I was wrapped up in my new job, a young family, and all the other responsibilities related to the new area and life in general. Another major issue that kept family from further pursuing the case was Mom's health. She was having some pretty serious health issues that were mainly caused by emphysema. She had smoked for sixty years and it had taken its toll and she was in need of a lot of personal attention.

While Nebraska was considerably closer to Florida than Alaska, I was still fifteen hundred miles away, and wasn't able to provide much help with her care. Thankfully Guy and Kandy were just a few miles away, so they were the kids tasked with her care. I really appreciated the time and effort they put in, and I felt guilty I couldn't do more. Mom and I had grown very close, especially during the years we lived together after Dad's death, and I wished I could have been there more when she needed assistance.

Although Mom and I had been very close, there was an issue that drove a temporary wedge in our relationship, and it was about religion. I debated sharing it in this book because it could be taken out of context; however I included it because it perfectly demonstrates one of the main topics of this story. It's a great example of the power of beliefs, and how they affect lives. With that said, I share this with the intent to honor Mom, not to embarrass or belittle her. And while this brief emotional flare-up caused temporary friction, it led to a discussion about beliefs that we both needed to address. It also helped us both delve deeper into our beliefs to question and discover not only what we believed, but why we believed it. That's an important step to take.

While this book is not meant to be an argument about religion, that topic seems to be one of the most contentious subjects in the world. It's that same old struggle over religious beliefs that has continued since worship began. It's that ugly, unwinnable argument about God and his plan that can eventually lead to the inevitable, "I'm right and you're wrong."

Mom's and my disagreement was about the fact that I had left the Catholic Church and had begun to worship in Protestant churches. I had left the Catholic Church and was excited to share details of my closer relationship with Christ. My zeal for my newly acquired knowledge of scripture, the good news of salvation, and the gift of grace was not received with the warmth and welcome I had hoped for; that was partly my fault. Mom had been raised a devout Catholic and loved the traditions and ceremony of the Church. I on the other hand, was a newly saved, Born Again Christian who simply wanted to share the good news with my family.

I sent Mom a video that questioned several of the tenants of the Catholic faith, and challenged their parallel to scripture. While I thought I had clearly prefaced the tape with a detailed monologue explaining I wasn't condemning the Catholic Church, but instead was questioning certain doctrines and dogmas, the tape went over like the proverbial fart in church. Mom took it as a very personal attack on her beliefs and she responded in a way I never expected.

As I look back, the tape was probably a bad idea, and she had the right to be upset with my approach. In her anger she blurted out I was no longer invited to her funeral, which we all knew was not too far away. While her statement was actually just an emotional outburst, I was crushed. In a moment of passion, the woman I loved so dearly had excommunicated me from her life's end, and the quarrel was over religion. I knew I had to further explain my intentions and apologize for upsetting her, but I had to do it in a way that included truth and led to an honest explanation of what was on my heart.

Just before Christmas of 1998, I wrote her a letter. I shared that letter with my siblings a year later, just before Christmas of 1999. I'm sharing these letters with readers because their theme resonates throughout this book. This spiritual revelation and relationship moment between Mom and me played a huge part in forming my adult years, my values, my beliefs, and my personal relationship with Christ. If you're Roman Catholic, please understand this is a story involving my personal questions concerning my understandings and individual struggles with my Catholic experience. It is not an aspersion cast against the entire Catholic Church and I mean no offense.

"Dear Family,   *21 Dec 99*

Since we're in the holiday season, and about to celebrate Christmas, I feel compelled to write and share the following. It's a letter I sent to Mom last Christmas after a falling-out we had. I made a video, which contained some less-than-flattering things about Catholicism. I shared it with her in November of 98. My intention was to share some truths about salvation, because after some discussions with her, I was concerned about some things she said. I was concerned because she basically said Jesus Christ was a nice guy, teacher, and moralist, but she didn't feel he was God, Creator, or Savior.

After seeing the tape she informed me I was not invited to her funeral because I was no longer Catholic. We've since reconciled and I think she took my motives as intended. The letter is pretty self-explanatory and I hope, as earlier you don't take offense to it. It's important because Mom like the rest of us is going to die someday.

The Bible (which claims, and I believe, to be the truthful word of God) says we receive salvation and eternal life by placing our faith in Jesus Christ.

I've spoken with some of you and we disagree on religious beliefs and what the "truth" about salvation is. Whether Catholic, Protestant, Buddhist, Agnostic or Atheist, there is a Truth, and we'll all encounter it someday.

I hope you take a few moments and ponder the points raised in this letter. It's the most important thing I've ever said to Mom. I hope it touches your heart.

Merry Christmas and Happy New Year!
DAN"

My letter to Mom…

"Mom,   *20 Dec 98*

I don't know how to start this letter. After we spoke I just went numb and felt I had to write you. I thought I prefaced the tape with a very thorough disclaimer about what was in it, and that I wasn't the judge and jury. Just that I had learned a little about the bible, salvation, and different religious beliefs. I'll be the first to admit there were some unflattering things about Catholicism in the tape. I thought my monologue explained my intentions.

This letter is not intended to upset you further. My intent is not to prove Catholicism wrong. I want to share with you a truth I've learned. I don't want this to be an intellectual battle of minds, but a message from my heart to yours. Please keep my intentions in mind as you read.

You brought me up to do what's right and to tell the truth. What confuses me is now is, you tell me what ever a person believes is the truth. I'm sorry I don't agree. I don't believe every opinion is the truth. I believe in universal right and universal wrong. I believe an almighty God created them and set them in place. I believe this God used mortal men to record the scriptures, which were divinely inspired by the Holy Spirit. I believe the whole scripture, not just parts I'm comfortable with. I believe God is smarter than I am and that it's not my job to pick the parts that are true and discern where God was inaccurate. I don't believe He would toy with us that way. I believe His Word tells us what is right and wrong. I believe, as He said, He sent His one and only Son as the final sacrifice for my sins as well as yours. I believe salvation is a gift and not of works, so that no man can boast. I'm surprised you believe you can save yourself from sin, and that you have no need for Jesus Christ. The Lord says All fall short of the glory of God. That's why he sent the Christ.

I'm also surprised you don't believe that God is the author of the Bible. I thought that's why you sent me to a Catholic school and why I attended church nearly every day where the Bible was a source document. Every Sunday we read from it in church and proclaimed it's authorship after each reading. I still believe that the Holy Spirit is the author of the Bible, not mere men.

History shows men created religions, and they're still creating them today. I don't believe there is a perfect religion anywhere. I don't believe any religion can offer salvation; not Catholicism, Protestantism, or any other ism. I believe God's words about Christ are true. After hearing you recite them year after year, I thought you believed them too.

I believe these things because I decided to look at scripture, religion, and secular explanations objectively. I was looking for the truth. I started with secular explanations; you know ... We came from nothing, we don't know why we're here, we don't know where we're going, and everything is fair game ... life's short, play hard get what you can for yourself. That just didn't make sense. It's obvious there's something special that makes us different from the animals and there's tons of evidence that support the claims of the Bible. Each new archeological dig provides names and facts that support the true history of Old and New Testament.

I tried religion most of my life and I'm sorry, but Catholicism taught me how to be a good Catholic, not God's plan for salvation; at least not salvation based on scripture, which is where I turned. When I did read what God says in the Bible, my heart and eyes were open to the simple truth. No unreachable performance of perfection required. Christ was the only One capable of that performance. And He asks us to count on His sacrifice to save us ... because we do need saving.

I'm grateful for my Catholic upbringing, it taught me a lot about Christ, religious beliefs, and the importance of God in our lives. It taught me the Bible was important. As a lector I would process down the aisle holding it above my head while the congregation would sing and worship. Then I would recite a reading and close with the words, "This is the word of the Lord." And for years you confirmed that with your response, "Thanks be to God." Now you tell me you don't believe that.

Thousands of times you've made the sign of the cross and proclaimed, "In the name of the Father, the Son and the Holy Spirit", to honor the Godhead, the Trinity. Now you tell me Christ is not God but just a man, and although he was an important person, you don't need him or consider him God. All these years I thought the Bible was important to our family. That we believed it was the word of God. Now you tell me it's all a hoax, just a book or a guide, like directions to put together a bicycle. Leave off the handlebars and you still get a bicycle. Leave off one pedal and you still get a bicycle. Choose not to put the chain on and you still get a bicycle. Problem is, the bicycle goes nowhere. I'm sorry, I want the whole bicycle. I want all of what God has to offer. I believe in the God of the Bible. Not a Bible written by men, but the one authored by the Holy Spirit, which God himself wrote.

Saying the bible can't be trusted because men wrote it, is like saying the authority of your marriage license comes from the secretary who typed it instead of the state who issued it. The day Dad died he was planning to lector once again at church. That very last day he was going to close the Gospel with, "This is the word of the Lord." I believe he meant it. When the lector reads from the Gospel, and closes with those words of authorship, "the word of the Lord", are you telling me we don't believe that? If not, why do we respond?

If we start to pick and choose which parts of the Bible are true, we negate the whole book. If every part of it isn't true, the whole book becomes a lie. If the miracles, from creation to feeding the 5,000 aren't all true, then the Bible is a cruel book, which deceives and lies. If you believe God created Adam and Eve, but you don't believe Eve was tempted by Satan, and brought sin into the world, then you can't believe Christ was sent to save the world from sin, and the whole book becomes a lie. If Christ is not the Messiah sent to save us from sin, then his death was a waste and Catholicism, Protestantism and all of Christianity is a sham.

I'm really confused as I sit here and use the Bible as the source document knowing you don't believe its claims. It makes my whole argument baseless. What confuses me is trying to understand what you use as a source for your beliefs. I really thought Catholics believed Jesus Christ is Lord. If Christ is not God, why the belief in the trinity? Why the sign of the cross? Why the mass? If Jesus is God, then the whole Bible is true because He claims it is down to the last jot and tittle. If He is God he didn't lie about that, and His claim to be the only way to Heaven is accurate. If any of it's fiction, then we're both totally off the mark and salvation is a moot point. I personally think the choice is a simple one. This is not about you or me being right or wrong. I'm not the judge, so please understand I'm not trying to be ... but here's a pretty simple choice ...

If you're right, and I'm wrong, and this whole bible thing is just a book of half-truths, no universal right or wrong, and Christ is not our Savior, then we both live good lives and we die forever. Neither of us wins nor loses and I'm no worse off. But if I'm right and you're wrong and the bible is what it claims, and to enter heaven we must accept Christ as our Savior, then those born again gain everything, and those who aren't lose it all. Quite a risk I don't want to take, and I don't want you to. If you accept that gift, it's a win-win situation. Regardless of interpretations or opinions of men, the Bible states there is an eternity, we get to choose where we spend it. I didn't make up the rules, God did. Please don't take that as a personal dig, it's simply a picture of the cost of our decisions.

You say I'm wrong to confront this issue. You feel I'm trying to impose my belief on you, and that I condemn your belief. You say I'm being judgmental and narrow-minded. I know I don't have all the answers and I'm not judging your belief. I'm trying to share a truth that was shared with me. If it is the truth and you disagree with it then you are wrong, not according to me but to the definition of right and wrong. If I believe the earth is flat, or that the sun revolves around the earth, then I'm wrong. There is such a thing as being wrong. I didn't create the truth, I didn't make the rules, and it doesn't matter what my opinion is. Whatever the truth is, it's going to reveal itself to us one day, regardless of what you or I think.

The Bible says we can know if we're going to heaven. We don't have to wonder, or hope we were good enough. At some point in our lives we all have wondered if we're going to heaven. I simply wanted to share what I've learned because the stakes are so high.

I tried to explain in the tape how much I cared about you all, and that I wanted to share with you something I learned. Now because I shared a tape and an idea that challenges your belief, I'm not invited to your funeral because we disagree. I thought we were much closer than that. My beliefs don't diminish the love and respect and honor I have for you. I'm really sorry and hurt that you don't want me at your funeral. That you would excommunicate me from a chance to honor you and all you've done for me.

Five years ago you said I should have been a priest because I had a caring heart and a gift with words. Now that I have a closer relationship with Jesus Christ, I share some biblical truths you're uncomfortable with and you don't even want me near you.

I'm very sorry you reacted to this information so negatively. It was not meant to be hurtful or judgmental. It was meant to be a witness to God's word, which He commands all of us to do. I respect your right to believe what you want. God gives us all that choice. But just like you taught me, and I teach my kids, there are consequences for every choice we make, both right and wrong. This issue generates the mother of all consequences, our eternal destination.

I pray you'll open your bible today to any page, read a passage or two, and then try to tell yourself it's just a bunch of guys' wild imaginations. If you feel that way, go through the book and tear out each page you disagree with or don't believe. You'll soon have a bicycle that goes nowhere. If you believe God is who He says He is, capable of forming a universe or a baby's fingers, why is it too hard to believe His Son is our Savior?

You said I'm welcome in your house but not at your funeral. If I die today or next week, I'd want you at mine. Every day I pray for you, I pray for your health and happiness. I also pray for your salvation. I do it out of love for you, not self-righteousness, or pride, but simply out of love. If I'm wrong, I sure hope my kids find the truth and spend eternity with God.

*We just returned from a Christmas cantata where we sang all those old hymns and carols that you taught me as I was growing up. Silent Night, holy night…**Holy** infant, so tender and mild…**Christ the Savior is born, Christ the Savior is born.** Joy to the world, **the Lord has come.** O come all ye faithful, joyful and triumphant…Come and behold him, **born the King of Angels,** Oh come let us adore him **Christ the Lord.** God rest ye merry gentlemen, let nothing you dismay, remember **Christ our Savior** was born on Christmas day. Are these all just quaint little tunes or are they true proclamations of Christianity? I thought this whole thing was supposed to be real.*

I'm really quite confused. Do you believe the beliefs you taught me or not? Do you believe those songs and prayers about the trinity, Christ the Lord, and Christ the Savior or don't you? I took them as truth, and I still do today. Now you tell me it's all a hoax and you never believed it. You tell me we earn salvation. We don't need Christ we just need ourselves. Salvation is just a state of mind...be good and you'll go to heaven. If you're right, how good do I have to be to be sure I'm going? Christ says we are saved by His grace, and rewarded in Heaven for our works, not that our works get us there.

This next question is not sarcasm. I'd really like to know your thoughts. If a Satan worshipper is really nice to people and is the model citizen; member of the Rotary Club, gives to charities, helps the less fortunate but denies Christ and worships Satan, does he go to heaven? This guy is a very nice Satanist, all you could ask for in a neighbor...is he going to heaven? God says we are all sinners and fall short, but you tell me we all just have to do good and we'll make the cut.

Last night at church I celebrated the birth a child born 2000 years ago, who God sent to pay for my sins. You paid good money to send me to a school that taught me the same thing. For decades you attended a church that I think claims the same truth. You now receive communion at your house and believe you are receiving the body of Christ, I assumed because you thought He was your Savior. But now you say that's not the case. If Christ was not God and Savior, why do you receive communion at all? To remember some guy named Jesus, or our Savior's death to appease our sins and provide us a chance at salvation?

I really want to know what you believe...is Christ all that He claimed to be or is it a lie? If He is, then I'll place my faith in Him and His Father's word. If He's not, then it really doesn't matter what we believe because the Bible can't be trusted and Christianity is a joke. I know in my heart that the latter is a lie. I pray you come to the same conclusion. That's the whole reason I sent the tape; because I love you tremendously, not to dishonor you in any way.

If you really don't want me at your funeral because I believe Jesus Christ is our Savior, I'll honor your wishes, but I won't deny Christ. Peter tried it several times, but in the end came to face reality and spread the word of Christ throughout the nations. I'm truly sorry the tape offended you; no judgment or offense was intended; just trying to give back to one who gave me so much.

As you can see I've opened my heart and soul to you. I've told you my feelings and why I feel the way I do. I didn't hold anything back and I may have again ruffled some feathers. If so I'm sorry; it really is not my intention. If it weren't the most important thing to me I wouldn't even bother. My goal is not to get you to leave the Catholic Church. I know you love it and you're comfortable there. But I pray you'll recognize Christ for what He is and you'll put your faith in Him and not in your works.

I pray religion doesn't drive a wedge between us like it has all over the world. Seems religions have a way of doing that. I'm still your son and I hope you can see my true intentions. I also pray that you say a prayer and ask the Lord to reveal his truths to you, whatever they may be. Please believe me that the truth is all about you knowing Jesus Christ personally. It really happens when you say a little prayer and ask him into your heart. There are no special formulas or magic words, just a simple prayer that you know you need him and you accept His gift. It's too easy to not do it.

If I don't die before you I'll be at your funeral, either inside or outside, that's your call. If I do die before you, I want you to know that I found an absolute truth that the Lord promised us all. He offers us a gift and I accepted. I hope you do too. I love you very much!

With Sincere Love, Dan"

As I look back over this letter twelve years after writing it, I realize this whole encounter was a brief, unpleasant episode that happened in a way I wish were different. The video came across as confrontational and my heart-felt letter at times may have bordered on the edge of insult and offense. While I wish my method was different, I'm glad the message was shared.

As an older, and hopefully wiser adult, I now realize arguing with someone about religion rarely, if ever wins them over. As newly saved Christians, sometimes we can get a bit zealous wanting to share the good news. And as I assumed, believing that arguing our points louder and longer we can win people over and change beliefs. Beliefs are powerful, and they can be changed, but as I've aged, I realize I don't change people's beliefs, they do. When it comes to salvation, I'm now content to plant the seed and let the Holy Spirit do the rest.

This experience with Mom was an eye-opener for me. It led to a lot more prayer, a lot more asking for help, and the hope she would discover what I was trying to share with her. After spending some time in an assisted living facility, she took a turn for the worse, and in January 2000 she went into the hospital with severe breathing problems and she began to physically shut down. My siblings and I took turns sitting with her. When I was with her I would read scripture about salvation with the hopes she could hear the words, but more importantly the message. On January 15th, 2000 she took her last breaths of this world and passed away; a few days later she was buried next to Dad, and they were once again together.

Chapter 11

New Life, New Hope, New Blessings

I joined the Air Force on March 10, 1983. As of April 1, 2003 (April Fool's Day) I was discharged and again entered the world of civilians. It was a new fork in the road; one that brought with it a bit of fear and trepidation. A sense of lost security and the reality Kim and I were responsible for our lives and our future. But it also brought an exciting prospect that we were moving back to Alaska to start those new lives.

That excitement however was laced with a bit of sorrow since DeeDee, our eldest, was not going to be coming with us. She had decided to stay in Omaha to attend the University of Nebraska Omaha pursuing her teaching degree. She also had a serious boyfriend named Rob, and they felt Omaha was where their roots were taking hold.

In December of 2002, I began terminal leave preparing to retire from the Air Force, and on January 11, 2003, Kim, Shelbi, R.J. and I loaded up the Suburban, put the Jeep CJ-7 on a trailer and headed for the Alaska Highway…again…this time heading North…in January. No job, no home, no sense of security that I had come to expect; just a dream. We knew Alaska was where we were supposed to be and had faith everything would work out fine…and it did.

Nothing had happened with Dad's case for quite some time. But in March of 2003, Kandy was watching the news and caught the tail end of a story about the local Medical Examiner, Joan Wood. Over the years Kandy had saved some clippings from the newspaper that were about Dr. Wood, and how she had played a major role in a 1995 high profile Scientology case in Clearwater. The case centered on the death of a Scientology member named Lisa McPherson, who died in the care of Scientology staff. Wood was the coroner and originally ruled that McPherson died of a blood clot complicated by too much bed rest and severe dehydration. The Prosecution's case was based primarily on Wood's testimony which supported their claims that Scientology staffers failed to properly care for the woman, and were responsible for her death.

After years of judicial actions, proposed plea bargains, and promises to pay hundreds of thousands of dollars in restitution if charges were dropped or reduced, the Scientologist's attorneys received a huge break when Dr. Wood changed her opinion and autopsy findings. Her new opinion said nothing about the blood clot, bed rest or the severe dehydration. Her new opinion was that McPherson's death was accidental. This major flip by Wood doomed the prosecution's case, as the credibility of their expert witness was now in question.

In 2000, news stories began to surface about the District Six Medical Examiner's office that would shed even more light on the problematic agency. Wood had been promoted to Chief Medical Examiner and had hired an assistant named Dr. Richard Eicher. After evidence came to light that Dr. Eicher may have been incorrect and determined the wrong cause of death during more than one autopsy, Wood ordered her staff to review the one hundred seventy-eight autopsies he had conducted. After it was determined Eicher had confused a bullet entrance and exit wound in a man's head, Eicher resigned on March 13, 2000. After double checking all of Eicher's autopsies, it was determined he had significantly erred on at least seven cases.

Joan Wood was responsible for hiring Dr. Eicher and she eventually admitted he was not qualified for the job. Wood too was on her way out as her credibility put the entire ME office at risk. But people were hearing about the problems with the District Six ME's office and several families began hiring attorneys to challenge cases of their loved ones. Wood herself had misread pathological evidence in at least two children's autopsies, and her expert opinion had wrongly doomed two innocent men to prison.

On November 21, 2002, an ABC Action News Report claimed Wood's flawed autopsy incorrectly determined an infant named Rebecca Long was shaken to death. Law enforcement arrested her father David long, and jurors convicted him of murder…based primarily on Wood's flawed expert testimony. Fortunately the forensic evidence was reexamined and David Long was found to be innocent after spending forty-nine days in jail. Five other pathologists reviewed the case and evidence and determined the actual cause of Rebecca's death was bronchial pneumonia.

On November 23, 2002, another ABC Action News report was released. It described another case of shaken baby syndrome, but this time it was an eighteen-year-old father named John Peel who was locked up for four and a half years for murdering his young son. Again there were problems with Wood's autopsy that stated there were "no signs of retinal hemorrhage", but in other parts of her report she contradicted herself stating she found "gross retinal hemorrhage."

Remember her contradicting statements in my father's autopsy concerning his neck revealing no abnormalities, then in the same paragraph noting there was a three-inch incision? There was evidence mounting that her oversights and contradicting facts had affected numerous other families, resulting in erroneous murder convictions and prison sentences. Maybe now our claims and concerns of investigative negligence would be taken seriously.

The New Chief

Dr. Wood retired in 2000, and a new Chief Medical Examiner named Dr. Jon Thogmartin took over the agency, and as I write these pages he is still the Chief ME of District Six. Thogmartin was swamped with the task of reviewing numerous cases where Dr. Wood's botched autopsies and expert opinions were questioned. Perhaps he would be able to clear up the problems with Dad's autopsy?

I figured it was worth a shot, so in June of 2003, I sent a long detailed letter about our case to Dr. Thogmartin with the hopes he would take an interest and perhaps find enough cause to amend the death certificate; I received no response back. Apparently Dr. Thogmartin was too busy, or too burned out reviewing Dr. Wood's cases to take on a twenty-six year old mistake.

More time passed and there was not much accomplished on dad's case. In 2006 the family and I headed to Florida for a family reunion and there was discussion about initiating litigation in order to have the death certificate changed. While that seemed to be the most logical option, nobody was anxious to take the county to court so we delayed and did nothing. By this time, all the Dirscherl kids had reached our own levels of closure...whatever that means. We'd experienced so many emotional highs and lows, and time had worn us down; it seemed fate meant for the case to remain closed as a suicide. And for whatever reason, the justice we had searched for still seemed out of reach.

Years before, I had personally reached a point where my whole approach to the case changed. Looking back I noticed how I had tried to find answers and solve the case through my own works and worries, instead of doing what scripture says. At some point over the years; I can't say exactly when, I simply turned it over to God and I quit worrying about it. I prayed God would provide the answers we were looking for, but I realized He worked on His timeline, not mine. When I released the worries and pressures of dealing with the case, I encountered a new peace; more than mere closure with the case, but also a content belief that this was the right way to go about it. There was a unique sense of confidence that what was supposed to happen would happen, and I wasn't in charge, or responsible for it.

After leaving the Air Force and returning to Alaska in 2003, I was planning to pursue a city, state, or federal government job, but in the interim took a security job in downtown Anchorage. It was a good-paying armed security position with a federal union contract. In six months I was promoted to Lieutenant and was doing all the scheduling, and providing all the firearms and ancillary training. I enjoyed the work and met some really great folks along the way.

In May of 2005, our Contract Manager, who also held the company position of Alaska Field Service Manager, resigned to move out of state. The company was looking for someone qualified to fill the slot, and I was honored they were thinking of me. Shortly after being selected for the position, my boss informed me that due to a quick burn-out rate, the average career length for a Field Service Manager was one to three years. Wish I would have known that before I took the job.

I soon realized my new responsibilities were daunting. Not only was I the contract manager for the federal contract, which included seven federal buildings and over fifty security officers in Anchorage, Juneau and Fairbanks...as well as union collective bargaining, arbitration, and the like. I was also the contract manager for twelve other security contracts which included the Municipality of

Anchorage, Ted Stevens International Airport, and the cruise ship port security in Whittier and Seward, just to name a few.

I was still conducting the firearms training and was now responsible for about 300 employees. I don't want to sound too whiney, but the job was more than one person could handle well...at least this one person. I was used to seeing jobs and missions completed and feeling a sense of accomplishment. I believe my new job title should have been Fireman, because all I did was put out fires. There was never any sense of accomplishment, and each day entailed hopping from one problem to the next. I had also switched from Union Member to Management, so I now dealt with every union grievance that was filed, and there were dozens.

The ugliest aspect of the job was this small electronic device I had with me twenty-four hours a day...the cell phone. I cringe every time I think about it, and to this day jump when I hear the same annoying ring on someone else's phone. The beast usually rang in the middle of the night, especially during the long Alaskan summer nights. If we didn't have our security in place for the cruise ships to dock...they couldn't. This meant maritime fines and contract penalties could get a little expensive for the company. Many of the problems were out of my control, yet I was expected to handle them, like when security officers would miss the last tunnel to the small, scenic port city of Whittier.

The tunnel closed down at 11:00 p.m., cutting off the town from the rest of the civilized world. If our officers didn't get through the tunnel to Whittier for whatever reason, my phone would go crazy with angry clients and panicked supervisors. When the tunnel was closed, the only way to get the troops to the Whittier port would have been to helicopter them in; unfortunately the company had not issued me a helicopter.

The phone, the stress and the lack of sleep began to take their toll and were affecting my health and my personality. I was not loving life, and I wasn't fun to be around much of the time. Fortunately I recognized the problem and knew I had to make a change. I had stuck out the two years as Alaska's Field Service Manager and it was time to do something else...but what?

I had been praying a lot, knowing God had a plan, but didn't know what it was. I began to look at business opportunities and wondered what kind of business I could start that would provide the income I needed and allow my wonderful, charming, easy going personality to return. I didn't have a bunch of cash to invest, but I had a strong work ethic, the values my parents had instilled in me, and the discipline and communications skills developed in the Air Force.

I prayed some more, did some research, and began to build a business plan. I decided I was going to become my own one-man residential cleaning company. I made a bunch of flyers, and the family helped me hang them throughout Eagle River. I picked up my first client, and they told a friend, and they told a friend, and pretty soon I was too busy to handle it by myself. Kim and Shelbi joined me, and for the last five years Scrubs Cleaning Service Inc. has become one of the most sought after cleaning companies in Eagle River. We're keeping it small and personal, not trying get rich or too big for our britches.

In the spring of 2007, peace and happiness were again part of my life. All was back to normal...except for that little twitch when a cell phone rings.

This business turned out to be much more than a job, or a career. I now work half as many hours per week as I did with my previous job. I cherish those extra free hours because I get to spend them with Kim, Shelbi and R.J. This free time spent with the family can be so much more rewarding than a bigger paycheck.

I eventually realized I was using the new business, shortened work-week, and free time as a sort of surrogate life that I had missed with my dad. While I didn't comprehend it when I was young, looking back I realized that since Dad traveled so much, I really only saw him on the weekends and during vacations...and then when I was fourteen he was gone. I began to understand the correlation between missing my father, and my desire to spend as much time with my family as possible. Perhaps it's a compensation method, or some other Freudian rationalization, but I now recognize in some strange ways Dad's death is still impacting my life with my family; the butterfly-effect is still in motion.

While the cleaning business blesses our lives and provides me more control of my life, it also occasional reveals my human prideful sense of self, as I occasionally rationalize that I was able to create all this on my own. Sometimes I forget the answered prayers. My Ego stroking can lead me to an uncomfortable prideful moment that just doesn't feel right. When I catch myself reveling in self praise, I realize it's not a pleasant place, so I leap from my congratulatory stage, say a quick prayer, and return to my comfort zone of respectful humility…and the reality I scrub toilets for a living. I'm thankful I don't try to live on that stage often, or for very long.

Is There Anybody Out There

One day in December 2007, while cleaning a client's home, I received a phone call from out of the blue. It was Jessica Fairbanks with Cosgrove-Meurer Productions Inc., the production company responsible for Unsolved Mysteries. She told me Unsolved Mysteries was coming back on the air in October of 2008 in an updated format. They were planning to air old shows and wanted to add narrative updates if there was anything new to add to the story. When I told my siblings of the call and the news, we discovered there had been a strange coincidence concerning our involvement with Dad's case. I hadn't touched my "Dad files" in months if not years; neither had George or Kandy. Yet all three of us had strangely been drawn to our personal files the week prior. None of us knew why we had pulled our files out; it just happened.

As Unsolved Mysteries was revamping our story, another fork in the road strangely manifested. Guy informed us that his wife Barb had a coworker named Chris Dahl who was a published author and had taken a keen interest in our story and wanted to write a book about it. Guy and Barb filled him in on the case details, and Chris began deeply investigating and writing the story. He put a lot of work into his research and met with numerous psychics to see what else he could learn about Dad's death. I sent him the Mauser shotgun so he could conduct some of his own research with a key piece of evidence. Chris updated his manuscript a few times and wound up with a final version titled, *Night of the Beast; A True Paranormal Investigation* which was released in the spring of 2011.

I have to admit, when I read the manuscript the first time, I was a bit confounded with what I read. It was a fantastic tale that was based on Dad's death, but it wasn't at all what I thought it was going to be. While I was expecting to read a familiar chronology filled with facts we'd discovered and challenges we'd dealt with, Chris had used a more imaginative approach and developed a storyline that was created to be a paranormal thriller.

After rereading his book, I've become more comfortable with his concept. I understand it's meant to be a thriller based on our story, but written through his eyes, his imagination and his writing style. While it wasn't the book I was expecting, it's a remarkable story that gives the reader a glimpse into the realm of paranormal activities and criminal theories surrounding our case.

So Unsolved Mysteries had re-aired our story, and there was a book being written about Dad's death. Why was Dad's case coming back to life? None of the family had initiated what was happening, yet something or "Someone" seemed to be fanning the glowing ember. It seemed there may be a chance that ember might reignite the flames of justice we had been seeking.

Months passed, then on February 19, 2009, my oldest brother Kook sent me an email with a link to an organization he had stumbled across. He thought it was interesting and may be worth a look. The link led me to the homepage of an organization called Parents of Murdered Children, Inc., (POMC).

I perused their website and was intrigued. Their homepage stated they provided emotional support, education and advocacy for families of murder victims. The organization seemed to be legitimate, but what was most intriguing was a service they offered called Second Opinion Service, or S.O.S.

Their website explained that the purpose of S.O.S. was to provide answers to questions and concerns regarding a death and subsequent investigation(s). They provided volunteer medical, law enforcement and investigative experts to provide an independent objective viewpoint based on existing evidence and/or records submitted to them for review. These volunteers evaluated materials looking for evidence that needed follow up, findings that may have been misinterpreted, as well as inconsistencies or conflicting information. They stated in most cases, families would receive a written opinion of their findings.

Wow! If this was for real it was exactly what I had been praying for; an independent and objective review of the facts by law enforcement, medical and pathology experts. I was encouraged and excited, but didn't want to get my hopes up. The service required three copies of all associated evidence, reports, photos, etc., and a fifty dollar processing fee to cover handling, postage, and overhead costs.

Over the next several months I put together three identical fact packages. Each included a hundred and five pages of police and autopsy reports, and our family's questions/critiques concerning the reports and evidence. I included photos of the gun, autopsy photos, CDs containing the Unsolved Mysteries story and all the local news stories, and newspaper articles concerning Joan Wood. If it was something an independent investigator might need, I included it. On October 3, 2009, I mailed the packages to POMC and included a check for a hundred bucks. All I could do now was wait for a response that would hopefully include a validating opinion provided by a qualified expert.

Over a month went by and no word from POMC. My hopes were fading and I was beginning to think I wasted many hours and a Benjamin on a shot in the dark. I knew up front I was taking a chance and it may just be a scam, but I still hoped there was a reason this was happening. Then on November 11th, while cleaning another client's home, I received a call from Bev Warnock at POMC. She told me there was a Forensic Pathologist in San Francisco named Dr. Judy Melinek who was looking at our case. Bev said the Doc requested a schematic of the house and photos of the test fire targets I created in the early nineties. I drew up the schematic that night and explained I'd have to perform more test fires as I had no good photos of the results.

November 28th temperatures finally crept above zero; a balmy four degrees…great shooting weather. Kim, Shelbi and I went to the Birchwood Recreation & Shooting Park to recreate the test fire targets. I took some photos of the targets and emailed them to Dr. Melinek through POMC. Two days later I received the following amazing email from the Doctor.

"Dan, these are excellent - very professional. The soot deposition is impressive and the ruler makes a comparison much easier. I need to look at these some more side by side with the autopsy photo, but I think I have what I need here. Let me see if I can get Dr. Thogmartin's attention directly. I think he might consider re-opening this and looking at it again if I wrote him a letter and included these photos and the packet you sent me. Give me some time: Holidays are always our busiest season, for professional and

personal reasons, and I want to get him when he's most receptive. Have a happy holiday and send my best wishes to your family. I think we have enough here to call this a homicide, or at the very least convince them to consider "undetermined" (which would mean that the physical evidence at autopsy can be explained by either scenario - suicide or homicide). After all these years, even "undetermined" would be an acknowledgment of sorts. I promise I will do what I can.

Judy Melinek, M.D. "

I don't know if it's possible to explain the emotional high I experienced after reading this short email. It had been nearly thirty-three years since Dad died and the rumors, stigma and legacy of his supposed suicide began. After all the years and efforts of trying to reach the objective minds of experts and those with the power to affect and amend the case, we finally found one helpful soul with expertise and a willingness to help. Perhaps the scales of justice would begin to tip back towards balance. Perhaps facts and evidence would at least have a chance to be objectively reviewed. Perhaps the elephant in the room would soon find its way out.

I wrote the doctor this short reply...

"Dear Dr. Melinek,

Thank you for the news! I understand this is a preliminary opinion and not the end-all, but it's so nice to finally receive a bit of validation concerning our case. I'm glad the photos are what you're looking for; I hope they add to the evidence that may help overturn the current ruling.

I passed on your email to my family, and we all are excited to see where this journey leads us next. We understand the holidays have a way of warping the time-space continuum, and that Dr. Thogmartin is a busy man. Our hopes and prayers are that he is open to reviewing the evidence, and ultimately that he agrees that suicide has not been proven and that Dad's death was a homicide. A finding of undetermined would be a victory as well. I'm not sure how our case wound up in front of you, but we are very grateful it did. I can't thank you enough for the work you've put into this case. Please keep us posted and let us know when you plan on contacting Dr. Thogmartin...we'll be standing by waiting for more good news. I hope you have some time to enjoy the holidays as well; we will keep you in our thoughts and prayers. Thank you again, your help is one of the greatest Christmas presents we could imagine.

Dan"

The next day, December 2nd, my birthday, I received a wonderful email from her that explained why she decided to help and how she got involved with POMC. Her email read…

"I will take your package with me when I go home for the holidays and write my letter to Dr. Thogmartin then. I hope to send it to him shortly after Christmas, and then follow up with a phone call a few weeks later.

I got involved with Parents of Murdered Children because another colleague does volunteer work for them. He mentioned the group on the National Association of Medical Examiners email list and I felt that it was important to volunteer my time for such an organization. My own father committed suicide when I was 13 years old, and it has taken me years (I am now 40!) to come to accept it. It is my mission in life to spread the word about suicide; that it is not shameful, that it is preventable and that people need to know what to do to prevent it. So when a doctor told me of this organization, and that families who don't believe a suicide occurred want closure, I knew that I would be the right person to review cases. I am not biased either way; if something is not a suicide I have no problem saying so. But if a death is a suicide, who better to explain it to the family than me? I know from my own work at the Medical Examiner's Office in San Francisco that when I tell families of a suicide victim that I too am a "survivor" and that suicide, by definition, does not make sense - for some reason they are willing to listen to me. Something about my own personal story makes it OK to not understand, to have some questions, but to still grow to make peace with it. Anyway, that is why I am here and that is why I am interested in helping you.

So far I have only gotten 2 cases from POMC. The first one was clearly a suicide and I hope my opinion helped the mother get some closure. Your case - well, it's not so clear cut. I am with you and I support your suspicions. In the absence of a suicide note and without a clear history of suicidal ideations, I would have demanded a more complete investigation, and I don't think I would have called this a suicide. It would help to know if anything was noted missing from the residence after he died: was the closet open? Was jewelry or other small items with some worth missing? Can you jog your mother's memory on this, or will that be too traumatic? I will trust your judgment on approaching her. Sometimes drug users (who succumb to AIDS years later) are just looking for something they can steal and fence easily. It may not have been obvious immediately at the time, but if she noticed that some small trinkets went missing around the same time, this might be an explanation why.

It might be worthwhile for you, in the meanwhile, to file a freedom of information act request of the police department for all police reports of break-ins and robberies in your neighborhood for the months preceding your father's death. There may be some pattern of cars and houses hit and times of day that may prove useful. Also what is reported stolen from others' cars or homes, might help in jogging your mom's memory. I would be more interested in what robberies occurred before the death than after, only because after killing someone, the culprit might be less likely to go back to the same neighborhood again, at least for a while... these are my thoughts for now. I have to also add that it really helps that you kept the gun, all these records, and that you are a firearms instructor, so you are familiar with weapons. Makes my job a lot easier. Happy Holidays and Best Wishes to your family,

Judy Melinek, M.D. "

Reading her email brought a warm sense of contentment. There was a feeling of goodness, righteousness, and nobility supporting her motives. I finally felt good about how things were shaping up. There was hope…our roller coaster was heading upwards again. Another angel had entered our lives bearing good news.

Music to My Ears

I don't know for sure, but I suspect some of you have had strange experiences of coincidence…a time period of moments, or minutes where things begin to happen and the longer they go on, the more you feel like you're experiencing some strange sort of ordered plan, almost like a scripted déjà vu; where one scene leads into the next and you know there is something or someone steering the plot.

The next morning while I was working and listening to music on my iPhone, I began to sense that strange feeling as a series of four songs played one right after another. *Calling All You Angels* by the band Train...then, *Running Out of Days*, by 3 Doors Down...followed by *Revelation*, by Third Day...and finally, *If Today was Your Last Day*, by Nickleback. If you've never heard these songs, I think you can probably sense the ethereal essence of their message just by the titles. If you have heard the songs, you listen to some great music, and you can relate to the eerie sensation I was feeling.

The songs were just melodies, rhythms and words, and their order was probably simply due to the random shuffle command on my iPhone. But for those fifteen minutes, I felt connected to something; a feeling that I really can't explain. I had given up my worries and turned my quest over to God, and had asked him to use me as he saw fit. Things I hadn't initiated were happening, and people were beginning to step forward to help. There seemed to be a calm sense of purpose.

The rest of that morning poignant music merged with incredible scenes in my mind's eye...like a movie with an amazing soundtrack unfolding before me. I interpreted this moving jam session as a suggestive nudge; I was convinced we were to continue our search for justice. And it was the day I knew I was supposed to write this book.

Was this a God-thing or just an iPhone shuffling coincidence? Guess we'll never know...but if this experience was due to Steve Jobs and not God, I'd like to sincerely thank Steve for the experience.

Three days before Christmas I called the Pinellas County Sherriff's Public Information section to request police reports of break-ins or burglaries in Dunedin from January, February and March of 1977. Shortly after Christmas I received a call and was informed that because those reports weren't computerized they could not research them without case numbers, names etc. If I wanted to pay $17.50 per hour, they would do a manual search reading every case, but the manpower costs could be significant. I decided to forgo the search for the time being.

On January 4, 2010 I received an email from Dr. Melinek containing the letter she planned to send Dr. Thogmartin. It read...

"Dear Dr. Thogmartin,

I wanted to call attention to a matter from your district that in my opinion warrants a re-evaluation, considering additional information that has been obtained over the years by the deceased's family. The attached folder is a packet I obtained from Parents of Murdered Children, a non-profit organization that arranges for pro-bono forensic evaluations in cases that family members or forensic experts have found difficult to accept or understand. Harry Bonnell, MD, a consultant from California who you may recognize from the NAME list server, put me in touch with this group about a year ago and I have volunteered my time since then. Previous cases I have received from them have been clear-cut suicides, based on the forensic evidence. This one, an old case from your jurisdiction, preceding your appointment as Chief, is not so clear-cut.

The deceased had no history of diagnosed clinical depression, suicidal ideations or attempts. There was no particular inciting event (a fight with a spouse, loss of job or other significant stressor) that would explain a self-destructive act. He left no note of intent. Furthermore, the forensic evidence indicates a close-range wound of the chest and a trajectory that would be difficult to be self-inflicted. According to the son, who as a child entered the room and witnessed the aftermath, the location of the weapon in the original police investigation diagram is incorrect; he remembers that the weapon had been moved to secure it, then placed back in a different position on the bed before the diagram was drawn. Many years later, the family received an anonymous confession note from a person who claimed responsibility for this death. This letter could not be traced, so after a brief re-opening of the investigation, the police closed the matter.

The packet enclosed contains letters from the family, a copy of the autopsy report and investigative reports, as well as other materials pertaining to the case. I have also included some of my correspondence with the son and additional material I requested he provide: a map depicting the layout of the house (so that I could visualize potential escape routes, and the correct positioning of the gun); and the results of range-of-fire tests done with the weapon used in the death. I have printed photographs of these test results, but if you want to see the original digital images he sent me, I would be glad to forward them to you electronically.

Based on the material contained herein, it is my professional opinion that this case is a homicide. I think the forensic data and additional information obtained over the years give sufficient support for a re-classification of the manner of death. I would greatly appreciate if you could take the time to look at this material and consider amending the death certificate to "Homicide", or at the very least to "Undetermined", if you are not as thoroughly convinced as I am. To my knowledge, there are no pending financial issues that would be influenced by your re-evaluation. This would just help the family with their grief and give them closure after many years.

I appreciate your attention to the matter. I will follow up by e mail in approximately 3 weeks time.

Sincerely,
Judy Melinek, M.D. "

Doctor Melinek mailed her letter and our patient, ever hopeful wait for answers ensued.

On February 5, 2010 I received a package from Florida's District Six Medical Examiner's office which contained copies of four death investigation reports conducted by Dr. Melinek, and a four page letter written by Dr. Noel A. Palma, The Deputy Chief Medical Examiner, who had been assigned to our case by Dr. Thogmartin.

I was anxious and excited to see someone at the ME's office was finally responding to our case. It was very well written, and incorporated what seemed to be a synopsis of a thorough review of our case performed by Dr. Palma. I wasn't immediately sure why there were copies of Dr. Melinek's cases included, but as I read the letter it became apparent; there was an underlying drift to the letter that would become a recurrent theme. The letter was dated February 1, 2010, and it read…

"Dear Mr. Dirscherl,

I would like to express my condolences regarding the unfortunate premature death of you father Robert Dirscherl. In particular, I have great regret in learning that for over 30 years your family has struggled with the manner of death certification of your father.

We have thousands of archived case files in our records department from the time of previous Medical Examiner administrations. Receiving the correspondence form Dr. Melinek was the first time that our office became aware of the dissatisfaction that your family has regarding your father's death. The death investigation was performed under the administration of District Medical Examiner Dr. John Shinner (now deceased). The autopsy was performed by Associate Medical Examiner Dr. Joan Wood who later became District Medical Examiner and held that position until the fall of 2000. Our current administration began in December 2000.

As we can tell from the documents sent to us by Dr. Melinek, your family is well aware that your father's case is not the first case we have reviewed from the prior administrations. Our philosophy is that no case is ever closed and any case will be reviewed when we become aware of additional credible information. We have no hesitation if we find, based on the new information, that a cause or manner of death amendment is appropriate. In our opinion, this philosophy is the hallmark of objective practice of forensic pathology. We approach any reports of new information or new awareness on any of the archived cases with open minds and evaluate them as if they were new cases. Like all our current daily cases, we base the death certification on all of the available credible information. Such evaluations have exonerated individuals from criminal liability wrought from previous certifications.

In Dr. Melinek's page and a half long correspondence, (she provided case information, photos, police reports, portions of the original case file, and new information provided by your family). She wrote that the manner of death in her opinion should be changed to homicide or at least undetermined. She based her opinion on the following pieces of information:

1. *No history of clinical depression, suicidal ideations or attempts*
2. *No particular inciting event*
3. *No note of intent*
4. *Close range wound of the chest with trajectory difficult to self inflict.*
5. *Son indicates location of weapon in diagram was incorrect*
6. *Anonymous confession letter received years later*

In evaluating all of the available information, we read the documents sent to us by Dr. Melinek, the entire case file out of our archives (including photos), interviewed the current investigating agency, and I spoke with Dr. Melinek on the phone. As is our habit in such cases involving outside experts, we requested and received death investigation reports that Dr. Melinek has performed on similar cases during her career as a forensic pathologist (San Francisco and Santa Clara County Medical Examiner Offices).

Allow me to first address the range of fire and the difficult trajectory. Since the Dunedin Police Department closed, the Pinellas County Sheriff's Office took over that department. We learned that the Dunedin P.D. reopened the investigation in 1994. From speaking to Detective Rob Snipes we know that he and his agency looked into the case in 1997. He reported that he met with your family discussing the letter, the range of fire, etc. Subsequent to the original and 2 additional police investigations, no action was taken. The determination was contact range and the shotgun wound could easily be self-induced.

We reviewed the photos of the gun as well as the test firing you performed that were included in the packet of info Dr. Melinek sent. We compared these to the photos in our possession, a similar shotgun, and the police reports. According to the investigation information the muzzle to trigger distance is ~30 inches and the reported weapon of death is a double barrel over and under shotgun. The autopsy report contains good detail, corresponds with the wound but does have some organizational shortcomings. The autopsy photographs are less than ideal by today's standards, and we would certainly prefer more, but they are good by 1977 standards. The height of your father was recorded at 5'10 ½ inches. The wound is over the heart and the direction of the pellets is reported as downwards.

The entry wound is a contact wound. The state of the clothing around the wound, the soot around the wound, the pink discoloration of the muscle around the wound (injected gas effect), and the outline of the non-firing barrel above the entry wound clearly and, in our opinion, unequivocally indicate a contact range of fire.

In regards to the distance and ability to reach the trigger, at 5'7" I am significantly shorter than your father. I have little difficulty reaching and activating the trigger of a shotgun of similar length. Of course, others closer to your father's height had no difficulty. The trajectories were easily duplicated and understandable in the act of reaching for the trigger.

We did find something that had not been apparently noted before. The top barrel of the gun had the fired shot shell and the bottom barrel was not fired. The outline of the non-firing barrel above the entry wound indicates that the shotgun was oriented upside down when firing relative to orientation of your father's body. When reenacting the shooting scenario with this in mind, it was much easier to reach the trigger and actually one could see the trigger clearly. If this was an act of homicide, the assailant would have had to fire the gun while holding it upside down relative to orientation of your father's body. Although, one could imagine scenarios where this could possibly occur, this orientation along with the other factors makes homicide unlikely in the extreme.

In my conversation with Dr. Melinek, she clearly did not notice the orientation issue, had not evaluated the reach to trigger issue, and had not noted the pink tissue discoloration of the chest tissue clearly described in the autopsy report. All of these facts can be easily discerned from the material she sent to us. In our opinion, this investigation omission is possibly explained by Dr. Melinek's relative lack of experience with self inflicted shotgun wounds and gunshot wounds of the chest in general. According to the offices in which she has worked or works, she personally certified only 3 shotgun wound/suicides (head only, no chest) and only one gunshot wound of chest/suicide (see attached reports and correspondence).

Regarding the reports of no history of depression, ideations, etc., inciting events or notes, it is relatively common in our daily work to have cases where none of these are present, yet the cases are certified as suicidal manner. In fact, such events and evidence are present as often as not present. Most Medical Examiner and Coroner offices have similar experiences in death investigations. Examination of the 4 cases above from Dr. Melinek's forensic pathology career indicate the 3 of the 4 cases did not have notes and 2 of the 4 cases have no inciting events, depression etc. Thus her real world work experience undermines the veracity of her first 3 points arguing against suicide.

Regarding the anonymous letter: we cannot evaluate the veracity of this letter based on the information at hand. The letter is unusual and the investigating agencies worked this lead and report that they doubt its authenticity.

The gun position being described as different appears in conflict with the investigative reports. Unfortunately, due to the long remote nature of the case, the involved law enforcement agencies could provide no scene photographs. This is unfortunate and beyond our control.

I sincerely regret that, at this time, we cannot offer a scientifically valid alternate conclusion based on the information at hand. I regret that you were unfortunate enough to employ the services of an expert who, in my opinion, has insufficient experience in this specific type of case and, as apparent in my phone call with her, has personal experience that may have clouded her objectivity in the evaluation of your father's case. I would be happy to refer you to those who are published experts in the area of shotgun wounds, and I would certainly pay attention to any credible opinion on the matter.

Sincerely,
Noel A. Palma, MD
Deputy Chief Medical Examiner"

After reading the letter and digesting its information, I believe Dr. Palma reviewed the case information. But it seemed the main effort of his letter was to discredit Dr. Melinek and to show that the wound could possibly be, and therefore most likely was self-inflicted. While I hoped the case review would begin with the claimed level playing field, I was left with that familiar nagging feeling that I was just patted on the head again, and that we were petitioning an agency that seemed to have a dog in the fight. It seemed none of the facts that challenged the suicide or supported a possible homicide were considered to be relevant. Every time we brought questions to an agency that had some accountability or involvement in the initial investigation, their attempt was to prove the possibility of that initial suicide finding instead of seriously considering the very real probability of a second person being involved in the death.

Dr. Palma's letter seemed to imply Dad could have fired the shot, so therefore he must have. Yet he didn't explain how he held or positioned the weapon during his testing that would result in the wound characteristics and pellet path, and more interestingly the position of the firearm back in the middle of the bed, and Dad's body winding up six to eight steps away from where he supposedly shot himself. The goal once again seemed to be to prove our new information and expert were not credible and that a self-inflicted wound was the most likely explanation.

Although Dr. Palma stated they approached the case with open minds, the remarks that they and law enforcement doubted the confession letter's authenticity seemed to be an indictment that we were still chasing ghosts and that there was no possibility someone else pulled the trigger.

What if they were wrong and the letter was real, and it was an honest confession to the murder…was that considered? Apparently not; since police could not find the author of the note, this death had to be a suicide. This new fifth theory of holding the shotgun upside down mentioned by Dr. Palma seemed to bolster their beliefs. But since the case was closed based on the phone book or toe theory decades ago, we didn't know what to believe.

I wrote Dr. Melinek and gently explained how her investigation was received and what Dr. Palma thought of her qualifications. She knew how he felt as she had spoken to him on the phone. She apologized that her father's suicide was perceived as hindering the case. I personally believe her volunteer efforts with POMC and her calling to help people deal with suicide prove she's not one to try to fraudulently overturn actual suicide cases, but instead to help folks accept the truth. Instead Dr. Palma used it as a way to discredit her.

Dr. Palma seemed to allow a window for justice to prevail when he stated, *"no case is ever closed if we become aware of credible information"*…and closed his letter with *"I would certainly pay attention to any credible opinion on the matter."*

I intended to continue the discussion, so I wrote him back asking for a bit more clarification. I was hoping to find out more about the wound and if his theory offered evidence of Dad leaning on the barrel, thus being a hard contact wound, or did the wound evidence reveal a loose contact wound and a possibility someone else could have inflicted the deadly shot.

I felt another letter was necessary…

"February 18, 2010

Dear Dr. Palma,

Thank you for taking the time to review the information you received and for your professional response. Please understand my following questions and comments are not based in emotion or anger, but in a sincere attempt to ascertain what actually happened. Our goal as a family is simply to find the truth.

Your response concerning Dad's death provided new information, and a new explanation as to how the fatal shot was fired. This information is helpful and confusing for us at the same time, since we have now been given five different explanations as to how Dad shot himself. These varying theories seem to imply the more we question what happened, the more information is revealed.

As far as this being the first time your office became aware of our concerns...on June 5, 2003, I sent a Certified Mail package to Dr. Thogmartin which contained police and autopsy reports and a 4-page letter that explained our concerns and asked for a review of the case. I received nothing in reply.

Your letter conveys the importance of investigator competence, credibility, and objectivity. You stated Dr. Melinek may not be a qualified expert as she has few shotgun suicide investigations under her belt, and that she misread the orientation of the upside-down barrels. Apparently Dr. Joan Wood, who is touted as being a highly qualified gunshot wound expert and the ME responsible for the current death certificate, missed this call as well.

I hope you can see why we are concerned, as the conclusions provided by law enforcement in 1977 closed the case based on "gut feelings" and impossible methods (toe & phonebook). The second investigation was overseen by Captain MacKenzie, who was responsible for the initial suicide finding, and seemed a bit biased. After reopening the case, we were told by Captain MacKenzie the confession letter was probably a hoax, they had no suspects to prove a homicide, and could not afford to spend any more time on the case. He then suggested we "forget about it or come up with the little green men from Venus who had committed the murder."

The subsequent investigation conducted by the Pinellas County Sherriff's office was appreciated, as they followed up on the confession letter and other possible leads. After receiving no feedback on the handwriting samples, we inquired again to discover the letter had been misplaced for 4-5 months and had not even been sent out. Eventually results were returned as inconclusive. Again, we appreciated the investigation, but it still didn't answer the questions about the evidence and how this supposed suicide outweighed the evidence supporting homicide.

Since little physical evidence is available and 10-12 crime scene photos were lost by the investigating agency, the wound photos and autopsy reports are very important in determining what happened.

Could you please help us understand a bit more about the wound characteristics, orientation of the shotgun, and how the shot was believed to be fired? We still aren't clear on the following issues:

1. *Is it your opinion that the muzzle was placed/held against the chest with the butt of the weapon overhead, or does it appear to be a hard contact wound, indicating Dad may have leaned onto the muzzle?*

2. *Does soot and powder residue above the wound, indicate more of a seal between the muzzle and the bottom edge of the wound, versus a seal at the top edge of the wound?*

3. *Is the wound characteristic consistent with a contact wound or a hard contact wound?*

4. *Is there any indication what caused the linear marks outside the wound at the ten o-clock position in the photos?*

I don't know if you had all the facts about Dad's left arm limitations, but due to his previous cervical damage and significant left tricep atrophy, he was not even able to support the weight of his left arm if he tried to lift it over his head. If he were to attempt to raise/swing his left arm above his head, his forearm would immediately drop due to the muscle problem. His left upper arm was noticeably smaller than his right. This however was not noted by Dr. Wood in the autopsy, and may be very critical information. This information was discussed with Captain MacKenzie of the Dunedin Police Dept., who then told us he could have used his right arm to support the weapon. Is that a plausible explanation that correlates to the evidence? I find it extremely awkward to duplicate and achieve the pellet trajectory without the use of my left arm.

We're trying to visualize how the shot was produced. It appears the first two Dunedin PD investigations were incomplete, inaccurate and biased as they seemed to try to prove suicide. Your response was refreshing in that you at least considered the possibility of homicide. We're hopeful this case will be solved based on objective research and accurate data. Your professional forensic opinion on the numbered questions above would be greatly appreciated.

Another very important issue is the location/position of the weapon. It appears the on-scene investigators handled the shotgun to clear it and make the scene safe. Unfortunately they did not place it back where they found it before they drew their sketch, and possibly wrapped the case around it to keep their fingerprints off the gun as they handled it. I was the second person in the room after the shooting and distinctly remember the gun lying in the middle of the bed; muzzle pointing east towards the headboard. The gun case was not wrapped around gun, and the gun was not near the edge of the bed prior to the police arrival.

I understand Doctor Melinek's credibility and objectivity may be a concern to you, and I respect your opinion. But to clarify...we did not hire, pay, or employ Dr. Melinek. I contacted a non-profit organization called Parents of Murdered Children (POMC). They assist families who have questions and concerns about the death of loved ones, and they offer a service called Second Opinion. I sent them three copies of our information, a small donation, and handling fee. We were hoping for an objective review of the evidence. They sent the case to Dr. Melinek who reviewed the case and rendered an opinion. It was the first opinion rendered by an outside agency based on objective forensic evidence. We didn't buy an investigator we thought agreed with us.

I hope you see the irony of this issue, as our father's death certificate is officially closed by a Medical Examiner who was forced to retire due to her botching several autopsies, and was responsible for preventing justice to prevail in several families lives. When we explained our case and questions to her, she stated mistakes may have been made, but without further evidence from law enforcement she would not change her finding...and that "If her husband could commit suicide, anyone could!" I hope you see why we are a bit concerned with competency, credibility and objectivity.

Since we received the confession letter postmarked sixteen years to the date of Dad's death, we have discovered through more thorough and critical questioning, that things did not happen as police reports state.

I know this letter at times sounds angry, and may sound like it's directed at you. That's not my intention, and I apologize for that, but don't know how else to state some of our concerns. We really are looking for the truth. We would greatly appreciate any answers you can provide concerning the numbered questions. We would also appreciate you sending a list of published experts as you offered.

Thank you again for your time and your concern with this case.

Sincerely, Dan Dirscherl"

I had been keeping POMC aware of my communications, and shortly after sending my second letter to Dr. Palma, I emailed Bev the following note...

"Hi Bev,

I just wanted to take a moment to thank you and POMC, for your help with my father's case. You put us in contact with Dr. Melinek, who objectively reviewed the evidence, and saw the same issues we did. 33 years after Dad's death our case is once again before the Pinellas County ME's office. Dr. Melinek's opinion gave us hope and validated some of our concerns.

I received a response from the Pinellas County ME's office, who read her opinion and reviewed the case. While he (Dr. Palma) believes this is a suicide, he provided a brand new theory about the shooting and the orientation of the weapon (The 5th different theory as to how Dad may have shot himself). I wrote him back to ask for further clarification, and I'm awaiting his reply.

An interesting aspect of his initial response was to aggressively attempt to discredit Dr. Melinek's experience and abilities. He erroneously implied we found an inexperienced pathologist who would agree with us, and basically bought the answer we were looking for. We find it interesting that Dr. Melinek, the first forensic expert not associated with Pinellas County is not so certain this was a suicide based on an objective review of the facts...thanks to you and POMC.

In her email below, Dr. Melinek recommends contacting other experts (Dr. Stuart Grahm in Florida and/or Harry Bonnell in San Diego) to see if they would be willing to get involved. I don't have the money to hire an attorney...Dr. Melinek said Harry Bonnell may take the case pro-bono if the request came from your agency. Is that something POMC is able to do?

If POMC cannot contact those two, could you again send the packages to other POMC expert volunteers to see what another objective review may net? I'd be glad provide more copies of our package and another $50 to cover required fees. If we can show two or more completely objective forensic experts have concerns about this supposed suicide, it may bolster our case for a judicial review or help us present a stronger case to the Florida State Attorney's office.

POMC has been a great help to us...I hope there is more good news to come. I look forward to hearing from you. Thank you again for your time and assistance.

Dan"

I waited for more news. I was hopeful Dr. Palma would understand our questions and the possibility Dad's death was a homicide. I was also praying that POMC would come through for us and provide a second opinion from someone Palma would consider credible. Within a window of ten days, two letters appeared in my mailbox; the first, a response from Dr. Palma which arrived on March 15th. The second letter was an opinion rendered by Dr. Harry Bonnell, which he wrote on March 15th. Prayers were again being answered.

Dr. Palma's letter was a response to my earlier questions, and was kind of what I expected. It read as follows...

"Dear Mr. Dirscherl:

I received your letter and questions. I have attempted below to answer your questions to the best of my abilities based upon the materials available to me.

1. <u>*Is it your opinion that the muzzle was placed/held against the chest with the butt of the weapon overhead, or does it appear to be a hard contact wound indicating Dad may have leaned onto the muzzle?*</u>

The shot pellets are described as being directed primarily downward at an angle of 20 degrees from horizontal. As I have written previously, based upon the pictures of the wound, the clothing, and the wound description, this is a contact wound. I have previously described the orientation of the gun in my last correspondence. Since the photographs were not taken with the blood and debris removed, I can't be any more specific regarding the range of fire than that.

2.   *Does soot and powder residue above the wound indicate more of a seal between the muzzle and the bottom edge of the wound, versus at the top of the wound?*

This is a highly specific question that I can't answer based on the available information.

3.   *Is the wound characteristic consistent with a contact wound or a hard contact wound?*

The wound is clearly a contact wound. The two types of contact wounds are generally considered to be loose contact or hard contact (and all variations in between). When not over flat bones such as the skull or sternum, the appearance of a hard contact wound is not as dramatic. Considering the location and without clean photographs, I can only opine that it was a contact wound.

4.   *Is there any indication what caused the linear marks outside the wound at the ten-o-clock position in the photos?*

Based on the photos, the linear marks to which you are referring to may be due to the edge of the barrel of the weapon, dried blood, debris, etc. Due to the nature of the photographs, I cannot give an accurate answer to your question. The linear mark may not be an injury or a mark of the skin but merely a collection of blood and debris.

I wish that I could give more satisfactory answers, and I know that this is frustrating as there is no going back to do the autopsy or photographs over again using today's standards. The information available is not sufficient to answer such highly specific questions about the entrance wound.

Regarding an experienced expert in the field of gunshot wounds, I would recommend Dr. Vincent DiMaio, MD. He literally wrote the book on gunshot wounds.

Sincerely,
Noel A. Palma, MD
Deputy Chief Medical Examiner"

The second letter I received was written by Dr. Bonnell and forwarded to me by POMC. I was about to read the opinion of the second objective and unrelated forensic pathologist who was looking at the same evidence as Dr. Palma and his Pinellas County crew. Dr. Bonnell's letter read...

"15 March 2010
Re: Robert Dirscherl

I have reviewed the police and medical examiner reports as well as photos and other materials provided by his son, Dan. The autopsy pathologist described a four inch area of bright red muscle under the entry wound; this coloration is due to the carbon monoxide exiting the muzzle as a result of the explosion of the gunpowder. This usually implies a contact or partial contact entry wound. The extension of soot upwards from the entry wound would imply that the muzzle was not in actual contact with the skin on the upper side of the entry wound and that the wound track would also be angled upward; however the wound track has a downward angle of approximately twenty degrees. Since the shotgun pellets were very small and there is a "billiard ball effect" with the pellets bouncing off each other, it is possible that the small pellets were somewhat re-directed by striking a rib and each other.

In measuring the inner dimensions of the entry wound, I found it measured 18 x 26 mm and the diameter of the shotgun barrel is 18mm. The elongation of the wound by 8mm is consistent with the effects of Langer's lines, or the orientation of elastic tissue beneath the skin. So my opinion is that this is a loose contact entry wound, but that is not to the same as saying self-inflicted.

The original misinterpretation by police as to where the shotgun and telephone book were found, versus where they had been at the time of the shooting, led to some quick conclusions. Subsequent events also cast doubt on this being a self-inflicted wound; and, certainly, the absence of forced entry does not preclude unlawful entry into a residence.

At this point in time, I would opine that the manner of death is undetermined, if it were my case. If the envelope containing the confession note is available, it would be interesting to see if any DNA can be recovered from the adhesive portion of the envelope and stamp; this should certainly exclude the note from being written from a family member.

Sincerely,
Harry J. Bonnell, MD"

Undetermined! Not enough evidence to conclude suicide. Certainly the District Six officials would consider this highly respected, credible expert's opinion relevant.

Chapter 12

The Plot Thickens

The involvement and assistance from POMC, Dr. Melinek and Dr. Bonnell had certainly buoyed our spirits, even though we were still encountering challenges. At least we were still on the track and our coaster ride seemed to now be plodding along another upward grade. While we had received positive news from outside eyes, we were still arguing details, theories and possibilities based on old photos, limited physical evidence, and fresh opinions of distant experts. What we really needed was some new evidence; perhaps some physical evidence, or more supporting evidence that there were serious problems with the DPD's original investigation. All I could do was pray, leave the outcome in God's hands and see what He had planned.

Then, on March 27, 2010, I was surfing the internet and decided to Google James Allen MacKenzie, and Florida State Attorney Bernie McCabe. I stumbled across a document written by the mother of a young Florida man who was killed by a gunshot wound to the head. I began to read the horrible story about an alleged cover up involving MacKenzie and the Tarpon Springs Police Department. The story was gut wrenching, but when I reached the top of page four of her document, my heart stopped, my mind seized and I couldn't believe what I just read.

The story was written by a Pinellas County attorney named Michaela Mahoney, and I was about to enter her world of loss, alleged conspiracy and cover up. Her story was familiar and upsetting, but when I reached page four, I knew I had not randomly selected this document…it seemed it had chosen me. As she explained her personal experience with then Sergeant James Allen MacKenzie, who was working for the Tarpon Springs Police, she wrote on page four that MacKenzie "*made reference to a family that has fought with him for ten years because he said their relative's death was suicide and the family believed it was murder."*

I knew God was at work again. The document I stumbled upon describes her horrible experience dealing with the experts, and the alleged corruption she encountered while trying to find the truth concerning the death of her son. The document written by Michaela that I coincidentally stumbled across follows…

"Looking for Answers in all the wrong places

On September 06, 2001, I visited Sgt James Allen MacKenzie at the Tarpon Springs Police Department. It was just four days after my son's horrible death and two days after he had closed the case. I was accompanied by Margaret Mackay who had come to Florida to help with the funeral arrangements. Ms. Mackay witnessed and heard everything Sgt. MacKenzie said that day. In addition, I took extensive notes while Sgt. MacKenzie gave us his version of the events that had occurred that night based on Officer Parson's interviews, the police report and what Sgt. MacKenzie referred to as his own "forensic" investigation. I was looking for answers and expected to hear truthful and factual information as to what had actually happened the night my son, Shawn was shot with Officer Dan Nordmark's laser sighted handgun.

Sgt. MacKenzie was quick to tell us that Officer Nordmark was not arrested after my son was killed because he did nothing wrong and nothing illegal. According to the Detective, Dan Nordmark and Shawn were alone at the Shades Bar located on Alternate 19 in Palm Harbor, drinking and singing karaoke when they got into a verbal argument with some other patrons. I immediately thought this odd since Shawn had never been one to engage in this type of behavior. He was always a gentleman and a peacemaker when confronted with troublemakers. MacKenzie said that while outside of the Shades Bar, the same group of males they supposedly got into an argument with started "messing" with them again. He said Dan Nordmark retrieved his gun from his car for "protection" then Shawn approached, observed that Dan Nordmark was intoxicated and asked to hold the gun. Sgt. MacKenzie said that Shawn was trying to keep Nordmark from doing something stupid.

Sgt. MacKenzie went on to say that Dan Nordmark gave the gun to Shawn (with the safety on) and observed a police type car drive through the parking lot. He said the group of guys messing with them saw the cruiser and left. Officer Nordmark then realized that he had locked his keys in the car and called his sister-in-law, Rita Nordmark at home just before 2:00 AM and asked her to pick them up. He went on to explain that as Shawn was telling Rita Nordmark how to get to his house, Dan Nordmark asked Shawn to give the gun back and accidently shot himself. Rita Nordmark had apparently told the same story telling the police that she was at home when he called and after picking them up at the bar around 2:00 AM, drove North on Alt 19 and stated that when Dan Nordmark asked Shawn for the gun it fired. Sgt. MacKenzie was in complete agreement with the explanation of Nordmark's sister-in-law, Rita Nordmark and the extremely inebriated (MacKenzie's words) Dan Nordmark.

Sgt. MacKenzie relayed that Shawn was sitting in the middle of the back seat and asserted that it would have been impossible for Nordmark to shoot Shawn from the front seat of the car. He actually set up two chairs to demonstrate and had Margaret sit in the chair which would have been the front passenger seat where he said Nordmark sat and the other one was set up for me as if I were sitting in the middle of the back seat where he insisted Shawn was sitting at the time he was shot. Then he instructed Margaret to see if she could aim an imaginary gun at my head. Margaret effortlessly turned and instantly put her trigger finger against my temple. Sgt. MacKenzie frowned at us and then mumbled that it would be a lot harder to do that inside a car. And besides, he said, he had conclusive proof that Dan Nordmark was not close enough to Shawn to harm him. He told us that four tests including visual, alternate light source, phthalien and Luminal test were done on Nordmark's shirt to see if there was any blood on it. Sgt. MacKenzie said all of the tests showed not one trace of blood on Dan Nordmark's shirts. (We now know this is false).

Sgt. MacKenzie went on to elaborate on how extremely inebriated Dan Nordmark was that night. When I asked about the results of his breath tests, I was told that he did not perform any alcohol or drug tests on Officer Nordmark because again, he did not do anything illegal and he did not commit any crime. When questioned about this further, MacKenzie impatiently said Nordmark's extreme intoxication was witnessed by him and by the other police officers and would show in the police report. He told us that Dan Nordmark was an off-duty corrections officer and he did not

*know if Nordmark was authorized to carry a concealed firearm but
that most agencies give blanket authorizations to carry them and it is
normal for off duty law enforcement to carry guns with the safety off
even when they go to bars and drink alcohol. When I challenged this
assertion, he angrily replied that Nordmark did nothing wrong and
that he had the right to carry the gun in public even if he were
drinking. (The next day when I had the Opportunity to review the
police reports I could not find any police statements verifying Officer
Nordmark's extreme drunkenness).*

*Knowing that Shawn was much too intelligent to shoot himself, I
asked Sgt. MacKenzie whose fingerprints were on the gun and was
told that he did not take any fingerprints on the firearm because he
had eyewitness testimony that both men had handled the gun. When
pressed, he told us his eyewitnesses were Rita and Dan Nordmark.
He told us that he had fingerprinted Shawn while he lay in the
hospital. He also stated that he did not perform any residue tests on
the gun, because again his "eyewitnesses" said both men touched the
gun. Thus according to Sgt. MacKenzie, a GSR residue test would not
show any difference if Shawn had touched the gun and Officer
Nordmark had fired the gun. I told him that Shawn would not have
handled the gun and GSR residue tests could have proven that Shawn
didn't fire or touch the weapon. Sgt. MacKenzie then informed us that
another reason no one tested Shawn's fingers was because after
Shawn was fingerprinted, "they" washed his hands. This seems
highly unusual that emergency room staff, police or anyone else
would wash his hands while they were focused on his brain injury.
When I arrived at Helen Ellis Hospital, Shawn's hands were not
covered and the Tarpon Springs police stood around and watched as
I held and touched his hands, head and body. I have been told by
intelligent and professional members of law enforcement that had
there been an honest and competent police investigation that night,
required police procedure would have mandated that the victim's
hands be covered to preserve evidence.*

*I asked Sgt. MacKenzie why he concluded that Shawn touched
the gun based on the Nordmarks' testimony? Why did the Tarpon
Springs police accept the explanation of this highly intoxicated
individual, Dan Nordmark and his sister in law, Rita Nordmark
instead of searching for and questioning the employees and patrons
of the Shades Bar, where they said they had been that night, the men*

in the alleged confrontation etc. How could they close the case just one and a half days after Shawn's death without ever seeking any witnesses? Why weren't the Nordmarks considered to be suspects in Shawn's death? How could either of these people be considered unbiased competent witnesses in a possible murder? The Tarpon Springs police clearly knew that Officer Dan Nordmark was so drunk, he could not even stand up that night and they knew that Rita was a family member of Dan Nordmark's. Again, Sgt. MacKenzie's angry reply was that Officer Nordmark did nothing illegal and he did not commit any crime. Sgt. MacKenzie then had the nerve to tell us he believed their story because if Officer Nordmark had shot Shawn they would have parked in a regular parking space at the hospital instead of pulling up to the emergency room doors. Where did this detective get his training?

Later Sgt. MacKenzie told the FDLE he did try to take fingerprints but if you look at the photos taken on September 04, 2002 you can see gun was clean and shiny although by late September when I requested that the FDLE get involved, the gun had been smudged and covered with grey powder. Richard Pyles, an FDLE agent said their crime labs could not find any fingerprints because all prints had been completely obliterated by the Tarpon Springs police. Mr. Pyles also told the State Attorney that the weapon was covered with black powder and smudged when the FDLE received it from the Tarpon Spring Police Department.

Sgt. MacKenzie went on to say that he was sure Shawn was alone in back seat and shot himself because the two blood splatters on the passenger side right door, one high forward and one low back indicates low probability that anyone was in the back with Shawn. He said that the CT scan showed that the bullet entered Shawn's right temple and fractured the left side of his skull but lodged there and did not exit actually remaining completely under the skin. He said that accounted for absence of evidence of material from an exit wound of the bullet. He said there was very little blood in the car which proved they were very close to the hospital, made a U-turn and came back to the hospital immediately. He also said the presence of blood drops on the car shade on the left foot well was consistent with the Nordmarks' story. Sgt. MacKenzie said Shawn was still sitting up after the shooting and fell over when Rita Nordmark, the driver turned the corner. The Police report says Rita looked back when she heard the shot and Shawn was lying down with his head toward the back door on the driver's side of the car.

Sgt. MacKenzie said that the wound was a contact wound -close or against Shawn's head and that the 25 caliber gun had a laser sighting device with a safety on the back of the gun handle. According to MacKenzie, you squeeze the safety ½ way to activate the laser and to release the safety and you squeeze a little more with your finger on the trigger and it fires (staging the trigger). MacKenzie said a person would have to have a lot of manual dexterity to activate the laser without putting his finger on the trigger. He also said that there was another very small safety on the side of the gun which Shawn could not have seen unless he was in bright sunlight or under very bright indoor lighting. Sgt. MacKenzie said the gun was set to fire and the alternate safety was in the off position contrary to the police report which says Nordmark stated that the safety was on when he gave the gun to Shawn. (Sgt. MacKenzie told the medical examiner's investigator there was no safety on the gun).

We were then told that the car was never impounded or taken to a crime lab to gather evidence. MacKenzie informed us that he had released the Honda Civic car to Rita and Dan Nordmark the same night of the shooting. He also told us there was blood on the back of the driver's head rest that appeared to be manually transferred but concluded that it was placed there when Shawn was removed from the car. The blood on the back of the driver's seat was not tested for prints.

Sgt. MacKenzie told us that he believed that the wound was self inflicted but was positive that Shawn absolutely did not commit suicide because Shawn was sitting in the middle of the back seat, leaning forward, talking and giving directions home when the gun supposedly fired. However, Sgt. MacKenzie said, he could not control what the medical examiner would say. (I later found out that Sgt. MacKenzie and Officer Parsons had already spoken to the medical examiner's investigator a few days before he met with us and had discussed their version of the events and the ME's determination of suicide).

MacKenzie then made reference to a family that has fought with him for years because he said their relative's death was suicide and the family believed it was murder. *It appears that he was trying to keep me from causing problems although he had apparently* *already indicated suicide to the medical examiner. A finding of suicide would of course re-enforce Sgt. MacKenzie's efforts to show that Dan Nordmark did nothing illegal that night and would relieve Officers MacKenzie and parsons, the Tarpon Springs Police Department and Dan and Rita Nordmark and any others who may have been involved of all blame and responsibility for Shawn's death and the subsequent lack of an appropriate investigation with interviews, mandatory drug and alcohol test, fingerprints, residue tests etc. and which should have resulted in Nordmark's arrest.*

Before Margaret and I left MacKenzie's office, he leaned forward, locking his eyes on mine and carefully explained that an internal investigation would be conducted by the Inspector General's office because Officer Nordmark is associated with law enforcement pursuant to his position as a prison guard for the Department of Corrections. He said if Officer Nordmark admits anything at all during that investigation, it could not be held against him in criminal court because he would have no fifth amendment right and it would be considered compelled testimony and alternative evidence would have to be used in court, however, MacKenzie and other officers failed to gather any physical evidence of any kind that could be used in criminal court.

Then as Ms. Mackay looked on, Sgt. MacKenzie warned me several times in a threatening tone of voice that if I spoke with the press or anyone else before the investigation was completed that I would be criminally liable with criminal sanctions against me. He did not arrest the drunken owner of the gun after my son was killed, but he threatened to arrest me the day after my son's funeral. He obviously was attempting to intimidate me. I have heard that he now denies making these statements, but he did make them and again, I had a witness with me who clearly heard him and is willing to testify in court if necessary.

In the days that followed, Sgt. MacKenzie behaved in an unprofessional, volatile and aggressive manner, shouting at Shawn's distraught younger brother, Daniel McMillan and at me on at least two different occasions when we came to the police department to request a copy of the police procedures which were normally followed in the event of a shooting. On another occasion after demanding to know why there was no reference to Officer Nordmark's extreme intoxication in the police report Sgt. MacKenzie pointed out that Shawn had said, "you are intoxicated, let me hold the gun." He incorrectly assured me that this was a "statement of interest". I told him this was not a "Statement Against Interest" and it could not be held against Dan Nordmark in Court. Daniel and I also wanted to know what is the required Tarpon Springs Police Department procedure when there is a death by gunshot and the owner of the gun is extremely intoxicated? Sgt. MacKenzie refused to give any written procedure to me or to my younger son when we requested it and said it's based on thirty years of experience and volumes of textbooks and everyone does things differently. He then yelled that I should just leave the poor man alone. He was going to have to carry the incident with him the rest of his life. What about Shawn? What about all of his family, friends and fraternity brothers who loved him and would never see him again? Obviously, Sgt. MacKenzie cared only for Officer Nordmark.

Later, when Daniel had called City Hall to ask for a copy of the police procedures, he was told to go to the front desk of the police department, which he did. Although he did not ask to see Sgt. MacKenzie, he was angrily greeted by him, shouted at and actually followed to the door by this irate and crude Tarpon Springs police officer.

I had gone to speak with Sgt. MacKenzie to get answers but all I got from him was the distinct conviction knowledge that Sgt. MacKenzie and other Tarpon Springs police officers failed to gather any physical evidence of any kind that could be used against Officer Dan Nordmark. They failed to obtain any fingerprints from the weapon (I believe that if my son had touched that gun and there had been one single print of his, the Tarpon Springs police would have found it and quickly informed the press). The Tarpon Springs police failed to take residue tests; failed to cover Shawn's hands, as is routine procedure with a serious or fatal gunshot wound; failed to administer mandatory alcohol or drug tests after observing Officer Nordmark's extreme intoxication and they failed to impound the car and properly process it for evidence. They failed to pursue even one lead or one credible witness at any time.

They failed to note in their report that there was a second bullet missing from the six round clip; failed to photograph the inside of the car's trunk; failed to interview any of the witnesses who saw the horrifying events unfold that night; failed to make any arrest and they did not request assistance by the Sheriff's office in their investigation, although they are obviously not equipped or qualified to conduct this type of investigation.

They failed to photograph or list Officer Nordmark's shirt in evidence which Sgt. MacKenzie misrepresented had been tested for blood. This shirt which was alleged to have been taken from Officer Nordmark on the night of the shooting was not sent to the Sheriff for testing for another two and a half days. We now know these forensics tests were never performed and the police report is falsified. They failed to note in their report that there was a second bullet missing from the six round clip (fired by Bernie Dillman in the parking lot of the British Pub minutes before the second bullet tore through Shawn's brain). They made no arrests yet Sgt. MacKenzie threatened the mother of the victim with criminal liability and criminal sanctions. Was he going to arrest me? Incredibly, the Tarpon Springs police closed the case one and one half days after Shawn's death (Monday was a holiday)".

After reading this familiar and horrible declaration of alleged injustice, I tracked down Michaela through a website she authored, and I sent her a detailed email explaining our story. I included the following paragraph.

"I recently discovered your case as I was searching the web for information on Pinellas County Medical examiners, attorneys, and Bernie McCabe. In one of your letters you mentioned a discussion between you and MacKenzie, where he mentioned a family that has fought with him for years over a relative's supposed suicide that they thought was a murder. I believe we are that family."

She responded to my email the next day and her opening sentence reveals the amazing connection that had just formed…supposedly by coincidence.

"Dear Mr. Dirscherl,

Thank God you have contacted me as I have been searching for you for many years."

While my family and I had been struggling all these years trying to understand why our case was stubbornly unfolding with no credible explanation; thinking we were the only ones trying to slay dragons and battle experts, here was a the story of a mother who had lost her son and was also living in our bizarre world of frustration and injustice. Her story is as remarkable as ours…and involves a familiar key player. Not only did her story validate our concerns about our poorly investigated crime scene, it generated more concerns about questionable police investigative techniques and serious integrity issues. Here is a synopsis of her horrible story copied from her website, www.copsliesandcoverups.com.

On September 02, 2001, at 2:26 A.M., my son, Shawn McMillan, 26, was driven to the Helen Ellis Hospital in Tarpon Springs, FL, by Rita Nordmark and her intoxicated brother- in-law, Dan Nordmark, an off duty Corrections Officer. A bullet from the officer's gun had ripped through Shawn's brain. Officer Nordmark alleged the wound was self inflicted. The facts indicate otherwise.

Sgt. James Allen MacKenzie of the Tarpon Springs Police Department began his official Police Report with these words: "At 2:39 hours on September 2, 2001, I was called at my residence in reference to responding to a shooting at Helen Ellis ER with 'Special Circumstances.'" "Special Circumstances" was the code used by Sgt. MacKenzie to identify the drunken owner of the gun as a fellow member of Law Enforcement.

When police realized the suspect was a cop, "Special Circumstances" apparently took precedence over the investigation and dictated the actions taken by the Tarpon Springs PD as they ignored routine police procedures; failed to conduct Gun Residue Tests; failed to administer alcohol or drug tests on Officer Nordmark, who was so intoxicated he could barely stand up; failed to question credible witnesses; and failed to pursue a single lead or to impound the car. Instead, they obtained peroxide from the hospital ER and instructed Rita Nordmark to begin cleaning out the blood (evidence) within two hours of the shooting. Although three police officers and the emergency room nurse searched the car for the missing weapon, no one could find it. It later mysteriously materialized on the back floorboards. Police declined to lift prints; instead, they obliterated them.

Tarpon Springs police began conferring with the Medical Examiner's office about the shooting even before Shawn died. The ME, Charles Siebert, Jr., (the same medical examiner who sided with police in the notorious Florida Boot Camp Case), immediately concluded the manner of death was suicide, although there was no evidence to support that determination.

Several experts have disputed that ruling. Crime Laboratory Analyst Supervisor, L. Parker reported that a determination as to whether the gunshot wound was or was not self inflicted could not be made from Shawn's clothing and other items; Forensic Expert, T.A. LaVoy, who worked for many years with the FDLE, stated that Dr. Siebert's conclusion of suicide was not valid. Stuart James, another well known Forensics expert, also found the determination of suicide invalid, and the Former Deputy Commissioner of the FDLE has continued to maintain his belief that Shawn's death was not suicide.

Even the Probable Cause Panel for the Florida Medical Examiner's Commission reported, after a thorough investigation, that my request to have "suicide" removed from Shawn's death certificate was not unreasonable due to the actions of the Tarpon Springs police.

Shawn was as far from suicidal as anyone could be. He had worked with me in my law office most of that day and was in high spirits. After we left the office, we went to a clothing store. Shawn was full of jokes and laughter while he tried on suits, ties and shirts for his new job with American Express. I dropped him off at the Ale House Restaurant at 5:30 P.M. to meet some acquaintances. They proceeded from there to the British Pub to play pool. That's where they ran into Nordmark, another casual acquaintance, who offered to give him a ride home. First, however, Nordmark and his best friend, Bernie Dillman, wanted to go to the Palms Bar and Grill for Karaoke. Shawn accompanied them there and then back to the Pub, still looking for a ride home.

The day after the funeral, Sgt. MacKenzie threatened me with arrest if I spoke to the authorities, press or attorneys about Shawn's death. By then, MacKenzie already had told the press that Officer Nordmark could not possibly have shot Shawn because sensitive blood tests conducted by the Pinellas County Sheriff's Office proved that there was no trace of Shawn's blood on Nordmark's shirt. Later the Sheriff's Office and their attorney determined that those Luminal and Phenolphthalien tests were not performed. At that point, Maximo Sanchez, the Tarpon Springs police officer who took the shirt to the lab, admitted that the only test ever conducted on Dan Nordmark's shirt was a visual exam. A forensic report to Tim Whitfield, the Sheriff's Office Forensics Supervisor, and Sandy Jacobs, who was alleged to have conducted the tests, also confirmed that the chemical tests were not conducted. Both stated that, if Ms. Jacobs had performed such tests, she would have drafted the required Forensics Report specifically describing her participation and all results and would have notified the FDLE regarding her use of Luminol.

When the TSPD learned that I had been given this information, Ms. Jacobs abruptly changed her story and tearfully claimed that now she suddenly remembered conducting the tests. She could not explain why she had not drafted the required reports.

I don't know whose shirt, if any, was submitted for testing, but if Shawn's blood wasn't on it, it could not have been the shirt that Dan Nordmark had been wearing. Shawn was a big man, and nurses couldn't get him out of the car, so Nordmark crawled into the backseat, reached his arms up under Shawn's arms and around his chest and dragged him from the car and up onto the gurney. Shawn's profusely bleeding head was pressed against Nordmark's shirt during that process. There's no way that shirt could not have been saturated with Shawn's blood.

This fact was confirmed when two of Dan Nordmark's friends, (one a Pinellas County Sheriff's employee), testified separately under oath that Nordmark told them that the police had taken his shirt after the shooting because it was covered with Shawn's blood. Although everything on Shawn's person, including his Chapstick and pocket change, was photographed and listed as evidence, Nordmark's shirt, (which was described by Sgt. MacKenzie as "the most conclusive piece of evidence in the investigation"), was not.

The police reports are riddled with lies and omissions that completely conceal the events of that fateful evening. Nordmark and Dillman had very good reason to conceal the truth. While at the Palms, the two inebriated men had become furious at Kimberley, the Karaoke lady. The terrified woman gave a sworn statement that she feared for her life and for Shawn's when he tried to protect her from the belligerent men, who followed her into the parking lot, yelling obscenities while she loaded her equipment. She and other witnesses described Nordmark and Dillman as violently angry and "evil." Chief Assistant State Attorney, Bruce Bartlett, brushed aside that testimony.

About twenty minutes later, at the British Pub, where they had gone after being evicted from the Palms, Dan Nordmark brought out his firearm and drunkenly waved it about in front of witnesses. He jammed the slide several times in his efforts to load and cock it. He then handed the gun to Dillman, who fired it at an adjacent gas station and occupied mobile home park. The frightened bar patrons fled the premises in fear of being killed.

The name of the British Pub, the events that took place there, and the identities of the witnesses to those events were withheld from police reports. The Nordmarks asserted that they had been at a different bar that night. Later, when caught in that lie, it was explained that they were confused about the name of the bar due to all the excitement at the hospital. It's highly unlikely that the Nordmarks would have forgotten the name of the British Pub. The Nordmark family owned the British Pub!

I naively believed the FDLE would expose the truth and seek justice. Instead, they followed the Blue Code and protected law enforcement. By then, Dan Nordmark and Bernie Dillman were claiming that they had been too intoxicated to remember their own actions. Between them, they came up with at least five versions of how Shawn supposedly ended up with Nordmark's gun in his hand. Later, when Nordmark was deposed, he took the Fifth Amendment literally hundreds of times, and Dillman never showed up for any of his scheduled depositions. Their many lies and conflicting statements seemed irrelevant to the FDLE.

The FDLE seemed to help them come up with new stories. Dan and Rita Nordmark originally stated that Shawn was seated in the center of the back seat and was leaning forward between them, giving Rita directions to his home, when he was shot in the head. However, an FDLE agent asserted that a hair found on a car window proved that Shawn was sitting by the back passenger window, out of range of the gun, if Nordmark had been holding it. That hair fragment was found one full month after the car had been scrubbed with peroxide at the hospital, scoured with Oxyclean at Rita Nordmark's home, then scrubbed with commercial cleaners and paint thinners and detailed by Carsmetics, Inc. Since the hair had no follicle, it could not be successfully tested for DNA. The best conclusion that experts could reach was that the hair came from a male, who probably was African-American. (Shawn was a blonde Caucasian.)

More than fifty friends and family members who knew and loved Shawn wrote to the State Attorney insisting that Shawn never would have killed himself. Many spoke about his keen intellect, kindness, integrity and happy disposition. Others described Shawn's dismay about people who committed suicide and how he could not understand why anyone would do that to themselves or to their loved ones. They told about conversations with Shawn regarding his plans for the future and his excitement about starting his new job. One of the attorneys that Shawn worked for wrote about spending time with Shawn just twelve hours before he was shot. He stated that Shawn was upbeat and happy and there was absolutely no indication of any depression or imminent suicide.

All of those people were ignored by the State Attorney's Office. None were interviewed or even acknowledged. Instead, the authorities portrayed Shawn as a loser and utter failure with no reason to live. They were so intent upon proving Shawn's "instability" that they went so far as to investigate which books he checked out of the library and triumphantly reported that he hadn't paid a fine for an overdue book. (He hadn't paid the fine because he was dead.)

Their hateful words about Shawn and our family have caused devastating sorrow in our lives. The manner in which this case was handled defies all reason. At night I dream about holding my beautiful blue-eyed son as he dies, with his younger brother's ear pressed against his chest, listening as Shawn's heartbeat grew fainter and fainter. I wake up with tears on my cheeks, crying out for my son, and I feel unbridled rage at what members of law enforcement did to cover up the truth. By the time the Tarpon Springs PD, the FDLE, the Medical Examiner and the State Attorney's Office were finished with our family, our hearts and lives were shattered forever. Any trust we had in law enforcement is gone. I will never understand why corrupt and dishonest police officers and violent drunks were protected by the authorities while my son's reputation was destroyed by their treacherous attempts to justify a determination of suicide without a single piece of credible evidence. The authorities have made a mockery of our legal process and violated the rights of all Floridians by protecting corrupt members of law enforcement in a shooting with "*Special Circumstances.*" *Michaela E. Mahoney*

Sound familiar? Kind of make your heart ache? As I write this book and reread the horrible experience suffered by Michaela and her family, I wonder how many other family's lives have been destroyed by unethical behavior of those sworn to serve and protect. Not only can misguided police abuse their power and pride to twist facts and hold lives hostage, the sole authority bestowed upon medical examiners to determine the cause and manner of death are unchallengeable.

By the way, my thoughts and comments are not a condemnation of all those honest and ethical servants who wear the badge. But law enforcement, like the military or any other occupational assemblage, is a microcosm of society which harbors a percentage of unethical supposed-servants whose pride, power, and inability to admit mistakes inevitably results in the devastation of innocent lives.

So...was this chance discovery of Shawn McMillan's death a God-thing, or just another coincidence, happenstance, fluke, twist of fate, etcetera? Was I coincidentally introduced to Michaela and her story and more evidence that validated our concerns about DPD's investigation and more errors by medical examiners, or was there a reason this was happening? I can't prove if this was a God-thing or just a coincidental payoff due to endless hours spent searching all things relevant to our case.

Michaela shared that she too is a follower of Christ, and that she prays daily. She explained that she prayed about finding the family that MacKenzie randomly mentioned during their interview a decade ago. She knew no details about our case or who we were...only that we were out there, and that we may be experiencing a parallel nightmare. Ten years later her hopes and prayers about finding us were answered, but it happened on God's timeline, not hers.

After years of investigation, thousands of dollars in attorney fees and endless battles with the Medical Examiner's office and law enforcement agencies, she finally received what she thought was the good news she had been waiting for. Her case went before the Medical Examiner's Commission, who determined Shawn's death certificate should be amended.

When she received the amended death certificate, it appeared the new medical examiner Dr. Thogmartin had made the proper correction. The manner of death had been changed from "Suicide" to "Undetermined". But as she read across the form, shock, horror and disbelief flooded her mind. Although suicide had been removed and no longer defiled the manner of death block, in the block stating the cause of death, Dr. Thogmartin or someone from his office retyped the words… "Shot Self."

Michaela was crushed. Her years of battle had all been for naught. Her long struggle for justice was dashed by two small words; the words that her family and mine have in common…the words that condemn our loved ones to legacies as killers…the words we both struggle to erase..."Shot Self".

Michaela and I continue to communicate, and our goals and missions have merged. While we are both trying to solve our personal cases, we've come to agree that more needs to be done to change current Florida laws concerning the omnipotent powers maintained by medical examiners. She has already contacted numerous state representatives requesting laws be amended to strengthen the appeals process and reign in medical examiners' powers, but that has yet to happen. Perhaps others will join our cause and let their legislators know this injustice is creating more victims and devastating more lives.

So the curious question remains; was this chance discovery of Michaela and her story a God-thing or coincidence? I still can't say for sure, but if it was not God's hand, and was simply a happenstance discovery due to the massive amounts of information available on the World Wide Web, I'm truly grateful to the Web creator, and I owe Al Gore a great debt of gratitude. (Wink;)

I had been conversing by phone and email with Michaela and in June 2010 finally got to meet her as I took my brood to Florida for another family reunion. Spending a few hours with Michaela was quite an experience. It was the meeting of a fellow seeker; a victim who was also trying to share the truth about her loved one. She had succeeded with part of her mission, but still wanted to do more so other families didn't have to live through our hell.

After learning so much about her struggles with certain law enforcement officials and the medical examiner establishment, after we returned to Alaska I felt it was time to send another letter to Dr. Thogmartin.

"*July 13, 2010*
Dear Dr. Thogmartin,

On or about January 10, 2010 your office received a letter/packet from Forensic Pathologist Dr. Judy Melinek, concerning the death of Robert Dirscherl Sr. Dr. Melinek informed you she had reviewed the above referenced case and had several concerns related to the status of the death certificate currently closed as a suicide. She listed numerous concerns and asked your office to reevaluate the case, and asked you to consider changing the status to "Homicide", or at a minimum, "Undetermined", as convincing evidence of a suicide was not present.

The case was referred to Deputy Chief Medical Examiner, Noel A. Palma MD, who reviewed the information and responded to our family On February 1, 2010. Although I sent you a certified letter of concerns in June of 2003, Dr. Palma's letter incorrectly stated this recent contact was the first time your office became aware of our family's dissatisfaction with the finding. Dr. Palma stated your office welcomes any and all credible evidence, and will amend any such death certificate to accurately reflect the cause and manner of death based on the available evidence. Dr. Palma's first letter goes on to address and refute numerous issues and questions posed by Dr. Melinek.

Based on initial 1977 investigative reports by Dunedin Police Dept. (James Allen MacKenzie), initial autopsy report by District Six Medical Examiner (Dr. Joan E. Wood), a secondary investigation in 1994 by Dunedin Police Dept. (James Allen MacKenzie and Stephanie Brown), and a 1997 investigation by the Pinellas County Sheriff's Dept. (Detective Rob Snipes), Dr. Palma stated..."the determination was contact range and the shotgun wound could easily be self induced." Dr. Palma stated that he and others had no difficulty reaching and activating the trigger on a shotgun of similar length, and that the trajectories were easily duplicated.

In my follow-up letter I informed Dr. Palma my father had significant nerve damage and considerable atrophy of his left tricep which prevented him from lifting his left arm above his head (a noticeable physical impairment that was not noted by Dr. Joan Wood in the autopsy report). While addressing this issue I also asked if his opinion was that the wound was caused by the lifted shotgun being held over head, or by my father leaning onto the muzzle while resting the weapon on the bed, as these alternate techniques would most likely produce different wound characteristics. Dr. Palma's answer was that he had previously described the orientation of the gun in his first letter. I find no information to substantiate this claim, or any description as to the weapon being held overhead or leaned upon.

In his next paragraph Dr. Palma theorizes the shotgun was oriented upside down when fired. This is the fifth theory our family has received as to how the supposed self-inflicted wound was produced. It seems to support the 1977 presupposed suicide finding, and Dr. Wood's cause/manner of death. While Dr. Wood, the expert responsible for the death certificate status failed to note this significant observation, Dr. Melinek is portrayed as a faulty rookie for not noting this proposed theory.

As recommended by Dr. Palma in his first letter, I requested the review of a second, more reputable Forensic Pathologist whose resume I hoped would meet Dr. Palma's expectations. Our case was forwarded to Forensic Pathology Consultant Dr. Harry Bonnell. On March 30, 2010 we received our second expert opinion from an independent, objective forensic pathologist. Melinek & Bonnell, the first two outside experts we contacted both concurred there was not sufficient evidence to determine a suicide, and the death certificate should be amended.

Please keep in mind both Dr. Melinek and Dr. Bonnell were contacted by the non-profit organization Parents of Murdered Children (POMC), and provided their assistance pro-bono; these were not two experts we paid to agree with us. Dr. Bonnell's opinion is attached, as is his curriculum vitae, including education history, academic appointments, employment history, publications, and other qualifications. A few of his pertinent qualifications follow:

Position
Forensic Pathology Consultant
San Diego, California 92119

Medical Malpractice/Wrongful Death

Dr. Bonnell has been consulted to review more than 200 wrongful death/malpractice law suits and has testified in court 60 times for the plaintiff and 54 times for the defendant. He regularly reviewed medical records as part of his job as Chief Deputy Medical Examiner for San Diego County. He compares physician notes to nursing notes to lab results to find inconsistencies or to substantiate the truth of the matter. He is able to determine what should be there but has been omitted. In some cases, he has pointed out to defense that there are issues even more serious than those claimed in the initial complaint.

Gunshot and Shotgun Wounds

A typical entry wound or atypical, shored exit wound. Research articles show that trauma and emergency physicians are no more accurate than 50% in determining which is entry and which is exit. They are trained to treat what lies between; but, forensic pathologists are trained to distinguish between entry and exit wounds. What was the distance between muzzle and target? Consistent with self-inflicted or obviously not a suicide? What was the position when shot? Dr. Bonnell has autopsied more than 750 shooting victims.

Medical Autopsies: More than 7000 personally performed. Court Testimony: Dr. Bonnell qualified as expert witness more than 470 times in 18 states, as well as federal courts and courts martial.

After explaining some law enforcement investigators doubt the authenticity of the confession letter, Dr. Palma stated "we cannot offer a scientifically valid alternate conclusion based on the information at hand." I contend the confession letter is authentic, and all physical evidence could have been produced by a second person in the room firing the fatal shot. We believe we can prove that possibility and that the concerns presented by the two objective Forensic Pathology experts are justified.

It's apparent to many that available evidence proves no clear conclusion as to how the fatal shot was inflicted. The poorly investigated initial crime scene, lost crime scene photographs, lack of fingerprinting, etc., coupled with subjective "gut feelings" provide no surety as to the cause and manner of death. Not to mention subsequent investigations conducted by the original investigating officer (MacKenzie), other law enforcement agencies and your office, have lead to five different theories as to how the fatal shot was fired; the last as recently as February of this year, by Dr. Palma of your office.

The closure of our father's case and status of his current death certificate are based on the inaccurate/incomplete investigations by retired Dunedin/Tarpon Springs Police Officer James Allen MacKenzie and retired Medical Examiner Joan E. Wood. While the facts and objective expert reviews show there is much doubt in the cause and manner of death, we are stymied by a system that seems to have no interest in accepting that the original experts made mistakes and got this one wrong.

Our family has attempted to work with authorities through the proper channels since 1993. The consistent response by police and the ME's office has been, "We solve and close these cases based on the evidence." Sir, that is all we are asking. We see no proof of a self inflicted wound. There is doubt (five different theories) as to how this death occurred. There is a plethora of circumstantial evidence that indicates a second person fired the weapon, and a confession letter which supports that premise. We see no objective reason why this death certificate should not be amended to accurately reflect these facts. All we are asking for is for you to amend the death certificate to Undetermined, based on the evidence. Proof of a suicide is simply not evident.

Although local newscasters have declared this "The most bizarre murder mystery in Tampa Bay history", and the story of our father's death became an Unsolved Mysteries television episode, national publicity and notoriety have not been our goal. We are not preoccupied with finding a killer. That individual has been forgiven by our family, and their fate lies in the hands of a Higher Power. Nor are we interested in defaming your office or the law enforcement community. We know you have a tough job, but at times mistakes are made.

We realize Law Enforcement is not likely to uncover new physical evidence which will lead to a killer or conviction. While that revelation would make the decision much easier for your office, it is not essential to amend this death certificate to more accurately reflect the truth based on the available evidence...all we are asking for is that the right thing be done.

This letter is our sincere attempt to contact you directly and ask you to review our case and to amend the death certificate. We do not seek public apologies, excuses for errors, or admissions of inaccuracies; we simply seek justice and request you amend the death certificate to accurately reflect that the cause of death is undetermined.

I look forward to hearing from you soon. Your time and assistance are greatly appreciated.
Sincerely, Daniel D. Dirscherl"

I included Dr Bonnell's several page long Curriculum Vitae, and mailed it to Dr. Thogmartin. Approximately two months after mailing Dr. Bonnell's opinion to Dr. Palma, I received the following letter from the District Six ME. The attempts to discredit our objective experts still seemed to be the strategy. The final letter I received from Dr. Palma on September 8, 2010 read…

"Dear Mr. Dirscherl:

I received your package July 13, 2010 including Dr. Harry Bonnell's opinion letter from the Second Opinion Services. In your letters you also mentioned that both Dr. Melinek and Dr. Bonnell were contacted by the non-profit organization Parents of Murdered Children and provided their services pro-bon and that both of these outside experts opine that there was not sufficient evidence to determine a suicide and the death certificate should be amended.

I took the liberty to request from the office of the Medical Examiner (County of San Diego) every gunshot wound involved case where the manner of death is undetermined as certified by Dr. Bonnell. Of the four cases, none were similar to your father's circumstance.

Being affiliates of the same organization, the alignment of their opinions is not surprising. Unfortunately in my opinion, Dr. Bonnell's correspondence mirrors Dr. Melinek's opinion in almost every way, and his correspondence does not address the gun orientation issue or any other additional issue that would cause me to conclude amendment is necessary.

Sincerely,
Noel A Palma, MD
Deputy Chief Medical Examiner"

When Dr. Palma stated in his first letter that he would "*certainly pay attention to any credible opinion on the matter.*", apparently that meant the credible opinion of anyone besides Dr. Judy Melinek or Dr. Harry Bonnell, since they both volunteered their time with the same non-profit organization, and had not investigated cases that were similar enough to our case. Apparently Dr. Bonnell's more than seven hundred-fifty shooting autopsies and seven thousand autopsies overall, didn't qualify him as credible. Apparently people have very different views of the word "credible".

It's apparent the current powers-that-be have no intention considering the opinions of outside experts if they conflict with their own.

Have I mentioned the rollercoaster ride analogy lately?

Chapter 13

...Know Your Heart

In October 2010, I sat down and began to write this book. I'd been encouraged by some friends and family to share our account, and I felt it was an opportunity to share the truth about Dad's innocence, and perhaps find another angel who may be able to help finally overturn this injustice.

While my siblings were encouraging me to write about our experience, they also indicated they were a little worried I had become too entrenched in the fight to clear Dad's name. There were subtle hints that I was spending a lot of time working on the case, and maybe I should take a break. While I appreciated their concern, I really wasn't spending that much time on it. Writing is a very soothing and cathartic exercise; it's a hobby and something I love to do. It also fit in well with my work schedule. Since I'm an early riser and we don't begin work until 9:00, I had a couple hours each morning to write if I chose to. Some weeks I might write for an hour or two several mornings before work; other weeks I wouldn't write at all. Each session was a comforting exercise and I felt I was being called to share the story.

I picked up on my sibling's concerns and tried to reassure them that I had truly given my worries over to the Lord and that I was not heading off the deep end or becoming fanatical about the case. I was really at peace and accepted the reality our case may never be overturned, or the death certificate amended. But that didn't mean I was ending a quest to see Dad's name cleared and justice achieved. I routinely stepped back and pondered that quote from the beginning of the book; that self-imposed mantra that reminded me I needed pursue this cause for the right reasons..."*The pursuit of justice without vengeance is a noble cause. The quest for revenge through the guise of justice is a lie...know your heart.*"

I truly believe my heart is at peace and this effort is just a small part of who I am…and that it's still a noble cause, not an obsession, overwhelming fixation, or quest for revenge; just a small part of my life that perhaps is part of my purpose. As I've stated, I believe we are all here for a purpose, and that God has plans for each one of us. I can't and won't attempt to prove that, but I believe it's true.

By March 2011, I had received the supporting forensic opinions of Dr. Melinek and Dr. Bonnell and had bantered back and forth with Dr. Palma at the ME's office, and spring was turning into summer. That could only mean one thing…baseball season in Alaska was about to begin.

Growing up in Florida where a baseball game can take place any day of the year made it difficult for me to get used to Alaska baseball. I've been coaching Recreational, Competitive and/or High school/Legion baseball in Alaska for the last eight years, and up here we have to wait for the snow to melt and the fields to reappear. It's not unusual to be shoveling the white stuff from ball fields in April or May, preparing to cram a season's worth of training and games into four months of daylight baseball marathons. Very few fields in Alaska have lights, but during mid summer, games can stretch past midnight with natural light. Since practice and games ate up much of my free time, I didn't do much writing during baseball season. But when the season ended and I sat down to type the last chapter; the book's ending…I realized I didn't have one.

Over the years we had shared our questions and concerns with the Dunedin Police, the Pinellas County Sheriffs, the Florida State Attorney's office, Unsolved Mysteries, POMC and finally the District Six Medical Examiner, who is ultimately responsible for the death certificate. The ME's office had made it clear they were done with the case and we had contacted everyone we could think of, short of hiring an attorney and initiating the dreaded "L" words, (Lawsuit, Lengthy Litigation, Lawyers, Loans). We had played by the rules and requested help from every official in the legal chain we thought could provide it. It seemed nobody admitted to seeing any flaws in the case, and the ME's unchallengeable power was all that was needed to keep the lid tightly shut.

But I had kept in touch with Michaela and remembered what she had been through. I remembered her tenacity at clearing her son's name and I realized we had one last hoop to jump through; one last opportunity available to give state officials the chance to review the evidence and a possible method to achieve an amended Death certificate. That option was filing a complaint through the Florida Department of Law Enforcement (FDLE) Medical Examiner's Commission, against Dr. Thogmartin for not using prudent judgment in this case.

This wasn't a preferred option, but besides litigation or going to the local media, it seemed to be the only opportunity we had. Michaela had filed this type of complaint against the ME in her son's case. The ME Commission determined there was justification to assign a Probable Cause Panel whose investigation provided evidence to the Commission, convincing the current District Six ME Dr. Thogmartin that the ME in charge of her son's case erred, and Shawn's death certificate should be amended to "Undetermined". While the suspicious evidence and questionable investigative processes surrounding Shawn's death were much more recent than ours, we felt the old, yet legitimate facts related to our case still carried enough weight to be seriously considered by the FDLE Medical Examiner's Commission.

When we previously requested Dr. Thogmartin review our case concerns and evidence, his decision was to assign the case to his Assistant Chief Dr. Palma, whose review didn't provide sufficient answers to the questions we posed. So in June I began to draft a complaint against Dr. Thogmartin; not out of anger or spite, but because it was the official avenue offered through the system.

The complaint was based on Florida Statute XXIX Chapter 406, also known as the Medical Examiners Act, which was enacted by the Florida Legislature in 1970 to establish minimum and uniform standards of excellence in statewide medical examiner services. I specifically stated the complaint was based on chapter 406.075, Grounds for discipline; Disciplinary Proceedings. I also identified and quoted subsection (1) which states, *"A medical examiner may be reprimanded, placed on a period of probation, removed, or suspended by the Medical Examiners Commission for any of the following:"* I specifically referenced subsection (i) of that section which lists the following reason… *"Negligence or the failure to perform the duties required of a medical examiner with that level of care or skill which is recognized by reasonably prudent medical examiners as being acceptable under similar conditions and circumstances."*

My goal was not to have Dr. Thogmartin removed or suspended, but to bring the facts before the Commission and have them convene a Probable Cause Panel who would seriously delve into the problematic evidence. Dr. Thogmartin was the Chief ME and was now responsible for the death certificate status. After reviewing all the evidence, we felt a "reasonably prudent" ME should certainly see there were problems with the investigation, physical evidence and impossible explanations of suicide; and the still very probable likelihood another person fired the weapon.

There was also the issue that no ME was sent to the crime scene to observe or investigate. There were the overwhelming concerns about our case medical examiner's and chief police investigator's previously alleged negligence and professional credibility issues, not to mention all of our case's misinformation, inaccurate facts and impossible theories. It seemed logical that all these problematic issues should set off alarm bells with the ME who was responsible for reviewing the case, and that a reasonably prudent ME should address these issues and take the appropriate actions to correct them.

On July 13, 2011, I sent the one hundred twenty-two page complaint package to the FDLE Medical Examiners Commission Bureau Chief, Glen Hopkins in Tallahassee. The package was signed for at 10:18 a.m. on Monday July 18th. On the next day, July 19th, Mr. Hopkins penned the following letter...

"Dear Mr. Dirscherl,

We have received your complaint against the District 6 Medical Examiner regarding the death certificate for Robert John Dirscherl, Sr.

The Medical Examiners Commission does not have the statutory authority to compel a District Medical Examiner to change a manner of death therefore we are unable to take any action in this matter.

If you have any questions, please do not hesitate to contact Mr. Doug Culbertson, Medical Commission Staff, at (850) 410-XXXX.

Sincerely,
Glen W. Hopkins,
Staff Director, Medical Examiners Commission"

So apparently after receiving my parcel on July 18th, the FDLE ME Commission intently studied the one hundred twenty-two page package, reviewed all the problematic evidence, carefully considered the complaint, and by July 19th, the next day, determined they were not in a position to help.

Or, as it appears, immediately found an easy out, and responded a few hours later by stating they didn't have the authority to force an ME to change his ruling. Even though my complaint clearly stated it was based on chapter 406.075 (1) (i) of the statute that gives them their authority to investigate medical examiner negligence, it seemed they chose not to look into the complaint.

This meant I could accept their quick-fire response or contact them again with a request for further explanation about the legitimacy of our grievance, and see if they intended to comply with the Florida statute that directed appropriate actions with all legal complaints.

On Monday August 1st, I mailed a certified letter to Mr. Doug Culbertson, a Government Analyst with the ME Commission. I hoped the letter would reach him by Friday, but as my luck would have it, there was nobody available to receive it, so it sat at the Tallahassee post office over the weekend and was redelivered and signed for on Monday August 8th. While I was a bit hopeful we might receive the good news that the ME Commission agreed that our concerns were justified and they were initiating a Probable Cause Panel to review the case, the odds were we were probably going to receive one more kick in the gut informing us unfortunately the FDLE was unable to assist us with our case. I'd gotten pretty used to that type of rejoinder and was prepared for the possibility of receiving another door-slamming response.

Why would a government agency want to get involved in a thirty-five year old case that might reveal negligence, unethical behavior and the ugly truth that several experts and professional agencies failed to perform as expected? Hopefully because that's the right and honorable thing to do, that's why.

On September 7th, my mailbox contained another letter from Mr. Hopkins with the FDLE Medical Examiner's Commission. I could tell when I lifted it from the mailbox it was only one page, which usually meant it was a short, concluding letter that I probably didn't want to read; and it was.

The letter explained Dr. Thogmartin was told about the complaint, questioned about the investigation, and agreed with Dr. Wood's finding of suicide. The letter also mentioned that ME Commission staff thoroughly reviewed all the information and determined the complaint was not legally sufficient in that there was no violation of any Florida statutes or administrative rule by Dr. Thogmartin.

While I appreciate their investigation, and respectfully disagree with Dr. Thogmartin's and Dr. Wood's finding, the last paragraph of Mr. Hopkins' response touched on the more troublesome issue at hand. It read... *"While most medical examiners take it upon themselves to reexamine cases when presented with new evidence, there is no language in chapter 406, F.S., or Rule 11G, F.A.C., that requires a medical examiner to reexamine cases investigated by a previous examiner in his or her district, and a current medical examiner should not be held responsible for the determination of cause and/or manner of death in a 34 year-old case. The "reasonable care" clause in statute 406.075(1)(i) does not apply, and we consider this matter closed."*

In other words, there is no rule, law, or obligation in the Florida statutes which govern medical examiner responsibilities, that requires a medical examiner review of a previous ME's case. Even if the previous ME was proven to be incompetent and negligent, there are no obligations to pursue obvious mistakes, glaring errors, unanswered questions or impossible theories. This type of unchecked ME power leaves Florida residents in a helpless position which forces unwanted litigation, or accepting lies as truth. One more State agency had closed our case and washed their hands.

Through the years, several family friends have recommended we take our case to the courts and make the experts show how they came to the conclusions they did. Lay out all the evidence and see where the preponderance of the evidence leads. Up to this point, my family and I have chosen to pursue non-litigious methods to see if we could overturn the injustice by using the system; so far no luck.

Along the way there have been a few cruel and ignorant accusations by some of the investigators, Unsolved Mystery bloggers, and detached passers-by that our objective to overturn this case is money. Since Dad's death was ruled a suicide, his $100,000 life insurance policy didn't pay any benefits and the insurance company kindly refunded his 1977 premiums after his death. While some can interject unfounded opinions and twisted motives, and theorize our quest is to recoup life insurance benefits; the truth is that our sole efforts have been to obtain an accurate death certificate and clear our father's name, simply because the truth should be told, a man's legacy should be accurate, and justice should prevail. I guess those cynical souls who think we're after money are entitled to believe any myth they wish. I'm confident most understand my family's true objective and honorable intent.

Money does at times find ways of tarnishing true and honorable intentions. History and current events reveal horrible examples of how money can corrupt and poison people; becoming the ultimate idol for some. The old saying "Money is the root of all evil" at times seems to ring true and confirm that money is wicked and serves no honorable purpose.

Hopefully, when one carefully searches for truth and has honorable intentions at their core, they realize money itself is just a tool to facilitate civilization's survivability. And that old proverb is just one more example of sloppiness, imprecise repetition and the product of inaccurate reiteration. As some of you know, the accurate quote is "For the *love* of money is the root of all evil", and it comes from Scripture, 1 Timothy,6:10. Seems God knows how to be accurate…He just needs people to get it right every now and then.

While the love of money may be at the root of evils, and money itself just a tool of man, the real problems surrounding money seem to lie in one's heart. My family's true intention behind our quest has consistently been bumped against that repeated message of this book…know your heart.

As we search our hearts for the truth in this matter, I'm comfortable that our objective and actions are based on honorable grounds, and refute the few cruel and baseless claims that we're looking for a monetary pay-off.

Chapter 14

The Never-Ending Ending

As this book nears its end, apparently our story doesn't. It's December 2011, nearly thirty-five years after Dad's death, and my family and I are still forced to accept unproven theories, beliefs as truth, and a story with no sensible ending. While a neat and comfortable finale to this book would be nice, I've come to understand that the muddled, painful struggles have been part of the plan all along. They've been a part of my family's life story that in ways has shaped us, defined us, and allowed us to grow and discover facets of ourselves that we may never have known.

This journey has been healing at times, and wounding at others. It's caused us to search deeply into our hearts and souls, and challenged us at every level of our being. It's introduced us to a myriad of people whose personalities and character run the gamut from hard-hearted to virtuous.

As a child growing up, I remember two very important lessons Mom taught me. They were more than just lessons; they were two of her convictions which she passed on to her children. She would never allow her kids to say they hated anyone. And she would never allow us to call someone a liar.

Anytime she would hear those detestable words leave our mouths she'd be on us in a instant, and with her eyes revealing a heartfelt distress, she'd sternly reminding us those words were some of the nastiest in the vocabulary, and they were not to be used in her house.

Her influence stuck, and helped me understand words can be very wounding. I compare malicious words to bullets fired from a gun…once they leave your mouth, or you pull the trigger, you can't call them back, and the pain is going to be inflicted. I also began to understand that like poisonous words, bitterness, grudges and resentment usually self inflict the same festering decay. While anger and hate may be directed towards others, I eventually realized the impacting effects usually wind up wearing on the one harboring the toxin. Resentment is like a cancer that spreads throughout a person's life, destroying the good and joyful things before us. It's an ugliness that won't go away until we realize it infects us, admit it controls us, and take the steps to remove the cancer that's killing us.

Over the years, I became very angry with some of the authorities involved in our story. In hindsight, through clearer eyes and a softened heart, I see how my anger negatively affected me, and had no effect on them. Thankfully, by the grace of God, I was able to release that anger, and it changed my life. I no longer harbored the personal bitterness, and I was able to forgive those who had caused me pain. What a freeing revelation...to be cancer free.

While I was able to forgive those who had perhaps erred, or wounded my family and me, that doesn't mean I'm giving up on attaining justice. I hope I've made the point that we are still attempting to set the record straight. And while I don't understand the details of how this whole crazy plan is supposed to work out, I've been assured there is "Someone" in charge who does. I pray this book is read by another "lower-case someone" who has the ability to provide a fact, or interpret a clue, or inject another bit of hope that might eventually lead to an amended death certificate and a redeeming and honest legacy.

While I'm optimistic we'll discover the truth and achieve the justice we seek, I have another desire concerning this book. I hope our story touches the hearts of some who read it, and helps them perhaps deal with their pain and suffering in a healing way. Life is too short to waste being angry or failing to forgive. I know there are folks reading this right now who are trapped in their own personal world of anger, guilt, vengeance or resentment...struggling with that personally imposed cancer that stands between them and real joy. I hope this book helps at least one person to recognize their burden and helps free them from it, perhaps bringing them to the point where they accept the gift of Grace, and release the anger and darkness in their life. It can be a life changing moment, or perhaps a slower gradual walk; but I can promise one thing...it's a genuine blessing that shouldn't be missed.

I know it's impossible to prove God exists or doesn't exist; we can't physically see or define Him, and it takes faith to believe. While neither can I see wind or gravity, or explain love or grace, I have seen their effects, experienced all of them, and trust they're real.

Throughout these pages I've shared some pretty amazing beliefs and experiences with you, and I know some may be hard to swallow. But as I stated in the preface of this book, everything you've read is true.

This manuscript ends with us still searching, our strange story still unfolding; and our hearts at peace. I hope and pray it brings new beginnings to those who read it.

The End?

Acknowledgments

I'd like to pass on my sincere thanks to the dozens of people who have been involved in this quest. To the law enforcement personnel and forensic experts who know deep down inside things didn't happen as the records indicate, and who support our search for the truth...thank you.

To my wife and kids...thank you for supporting me as I wrote and vented and theorized and vented and wrote and questioned and struggled and vented. When frustration tried to get the best of me, your unrelenting love and support gave me strength and encouragement to continue to search for the truth.

To my siblings; Guy, George, Kook and Kandy...thank you so much for your help and understanding. As a clan we've battled, and have yet to slay our Goliath. Your support throughout this endeavor is greatly appreciated. Your ability to press on and support my personal mission, even when it was painful for you reveals your love and caring hearts. I can't thank you enough!

To the wonderful folks at POMC...your organization is a Godsend that brought hope and optimism to this family after decades of hopelessness and despair; I'm grateful for your help and involvement. Special thanks to Doctor's Melinek and Bonnell for volunteering your time and expertise to complete strangers. Your hearts reveal goodness and your virtues are a wonderful example for others. You make a difference.

To the caring hearts at K-LOVE radio and the thousands of listeners who donate to keep the nonprofit station running...you've blessed me beyond measure. Your positive and encouraging words and prayers, blended with contemporary music and the message of God's love touch thousands of people each day. You are messengers of good news and your ministry changes lives.

Thank you to the extended family and friends who were there to listen to our crazy story and offer help, a sympathetic ear and at times a shoulder to lean on...you too have been pillars of strength through the last thirty-five years.

To Michaela, thank you for your boldness and your fight to change the system. Your efforts may help lead to legal changes that aid other families and perhaps help them avoid some of the nightmares we've experienced. Thank you for sharing your story.

To Nancy Durham...wherever you are...you rocked our world. Your strange message and stranger method introduced us to the reality of your gift. I can't wrap my head around it, but I believe you entered our lives for a purpose. I hope that purpose is to help us find the justice we seek, but I understand it may be for a purpose we'll never know, and may be intended for a person we'll never meet. Thank you.

To James MacKenzie and Dr. Joan Wood...after all these years I don't pretend to know your hearts or your thoughts concerning this case. All I can do is let you know I forgive you. I can't force you to accept that forgiveness or even compel you to believe it's necessary. The anger I carried for decades is gone and I pray you too have come to discover the truth through softened hearts.

To you...the reader; thank you for entering our bizarre saga and for caring enough to care. I ask that you pray for our family and other families out there who are experiencing the same injustice. I hope you consider taking the next step and forward a note to your legislators petitioning changes to Florida law. If you'd like to help my family, and Michaela's family, and the many other Florida families out there who are suffering the same injustice, please use the attached letter as a guide and write your Florida Legislator or Governor. Request they initiate new legislation that creates a check and balance of Medical Examiner powers. Printable copies will be available on the website www.IntelligentDesignInd.com.

To you, that special someone out there who may have a clue from decades past, factual evidence to share, or some ability to help...be it legal, forensic or judicial; I ask you to take that next step you're considering. I won't be specific, I'll let the Holy Spirit handle the details; you'll know if you're supposed to get involved. I continue to pray that you or another special someone will come forward with the last piece of the puzzle; that cloaked absent answer that will help us reveal the truth, obtain the justice we seek, and finally mend our healing wounds and our father's redemption legacy.

I Love You Mom & Dad!

In Memoriam

Since I began writing this book in October 2010, and closed my thoughts in December 2011, at least three of the people mentioned on these pages have passed away.

I recently learned that in July of this year, Dr. Joan Wood passed away. I didn't know her well, but I do know her high profiled career brought with it many challenges, much pain and anguish. I wish our personal/professional struggles and our battle over the truth had not manifested; but they did. I hope and pray her new journey provides her much comfort, joy and peace.

Another individual who played a major part in this story also passed away this summer; my close childhood friend Ingrid French. Ingrid was one of my best friends and is a part of so many of those old memories that include my father and my childhood. She lived a fabulous life even though she struggled forty years to overcome a brain tumor discovered when she was a young child. Her strength and tenacity are a shining example for many, and she memorably impacted the lives of all those she encountered. My thoughts and prayers go out to her father John and family.

Another loss: A famous stranger whose brilliant mind and incredible vision touched millions of lives and changed our world; Steve Jobs. His sister reports as he lay on his deathbed taking his last breaths, he opened his eyes, stared at her, his children and his wife...then gazed past them over their shoulders, locked his focus on something, and proclaimed "Oh Wow!" "Oh Wow!" "Oh Wow!" Perhaps someday we'll all understand what Steve was seeing. While I don't know for sure, I'm betting it wasn't an iPod, iPhone or iPad, but more likely the I Am.

Truth

All around us shines the Truth;
we see, yet still deny.
Each day it's there to reassure,
some glance and pass it by.

Truth shares life's answers, facts, and laws,
absolute, yet still forsaken.
Beliefs once strong, now decayed by doubts,
as time has our trusts shaken.

We've climbed the walls and searched the halls;
examined all the experts' books.
Some then invent a truth they like,
convinced it's not as silly as it looks.

To ease our minds we twist and change
the precepts we can't buy.
Then trust a soothing theory, opinion,
hypothesis, guess or lie.

Truth's always there to strengthen souls
when trials bend and break us.
A prayer to Him, our trust renewed,
His Truth will not forsake us.

DDD

Appendix

Dear Representative _____:

Please consider the critical issue explained below, as it appears to be an insurmountable obstacle for citizens who have lost loved ones in our State.

There is a glitch in our Florida law which allows a Medical Examiner to determine at his/her **sole discretion** both the "Cause" of Death and the "Manner" of death and all other information including how the injury occurred which is permanently recorded on a death certificate. This gives the presumption that the Medical Examiner is never wrong and no person or entity can successfully challenge their opinions and obtain relief under Florida law.

There is no recourse provided by Florida law to force a medical examiner to amend a death certificate, even when that medical examiner is dishonest or incompetent; or even when there is conflicting evidence, or new evidence indicating that his/her findings are inaccurate.

There needs to be some administrative procedure or appeals process giving the Court and/or the Florida Medical Examiner's Commission the right to overrule a Medical Examiner's findings and the legal ability to Order the Florida Department of Vital Statistics to amend the death certificate accordingly.

How many times has a Florida medical examiner sided with law enforcement or the State Attorney when a challenging investigation results in a flawed conclusion? How much longer will family members have to suffer because they are at the mercy of medical examiners who possess absolute power with no oversight and no means to challenge their decisions? It is devastating enough when families are coping with the violent death of their loved one. But then they are traumatized again and again after they learn that the Medical Examiner has the absolute power to make what can be arbitrary or capricious decisions and there is absolutely no legal or administrative recourse for citizens to challenge those decisions and seek an order to amend the death certificate.

Although you as a representative of the people, will most likely encounter strong opposition by medical examiners, state attorneys and law enforcement, please stand up for the people and make this right by filing a legislative bill to allow the public a fair and legal process to appeal a medical examiner's findings and to seek an Order for The Florida Department of Vital Statistics to amend any aspect of the death certificate when there is evidence that conflicts with the Medical Examiner's findings.

Thank you for your time and consideration.   Signature Block

Cover Art

I created the cover art to capture the many facets of this story in one shot. It includes a photo of my father, the weapon that ended his life, and a photo of the fatal wound. It also includes the cassette tape which contains the amazing story my Aunt Fran shares about her bizarre encounter with the stranger on the Amtrak train.

Also included is a sea turtle which represents the story of Gladys...the huge creature that for a few fleeting minutes became the pet I gleefully rode around the yard of a friend, moments before her throat was slit, and I was introduced to death.

The magnifying glass represents our search for the truth concerning our father's death. It's focused on a lost soul surrounded by an enormous wall which represents the barriers constructed by the experts...the wall we struggle to break through as we seek truth and justice.

The sketch also includes a crucifix lying on a hammer that appears to be falling into a hole. These items are a metaphor depicting how religion can at times be forced upon people, while some corporate beliefs may not be based on a solid foundation. The syringe injecting happiness and sadness into the hammer represents religious doctrine, and legalistic dogma some religions use to support communal beliefs...man-made crutches designed to fill the God-shaped holes in our hearts. The sketch is a collage inspired in part by Pink Floyd's album, *The Wall.*

Lurking behind the sketch is "the elephant in the room", quietly representing the stigma of my father's supposed suicide which silently lingered in the background of my family's lives.

Standing watch over the whole scene is an angel. A reminder that God is involved, has a purpose for the struggles we encountered, and is still in charge of this story and our lives.

Made in United States
Orlando, FL
14 February 2022

14791369R00129